The Gilded Curse

by
Marilyn Turk

HERITAGE BEACON
F I C T I O N

THE GILDED CURSE BY MARILYN TURK
Published by Heritage Beacon Fiction
an imprint of Lighthouse Publishing of the Carolinas
2333 Barton Oaks Dr., Raleigh, NC, 27614

ISBN: 978-1-938499-11-1
Copyright © 2016 by Marilyn Turk
Cover design by Elaina Lee
Interior design by Karthick Srinivasan

Available in print from your local bookstore, online, or from the publisher at:
www.lighthousepublishingofthecarolinas.com

For more information on this book and the author visit: http://pathwayheart.com.

Brought to you by the creative team at Lighthouse Publishing of the Carolinas:
Eddie Jones, Ann Tatlock, Leslie L. McKee, Shonda Savage, Brian Cross, Paige Boggs

Library of Congress Cataloging-in-Publication Data
Turk, Marilyn.
The Gilded Curse/Marilyn Turk 1st ed.

Printed in the United States of America

PRAISE FOR *THE GILDED CURSE*

Author Marilyn Turk uses both romance and danger to quickly draw us into this page-turning novel. When Lexie Smithfield's brother is killed in the attack on Pearl Harbor, she returns to the family's vacation home in Jekyll Island, Georgia, which she hasn't seen since she was a child. The old home still stands, though it is uninhabited—at least, as far as Lexie can see. Her mother believed both the house and the island were cursed, but Lexie finds that difficult to believe. With the help of her childhood friend, Russell Thompson (now an extremely attractive man), she dares to challenge her mother's belief—and quickly finds herself face-to-face with danger. This is a story I'd highly recommend, and one I hope has sequels coming along behind it.

~ **Kathi Macias**
Multi-award-winning author of more than 50 books,
including 2011 Golden Scrolls Novel of the Year, *Red Ink*

Driven by a story of "have nots" who once "had everything," *The Gilded Curse* magically takes us to an age of uncertainty by employing a cast of characters whose lives have been turned upside down by war and depression. With rich layers of description, this gripping suspense novel weaves romance, suspicion and intrigue into a dynamic wave of mystery.

~ **Ace Collins**
Author of over sixty books and
Christy Award-winning author of *The Color of Justice*

Take a trip to WWII America with Marilyn Turk in *The Gilded Curse*, where Germans off the East Coast are only one of the worries for the heroine in this entertaining mystery/romance mix. You'll get 1940s atmosphere, enough mystery to keep the pages turning, and a sweet little romance to boot!

~ **Linore Rose Burkard**
Award-winning author of Regency breakout novels for the CBA

The Gilded Curse is my kind of novel. I was totally drawn into the story from the very first page. I loved the setting and the entire cast of characters. It has everything you want in a novel: history, mystery, suspense, romance and intrigue. Highly recommended!

~ **Dan Walsh**
Best-selling author of *The Unfinished Gift*,
The Discovery and *When Night Comes*

Set just after the onset of WWII, *The Gilded Curse* gives us a glimpse into a society turned upside down by the war. Marilyn Turk's story is one of romance and intrigue surrounding a once grand old home where God's love breaks the curse and unites two hearts destined to be together.

~ **Martha Rogers**
Author of The Homeward Journey
and Winds Across the Prairie Series

Dedication

To Chuck, my husband and research partner.

Thank you for your patience, support, and effort to understand this writer's complicated mind.

Prologue

December 1941

"Mother, how do you like the tree?"

Lexie lifted part of the popcorn garland to make it drape on the tiny fir tree which perched on the small table. She glanced over her shoulder to see Mother's response.

Standing before the window of her room, Mother stared out. Nothing. No reply.

Lexie sighed. At least she was trying to bring Christmas into Mother's room at the sanatorium. Whether her mother actually understood or appreciated the gesture was doubtful. Lexie resumed her efforts to decorate the tree, humming along with Benny Goodman's Band playing "Jingle Bells" on the radio. Maybe the music would help Mother make the connection between the tree and the coming holiday. But so far, no recognition had registered.

She left the tree and joined her frail mother, once so lively and beautiful, at the window.

"Would you like to go outside, Mother?" Lexie noticed other residents and their Sunday afternoon visitors enjoying the bright winter day as they strolled the manicured grounds.

Was that a nod?

"Good, we could use some fresh air. I'll get our coats. It's chilly out. I see a light snow falling."

Lexie retrieved the garments and began putting Mother's hat, scarf, coat, and gloves on her while the woman stood like a mannequin being dressed. Next, Lexie donned her own wool coat and hat and gently grabbed her mother's elbow, leading her to the door. As Lexie opened the door, her mother's eyes widened and she stepped backward.

"Mother, what is it?" Oh no. Not this again. "Don't you want to go outside?"

Mother glanced at her, eyes filled with fear, her voice timorous. "I don't know you. Where are you taking me?"

"It's me, Mother. Alexandra. We're going for a little walk."

Mother withdrew back into the room, shaking her head. "I don't know if I can trust you."

"Okay, Mother. We'll stay inside."

Lexie closed the door and began taking their coats off. Why did she keep trying? Mother's fears consumed her so much that she didn't trust anyone anymore. But was it real fear or dementia, or had one caused the other? No one knew for certain. Yet the illness had taken its toll on her mother as well as on Lexie and her brother Robert. But now with Robert in the navy, an officer on an aircraft carrier in the Pacific, Lexie had the sole responsibility of dealing with their mother.

As she returned the coats to the closet, the music on the radio abruptly stopped. A somber male voice spoke.

"We interrupt this program to bring you some important news. The Japanese have attacked the American fleet at Pearl Harbor."

Before Lexie could comprehend the message, Mother started screaming. "They did it! They did it! I knew they'd get my family. They won't stop until we're all dead!"

Lexie's mouth gaped as nurses ran into the room and tried to calm down her terrified mother.

No. This couldn't happen. Not Robert too. Mother couldn't be right about the curse.

Chapter 1

"*N*ame, please." The burly boat captain checked his passenger list. Behind him, the shore of Brunswick, Georgia, receded in the distance.

Chilly gray moisture hung in the winter air. Lexie tugged the broad fur lapels of her coat together at her neck. "Alexandra Smithfield."

The captain's bushy eyebrows lifted. "Got someone meetin' you?"

Cold blew through Lexie's coat. "I booked a room at the clubhouse but didn't request assistance."

He eyed the single suitcase at her feet. "That all you got?"

"I don't expect to be staying long."

The captain shrugged. He picked up the suitcase. "You related to the Smithfields that own Destiny Cottage?"

"Yes. Robert Smithfield Sr. was my grandfather."

"Hmmph!" His brow furrowed, and he turned away to busy himself by placing her luggage atop the pile of bags.

Lexie frowned as he walked away. Did he not like her family? Maybe he was just surprised to find a club member traveling alone on the launch.

Lexie moved to the railing and gazed at the distant shore of St. Simons Island, squinting to make out the lighthouse, barely visible in the fog. She shivered. Her wool beret did little to keep her head warm, much less her ears. She'd forgotten how penetrating the damp cold of the South could be, unlike the dry, crisp winters of the North. She'd forgotten a lot in the ten years since she'd been to Jekyll Island.

The island held memories of her past. Most of them were pleasant— of Grandfather and Grandmother, Father and Mother, at Destiny, the splendid family cottage where she and Robert and their friends had played games. And pulled pranks. Once they'd given their cook Nadine a terrible fright when she opened the dumbwaiter and found them inside.

Robert. Could he really be dead? Her big brother, the one who'd protected her, the one she'd looked up to. So full of fun. And life. Why did his ship have to be at Pearl Harbor? And then Mother …

She shook her head as if she could shake the thoughts out of her mind. Tears pooled in her eyes threatening to freeze in the cold. She dabbed her lashes with her gloved hand, looking away from the water to scan the faces of the others onboard, searching for a familiar one.

She studied the six other adults and one child, observing their plain clothes. All staff members—probably housemaids and livery staff—they huddled together on the opposite side of the boat, keeping a respectful distance from her because she was a club member. A couple of them met her gaze and gave a sullen nod. Did they remember her? Perhaps they remembered the twelve-year-old child she'd been when she left, but who would recognize her as a grown woman?

It struck Lexie as odd that there were so few people on the boat. Of course. The rest of the staff must already be on the island. Had the other club members already arrived too? She'd never gone to the island alone before. Could she do this? Could she face the place her mother said had cursed her family? She steeled herself and took a deep breath. She could. She must settle matters once and for all, before her life, too, was destroyed.

The boat captain had taken over the wheel and stared straight ahead, a deep crease between his dark eyebrows. Didn't seem to be a happy fellow. In fact, no one seemed very happy today, or perhaps the weather just overshadowed their mood. The man gripped the steering wheel as if it would run away should he loosen his hold. Although he appeared to be her brother's age, his demeanor was that of a much older, craggy person. Surely, he hadn't been the ferry captain when she was a child. No, of course not. He wasn't old enough. Yet, he seemed familiar.

Someone touched her coat. Lexie glanced down to see a flaxen-haired little girl stroking the mink trim on her pockets.

"Evelyn! Stop that!" A woman in a loose-fitting, shabby brown coat grabbed the child and pulled her away.

"But Mommy, it's so soft," the girl whined.

Lexie guessed the petite child must be about eight or nine years old.

"I'm sorry, miss." The woman wore a floral scarf tied around her head turban-style, revealing a few tight brown curls around the face. She held the child close to her side.

"Oh, it's not a bother. Really." Lexie smiled at the child. "It is soft, isn't it? See, I have some around my cuffs and my collar too. It feels really nice next to my neck." Lexie pointed to her mink collar.

The wide-eyed child stared at Lexie's collar while her mother's expression changed from sad to sullen.

"Don't expect none of that on your collar, Evie." A man standing nearby snickered. "That's for rich folks."

"Maybe you'll get a coon tail on your'n." Another fellow guffawed, then the others onboard laughed as they joined in his joke.

Lexie felt her face warm despite the cold air. She turned away from the other passengers, chafing from the remark, and tried to focus on the approaching shore. She couldn't help the fact that she came from a wealthy family. Or rather, formerly wealthy family. Little did these people know she'd worn the same coat for three years. No doubt the other club members would notice the outdated style that showed its age. She'd be the topic of conversation among the gossips. They were the wealthy ones, the ones unscathed by the depression. Unlike her family, whose fortune had dwindled over the years.

Lexie's shoulders sagged. The Rockefellers, the Goodyears, the Goulds, the Morgans, the Vanderbilts—their children and grandchildren had been her playmates. At least they'd been while at Jekyll. But after Father's accident, all that changed. Back home in New York, none of them associated with her family anymore.

"Don't let it bother you," Robert had said. "It's not you. Or me. It's Mother and her strange behavior that makes them uncomfortable."

The cottage had stayed closed up the last ten years. She hadn't told the clubhouse staff to get it ready like they used to when the whole family arrived together. After all, she wasn't planning to stay there. She couldn't stay there alone—not with all the memories of relatives no longer alive, but she wanted to see it one more time. Her insides quivered with excitement like they used to when she was a child.

But apprehension quieted the child, warning her to be cautious and stay calm. This visit was not a social one. It was business—and a farewell. The cottage needed to be sold. Mr. Fitzhugh, the family accountant, could have handled the business from New York. He had informed her about the unpaid taxes on the property. However, Russell's telegram had asked her to come. It said, "Destiny needs you." She had no idea what that meant, but she had to find out. After all these years, a force tugged her heart and pulled her back to the island, and it was more than curiosity. Maybe she just needed to say good-bye in person.

As the island drew closer, Lexie observed the high turret of the clubhouse peering over the tops of massive moss-laden oaks. In the gray mist, the tower might be mistaken for a castle. No doubt the builders had this image in mind. A nouveau castle for American royalty—fitting for the members of the Jekyll Island Club. Visions of ladies in long white dresses holding lacy parasols aloft strolled through Lexie's mind. Yet, those were pictures she'd only seen on the walls of the Queen Anne-style clubhouse. Fashion had changed since the late 1800s when the first members arrived at the island. A weight pressed against Lexie's heart. So much had changed in her life too.

They're watching us, you know.

Her heart jerked. But the voice she heard wasn't audible. It was her grandfather's voice from many years ago as they rode the club launch to the island.

Who's watching, Grandfather?

Up there. In the tower. He'd pointed to the clubhouse turret. *They're looking to see who's arriving, so they'll be ready to meet us at the dock.*

Was anyone watching from the tower now? She squinted through the mist and tried to catch sight of someone up there, but the tower faded in and out of the fog like an apparition.

She let her gaze drop to the shoreline, hoping to glimpse Destiny where it sat near the water's edge. But ghostly forms became massive oak trees that blended together, blocking her view from any familiar landmarks on shore.

The boat horn blasted and Lexie jumped, her heart thumping.

As the vessel approached the dock, a tall man in a black fedora and grey overcoat stood waiting, his stare fixed on the oncoming vessel, then on her. An icy chill shook her. She glanced over at the other passengers to see if anyone returned his gaze. Perhaps he expected someone else on the boat. But as she turned back, she knew he waited for her.

Chapter 2

*R*ussell watched the club launch come down Jekyll River, searching the faces onboard to find hers. She must be on this boat. When she made her reservation, she didn't ask to be picked up, but he assumed she would ride from Brunswick with the rest of the staff.

Typical of her to go against the social customs of the island. She'd always resisted the pomp and circumstance associated with the wealthy, even as a child, playing with abandon and taking risks along with the boys. Never one to refuse a dare. He chuckled. Robert's kid sister had often been the victim in their shenanigans.

Would he recognize her now, ten years later? He'd seen a newspaper article in the Times that showed her standing among the Vassar tennis team with other girls of prominent New England families, her blonde curls standing out in the black-and-white photo. He remembered the look on her face—not haughty or giddy like her teammates—but serious. Was she contemplative or just bored?

So, she came to the island by herself. He had to admire her bravery. There had been a lot of changes in the past ten years. Many of the original club members had died, their property sold to newcomers or turned back over to the club. Some of the cottages had been abandoned, like Destiny. When he heard about Robert's death at Pearl Harbor, and her mother's subsequent passing at the mental hospital, Russell knew Lexie would be the sole heir. Now he had to convince her not to sell.

As the boat neared the dock, he spotted her. Pale blonde curls peeked out from under a fur hat, giving her away. Of course, she was the only one onboard dressed so well. But her posture alone declared her higher social position.

Lexie Smithfield had returned to Jekyll Island.

Whump!

Lexie stumbled and grabbed the railing, trying to collect herself as the launch slammed into the wharf. She glanced back at the captain, expecting an apology. But he just looked through her while he concentrated on docking the boat. Surely it wasn't a personal affront, but she sensed that it was. Or else he was just a bad driver.

As the gangplank lowered and men on shore roped the vessel to the dock, Lexie averted her gaze from the stranger standing nearby. He made her uncomfortable, staring at her that way. She moved to the rear of the passengers as they departed, hoping to get lost in the crowd. However, a crowd of six didn't provide much cover.

Head down, she hurried over to where her suitcase sat with the other baggage. As she reached for the handle, another hand gripped it first.

"Allow me, please."

Lexie dared not look up at the stranger.

"Thank you, but I can handle it." She grabbed the handle and attempted to wrestle it free from his hand.

"I see you haven't outgrown your stubborn streak."

Lexie halted, her temperature rising. Her head jerked hearing a voice that sounded familiar. Studying his face, her eyes widened.

"Russell?"

He laughed. "Yes, Lexie. It's me."

"Oh, my. You've changed." The club superintendent's son was no longer the teenager she remembered.

"Well, I believe you've changed even more." He grinned. "Why, you were just a child last time I saw you. And look at you now—a full-grown woman!"

Her cheeks flamed, and she shifted her gaze to the departing passengers.

"Russell Thompson." She spoke the name as her memory awakened. She faced him again. "How did you know I was coming today?"

Russell chuckled. "Lexie, we *always* know who's arriving. It's our job, ma'am." He proffered a slight bow.

"I didn't want to cause a fuss. After all, it's only me."

"But you're still a club member, and the staff always greets the members at the dock."

He motioned to a waiting car. "Come on. Let's get out of this cold. We can talk in the car."

It wasn't a long walk to the clubhouse, but Lexie welcomed the respite from the chill. She followed Russell to the car, noticing a slight limp in his gait. She didn't remember that about him.

When he opened the door for her, she climbed in the front seat. He went around to the driver's side and got in. In the past, a carriage would have met the family to drive them to Destiny, their cottage being farther from the others.

"Lexie, I'm so sorry about Rob. He was a good man and always treated me like a friend."

She nodded and stared out the window, the lead in her heart weighing her down. She blinked away tears that were all too ready these days. "You were his friend, weren't you?" She twisted around to face him.

"Yes, of course … we've kept in touch with each other over the years."

Robert and Russell were always together when they were on the island, even though Russell was the club manager's son. They were the same age, five years older than she. "R and R," her father had called the pair, like one of his railroads. How inconceivable that both Robert and her father were now dead. She shuddered and turned back to the window.

"Are you cold? I'm sorry the weather isn't more welcoming."

"I don't remember it being this cold here."

Russell laughed. "I'm sure it's been this cold before, but not often, and the good thing is, this is as cold as it's going to get. You know our winters are shorter and much milder than you have up north. I promise you it'll warm up before you leave."

She doubted that. He probably assumed she'd at least stay through March for the club season, but she wasn't planning on staying that long.

Encased in frosty fog, the clubhouse had a ghostly appearance. As they pulled into the circular driveway and up to the portico, the top of the building disappeared into the mist while the wraparound porch came into view.

"Where are your other bags?" Russell stopped the car in front of the steps and glanced over at Lexie.

"I don't have any others. I won't be staying long."

"You've been gone ten years, and you're not staying long?"

She smiled but didn't answer.

A bellman opened Lexie's door, and she climbed out.

Russell grabbed her bag and handed it to the bellman.

"Take this to Miss Smithfield's room, please."

The bellman nodded and turned up the steps. Russell took Lexie's arm and steered her toward the front of the building.

"Why aren't you staying longer, Lexie?" he asked as they entered the lobby.

Lexie started to answer, but noticed other guests nearby, warming themselves by one of the ornately carved fireplaces, and hesitated. She shot Russell a message with her eyes that she didn't care to discuss her business in public.

He glanced about and acknowledged her need for privacy. "I'll let you get settled in your room. When would you like to see the cottage?"

"Not today." Her answer came out more abrupt than she expected. "I do hope you haven't gone to any trouble opening it."

"No, we haven't, but only because you instructed us not to when you called to make a reservation. But I must warn you, the years have taken their toll on the old cottage." Russell shook his head. "Perhaps tomorrow the weather will be more suitable to go there. Would you like us to light the fireplace tomorrow to get the chill out of the house first?"

"That won't be necessary. I'm just too tired now. I'd forgotten how long the trip is from New York—hours on the train, then the ride over on the launch." Lexie stifled a yawn. "A hot bath sounds much more inviting."

"Tomorrow, then." Russell stopped at the front desk. "Miss Smithfield's room key, please."

The clerk nodded and retrieved the key, handing it to Russell. Russell studied the key before giving it to Lexie. "Room 214. Would you like me to show you to your room?"

"That won't be necessary, Russell. I believe I can find my way to the second floor." She glanced over her shoulder at the rich mahogany staircase flanked by twisted balusters.

"I'm sure you can, Lexie." He flashed a disarming smile. "I'll come for you at 10:00 in the morning so you'll have time for a leisurely breakfast."

Morning sunlight filtered through the tall windows of the grand dining room, trying to lift the weight from Lexie's chest. As she took in the scene before her, though, she felt an eerie sense of moving backwards in time. Well-dressed guests conversed at linen-draped tables arrayed in even rows reaching from one wall to the other. Imposing white ionic columns marched double-file down the center of the room just as they had so long ago. It was as if Lexie had stepped on stage in a familiar play, but with different cast members.

Huge pots of native palms flanked the columns while bouquets of fresh flowers graced each round table, competing with the lavish fashion of the diners, evidence that the island's greenhouse still functioned. One wouldn't know winter still existed elsewhere, with the tropical atmosphere perpetuated here. This was a world of man's creation, safe from the harshness of the outside world.

In this sphere of protection, did the members even realize the country was at war? Even the climate was controlled to keep the guests from any discomfort while here. Lexie drew in a deep breath, smoothing her hands over her slender gray pleated skirt as she scanned the room for a familiar face. Finding none, she headed toward an empty table a comfortable distance from the others.

"May I help you, miss?" The hostess attired in a crisp white apron rushed to Lexie's side.

"Yes, I'd like a table, please."

"Will anyone be joining you?"

"No. I'm alone." The sound of that admission reverberated in Lexie's mind. One more thing she had never done alone before—eat in the clubhouse dining room. There had always been an assembly of Smithfields at the table—Grandmother and Grandfather, Mother and Father, Robert and herself, and even Kenneth. Her heart twisted as the pain of her little brother's death renewed itself. Gone. Everyone was gone, except her.

"This way, miss." The hostess led her past couples and families enjoying each other's company. Several patrons nodded or smiled as she walked by, and she reciprocated. She had the impression of being on parade. Once seated, she wished she'd chosen to face away from the others. Several guests cast sideways glances her way and leaned close to their table companions, whispering about her, no doubt, and curious about the young single woman. Was this what a caged animal felt like in a zoo? Holding the menu up in front of her face, she tried to block out the other diners.

"Good morning, miss. Would you care for coffee or tea?"

Lexie jumped, unaware that the waiter had arrived. She exhaled the breath she'd been holding since she entered the room. "Oh, I didn't see you there."

"Sorry, miss." The tall, gray-haired gentleman bowed. "I didn't mean to sneak up on you."

She gazed up at the uniformed waiter and noted a slight smile on his face and twinkle in his eye.

"You're Mr. Mason, aren't you?" Her heart leaped at the recognition.

"I am indeed." He nodded then tilted his head, studying her. "Now let me guess who you might be."

Lexie fingered the pearls at the neck of her cream satin blouse, watching him. He'd been a fixture at the clubhouse forever, it seemed. How old must he be now? In his sixties?

"Ah … Miss Alexandra! Of course!" He snapped his gloved fingers on one hand. "I remembered those pretty blue eyes of yours. You've been gone a long time!"

"I have, Mr. Mason. In fact, I don't recognize a soul here." She glanced around the room. "It's a relief to see someone I know."

"Many of these folks are new to the club, which is why you may not know them."

"New? I thought the club was restricted."

Mr. Mason leaned over to whisper. "It used to be, but, unfortunately, the Depression forced many members to withdraw their membership. The club offered more affordable dues to entice new people to join."

"Oh, I didn't know." So her family wasn't the only one affected by the economy.

"Even so, the war has caused many to think of more important issues than vacation."

At the reminder of war, Lexie's mood sobered. Mr. Mason's eyebrows pinched together.

"Is everything all right, Miss Smithfield? Your mother and your brother are well, I hope?"

Her eyes began to fill again. "My brother Robert was killed at Pearl Harbor. He was an officer on the *Arizona*."

"I'm so sorry, miss. What a dreadful day that was. I'll never forget hearing the report on the radio."

She nodded and dabbed her eyes with the napkin. "Thank you. The shock of Robert's death seemed too much for Mother. Whether she realized he had been killed or not, she passed away a few days after Christmas." Mother's health had deteriorated at the sanatorium, but after Robert's death, she quit eating and just wasted away, the final blow to her pitiful existence.

"Bless your heart, dear." He placed a hand on her shoulder. "Let me get you some hot tea. And some extra honey and lemon slices, right?"

She lifted her tear-filled eyes. "You remembered!"

"Of course. Who could forget Miss Alexandra Smithfield?" He winked. "And I believe we have some of your favorite scones as well." She stared after his retreating form, her mouth agape.

"Excuse me, ma'am, did I hear correctly? Are you Alexandra Smithfield?"

Lexie jerked her head around to the heavyset matron standing on her other side. Oh dear. Of all people to run into—Mrs. Appleton—the one club member she had the misfortune of remembering. Did she still hold the dubious honor of being the biggest gossip on the island?

"Mrs. Appleton. Why, how nice to see you." Lexie stood and extended her hand. Inside, she cringed at the lie. "Yes, I'm Alexandra. It's been a long time, hasn't it?"

"Sit down, dear." Lexie obliged, and the woman plopped down next to her. "Why, you're all grown up. My, my. What a lovely young woman you've turned out to be. I just love the way your hair frames your face with those pretty blonde curls. Anyone ever say you look like Jean Harlow?"

Lexie's face warmed as moisture popped out along her hairline. How nice to know she looked like a dead actress. On the other hand, she'd also been told she looked like Shirley Temple, a former child star eight years her junior. How could anyone resemble such different personalities?

"How have you been, Mrs. Appleton?"

"Oh, just fine. But tell me about your family. How is your mother? I don't think she liked it here much, did she? Well, I can't say as I blame her, after your father's accident and all."

Lexie's stomach tightened. "Mother passed away last month. She had been in poor health for a while." The less said, the better, with this woman.

"Oh dear. I'm so sorry. Is your brother here with you? Robert the third, right?" She scanned the room as if she could find him. "What is he doing now?"

"Robert was killed at Pearl Harbor." How many times would she have to repeat it? Each time she spoke the words, her heart squeezed with guilt that she was killing him again.

"Oh, my. You poor child!" Mrs. Appleton reached over and squeezed

Lexie with her massive arms. "So who are you here with?"

"I came alone."

The woman drew back. "Alone! Don't tell me you're staying at that dreadful cottage by yourself!"

"No, I'm not staying at the cottage. I'm staying here at the clubhouse." Dreadful?

"Thank goodness. You'll be appalled when you see the place or have you already? It's in a terrible state. What a shame to let such a lovely place go neglected." She patted Lexie on the arm. "Of course, it's not your fault. Someone should have been taking care of it for you."

Someone had, before their accountant told the family they could no longer afford the upkeep. Lexie just smiled and nodded, revealing nothing. Mr. Mason returned to the table with her tea and scones. Her stomach grumbled as the scent of warm pastries wafted toward her. But the more Mrs. Appleton's chatter dragged on about other people Lexie didn't know, the more her appetite diminished. She sipped her tea and picked off tiny bites of scone, hoping to avoid talking.

"So, dear, have you a special gentleman friend? There must be many admirers seeking your attention."

Lexie gulped. "No, ma'am. I've been too busy with my studies at Vassar to even consider such things." Her studies, her mother, and her job, to be honest. More information she intended to keep private.

Mrs. Appleton's face lit up. "Well, isn't that a coincidence. My son Floyd is still unattached, as well. Do you remember him?"

Her stomach churned. Boy, did she remember Floyd. A mama's boy, to be sure. He never joined in with the other children, always afraid to leave his mother's side. Guess he never had.

"Yes, I remember Floyd."

"Well, you're in luck, because he's here too!" The woman began waving toward a table on the other side of the room. "Oh, bother, he doesn't see me. I'll go get him."

As soon as she left, Lexie grabbed a scone and stood to leave, hoping to get away before they came back. She'd eat in her room. Before she could make her escape though, she was intercepted by Mrs. Appleton and Floyd.

"Floyd, you remember Alexandra Smithfield, don't you?"

Lexie tucked the scone inside her sleeve unnoticed and extended her hand.

Floyd's dour expression changed little as he gave a slight nod. His pallid complexion reinforced Lexie's memory of the boy who never wanted to go outside and play. He extended a limp hand.

"Hello, Alexandra. How nice to see you again."

"Nice to see you again too, Floyd." His clammy, weak grip made her wonder if he had a pulse.

"Mother tells me you're not going back to your cottage. I wouldn't either if I were you." He lifted his eyebrows and nodded knowingly.

"I understand it needs some repair. When I go there today, I'll make a note of what should be done."

"You be careful over there." He leaned over, placed his hand beside his mouth and lowered his voice. "There's strange goings-on, I hear."

Lexie widened her eyes. "Whatever do you mean?"

Floyd glanced around to see if anyone else was listening. "Lights seen moving around inside the house."

Mrs. Appleton drew closer and cupped her hand over her mouth near Lexie's ear. "People say they've heard things too."

Lexie looked from the woman to her son. Taking a deep breath, she exhaled slowly. *Calm down, don't listen to them.* "I'm sure there's an explanation."

Both heads nodded agreement before Floyd smirked. "They say it's haunted."

Chapter 3

$\mathcal{L}$exie tried to steady herself. She had to get away from these people.

"Please excuse me. I have an appointment." She turned to go as Mrs. Appleton called out behind her.

"We'll see you at dinner!"

Not if she could avoid it. She hurried out, resisting the urge to run. As she rounded the corner from the dining room, she ran right into Russell.

He grabbed her by the arms to keep her from falling.

"Hey! I was coming to find you." He cocked his head with a broad smile. "What's the hurry? Is someone after you?"

Lexie's face warmed as she glanced over her shoulder, then back at him. "Of course not. I just needed some fresh air."

Russell threw back his head and laughed. "Then let's go outside, shall we?" He swept his arm toward the entrance. "Ladies first."

Lexie twirled and marched across the heart pine floors to the double doors, Russell following closely behind. He was teasing her, just as he had when she was a child. But now, she was a woman. How had he managed to make her feel like a petulant child again?

"Hey, wait up!" Russell hurried to her side in time to open the door for her.

She shot him an angry glare as she pushed through the opening. What was she doing? She stopped and waited for him outside on the veranda. He wasn't her enemy, so why did she get so offended?

"I'm sorry, Russell. I don't know what came over me. I guess I just felt trapped back there with the other guests."

"No apology necessary. Is there anyone in particular that you want to get away from?" His eyebrows rose as he crossed his arms.

Lexie studied his face. How handsome he'd become. *Lexie, it's just Russell, for crying out loud!* She might as well tell him. She lowered her voice.

"Mrs. Appleton. And Floyd."

Recognition registered on Russell's face, and his smile spread across it.

"Momma's Boy Floyd?" He nodded. "No wonder you wanted to get away. And Momma is probably going to try to get the two of you together."

Lexie grimaced. "She already has."

Russell burst out laughing again. She felt a tickle creep up from her stomach to her throat until her own laughter joined his.

"Do you remember when he said he couldn't get in the swimming pool because he might get measles?" She pictured the young Floyd shaking his head and refusing to get in the water while the rest of the children swam and played.

"Ha! I do remember that." Russell pointed a finger. "And he wouldn't climb trees because he might tear his britches."

"That never stopped me." Lexie recalled climbing alongside the boys.

"No, it didn't. Nor did a skirt."

"Much to my parents' embarrassment, I'm afraid."

"You've always been a swell sport, Lexie. Whatever Rob and I did, you tried to do too."

"What do you mean—tried? I could do anything you two did and just as well!" Lexie crossed her arms.

"Probably so, even though I would never have admitted it then."

"No, you never would say a girl could do anything as well as you!"

Russell's warm, inviting grin made Lexie let her guard down a little. She enjoyed the comfortable rapport, and it'd been a long time since she'd felt that way. She reverted back to the days of her youth when life was fun. And this is where it took place. So why did a pall exist over her memories?

Russell's gaze traveled across the grand lawn where the attendants were setting up for a game of lawn bowling, then returned to her.

"I do hope you'll have time for some fun and games while you're here. I'd enjoy the competition."

Fun and games? It sounded so inviting. But that wasn't her purpose for being there. This was business, serious business, and she had to act like an adult to handle it. She shook her head.

"No, I don't think so, Russell. As I mentioned before, I'm just here to take a look at the cottage—get it ready to sell."

A cloud passed over his features. "Yes, of course. Are you ready to see the cottage now?"

Lexie nodded but paused. "Let me run up to my room first and get my sweater."

"Go ahead. I'll wait for you here." He motioned to a row of white rocking chairs on the veranda. "At least it's much nicer than yesterday, even though it's still chilly."

"It's lovely, and even better, there's no snow here."

"No, ma'am. Don't think we have to worry about that. Although I believe it may have snowed here once or twice in history."

"I'll be back in a jiffy."

Lexie hurried inside and climbed the stairs to her second-floor room. Taking her room key from her bag, she placed it in the keyhole and grabbed the doorknob. But the door inched open from her grasp. It wasn't locked, much less shut tight. She distinctly remembered pulling the door closed and locking it. How odd.

She glanced up at the number—214—yes, that was her room number. Then who … Someone had been in her room. It must have been the housemaid. She looked up and down the hallway for signs of the cleaning staff. Seeing no one, she shrugged. Obviously, it'd been an oversight on the maid's part. As she pushed the door open, she scanned the room to see if anyone was there. Finding the room empty, she allowed herself to exhale.

Her stomach rumbled, reminding her of the scone she still had hidden in her sleeve. She smiled at herself for putting it there. A carafe of water sat on the nightstand, so she poured herself a glass and sat down near a small table to eat her hasty breakfast. She closed her eyes with the first bite, savoring the citrus tang of its lemon glaze. Still as good as she remembered, even though no longer warm. She hurried to finish and not keep Russell waiting. She took another sip of water before crossing the room to the dresser to retrieve her sweater.

As she leaned over to pull out the drawer, something caught her eye. Her toiletries on top of the dresser had been moved. Her brush and comb were previously parallel to each other on the right side, her perfume and powder on the left. Now they were reversed. Of course, the maid would move them to dust, but usually they would be put back the same way they'd been found. It wasn't that important, but perhaps she needed to speak to the head housekeeper about the negligence of the maid—leaving a room unlocked and rearranging a guest's personal items.

She opened the drawer and gasped. Her things were scrambled, not folded as she'd left them, as if someone had rummaged through them. But why would anyone do such a thing? Were they looking for valuables?

A chill shook her. Maybe someone was still in the room, hiding. That would explain the door. She turned around and knelt down to look under the bed. Holding her breath, she lifted the bed skirt, hoping another hand wouldn't grab hers. She exhaled a sigh of relief when she found the space empty and open through to the other side. She straightened as she scanned the room for another possible hiding place. The wardrobe door beckoned. She tiptoed across the room, grabbing an ornamental vase off the dresser for a weapon. Hoisting it over her head, she jerked open the door.

But only her clothes greeted her, the dead mink on her coat the most menacing, staring at her with glass eyes. She shoved the hangers apart to make sure no one was behind them. No one there. She blew out a breath, closed the door, and leaned against it, her body shaking. Had she imagined these things? Was this how her mother had felt?

No. Someone had definitely been through her things. Perhaps a thief had been looking for valuables. Well, they must have left disappointed. She wore the only valuables she'd brought.

Russell must be told about this. She grabbed her sweater and left the room, then made sure she shut the door and locked it. As she scurried down the hallway to the top of the stairs, she heard a door close behind her. She spun around and recognized the woman from the launch, the mother of the little girl. Dressed in a housemaid's uniform and carrying a feather duster, she appeared to have come from the end of the hall where a door led outside, probably to the servants' stairs.

As they exchanged glances, Lexie offered a smile. The woman nodded but didn't return the smile. In fact, she averted her eyes. Perhaps she had been the maid in Lexie's room. Lexie decided to ask her, but as she took a step in that direction, another guest room opened beside the maid, and the voice of Mrs. Appleton rang out.

"Oh, there you are! I wondered when you'd come. My room needs some attention."

Lexie whirled back around and headed down the stairs, hoping to once again escape the annoying Mrs. Appleton. She rushed outside to find Russell standing on the veranda engaged in an animated conversation with another man, a distinguished-looking gentleman dressed in a white V-neck tennis sweater and white slacks. As she approached, the men turned to face her and halted their conversation.

Russell held out his hand to her and beckoned.

"Alexandra Smithfield, this is Bernon Prentice, our club president."

Mr. Prentice offered a broad grin and extended his hand. "Miss Smithfield, how nice to see you. I remember your parents."

Lexie shook his hand, noting his lean form and tanned skin—in good shape despite his age. She pegged him to be in his fifties.

"Please call me Lexie. I remember watching you play tennis when I was a little girl."

"That right? Your mother played, too, didn't she? Do you?"

"I do. I played at Vassar."

"Then perhaps you'd join me for a game sometime?"

Lexie's stomach wrenched. She would love to play with this man, former captain of the Davis Cup team. Who would turn down such an invitation? She smiled and mustered the courage.

"I'd love to. However, I don't know that I'll have a chance to play."

"No time for tennis?" Mr. Prentice cocked his head. "Of course, we have many other activities to choose from, but perhaps you could squeeze a game in." He gave her a wink.

"Lexie's here to check on Destiny Cottage." Russell offered to help her with an explanation. "She plans to put it up for sale."

Mr. Prentice rubbed his chin while his smile changed into a frown. "I see. Have you seen the place yet?"

"Not yet."

"We're going there now." Russell moved to Lexie's side, an action which felt possessive. Or protective.

"Yes, well, I'm sorry to say the old place isn't what it used to be. Like several cottages on the island, it's showing its years of neglect."

"I expect to make some repairs before I put it on the market."

"Well, that's good. Fine, then. We'll be seeing you later. Very nice to meet you, and that invitation to play is still open if you change your mind!"

Mr. Prentice gave a nod to the two of them, then raced down the steps and strode toward the tennis courts.

Russell took her arm and led her down the steps. "My car is right over here." He nodded to his right.

Lexie stopped and pulled back. "Russell, do you mind if we walk? It's a lovely day, and I'd welcome the exercise."

"Sure, if that's what you'd rather do, we can walk. I guess I'm used to guests who prefer to be driven around."

"Russell, please stop treating me like a guest. For crying out loud, we played together!"

Russell laughed his easygoing laugh. "All right, I'll try. But it's my job to look after our guests, and it's been a long time since we played together." He cocked his head at her. "Hard to believe you're that same little tomboy who tagged along after us."

Lexie's face warmed. "Well, I am, and I won't have you fussing over me like some old lady."

Russell shook his head. "Never one to embrace frivolity, were you? No matter how hard your mother and grandmother tried to dress you up in girly clothes, you ended up getting them torn or soiled."

"They just weren't practical for tree-climbing, that's all."

"Ha! I remember the time you fell out of the oak tree in your yard right into a mud puddle! I don't know if your folks were more upset about you ruining your pretty dress or getting hurt. Thank goodness, you didn't get hurt."

"I wouldn't say that. I did get a spanking for disobeying and climbing that tree in my new dress."

As they strolled down the road, Lexie noted several gardeners working the club grounds. Russell waved and they nodded. One man though, an older man with leathered skin, scowled at them as he leaned on his rake. Lexie turned to see Russell's reaction.

"Whatever is the matter with that man? Did the two of you have a disagreement?"

"That's Abner Jones. It's not me he's got a beef with, though. It's you."

"Me? Why on earth would he have anything against me?"

"He was the gardener for Destiny before your family fired him."

Lexie gulped, her stomach churning. "We didn't mean him any harm, you know. Our accountant didn't think we needed the additional cost for a place we didn't use." Not with the rising costs of Mother's care. "Should I go apologize to him?"

Russell placed his hand on her arm, holding her back. "I don't believe that's necessary. You better just keep your distance. Some people hold grudges a long time."

Lexie shook off the chill from the gardener's gaze. "I hope he didn't suffer any hardship."

"Fortunately, we found him a place on our grounds crew. Don't let it worry that pretty head of yours." Russell gave her a wink. "Besides, I don't think I've ever seen the fellow smile, anyway."

Her face flamed and she turned away, focusing on the stately Crane Cottage on their right with its formal gardens. She remembered her grandfather complaining about Mr. Crane building the massive Italianate-villa style home, the largest cottage on the island, which wasn't in keeping with the other more "modest" homes of the compound. She noted the red tile roof, unique to the neighborhood, and admired the arches and wrought iron railings as they walked past.

Once past Crane, Lexie jolted to a stop. She stared, covering her open mouth with her gloved hand.

Instead of seeing Chichota Cottage, which used to be the next house on the street, two stone lions glared at intruders as they stood alone guarding steps that led to nothing. No grand front door and foyer greeted visitors anymore. Instead, all that remained of the Gould's former cottage were the foundations and the palm-lined courtyard with an empty swimming pool—the only evidence the impressive home had ever existed.

"What happened to Chichota?" she asked Russell as she struggled to comprehend what she saw. Where was the grand home where she had played with Mr. and Mrs. Edwin Gould's grandchildren?

"It had to be demolished last year."

"But why? Where are the Goulds?"

"Their other son Frank still lives here with his family at his cottage, Villa Marianna, but his mother refused to return to Jekyll after Edwin Jr. died here in a hunting accident. Mr. Gould Senior only came to the island a few times after that, and when he died, the house fell into very poor condition. Plus, even with our patrols, vandals managed to cause more damage in the off-season. It became an eyesore and a potential fire hazard to the other homes, so it had to be torn down."

Hunting accident? Lexie barely heard the rest of what Russell said. A shudder coursed through her body. When Father was killed in a hunting accident, her family had quit coming to the island too. Maybe it really was cursed.

"Lexie, are you all right?" Russell searched her face before a look of understanding crossed his. "Oh dear. I shouldn't have mentioned the accident. I'm sorry, Lexie. How inconsiderate of me."

Lexie shook her head. "No need to apologize, Russell. I'm just surprised to hear about another hunting accident. Have there been many here?"

His gaze drifted away to a place she couldn't see. He answered in a monotone voice. "No. Only two."

Was he there when the accident happened? When her father's accident happened? She didn't dare ask. She really didn't want to know. Maybe someday she could bring herself to ask about it, but not yet. She closed that door in her mind and focused on the task at hand.

"Russell, is Destiny in as bad a shape as Chichota was?" Her steps slowed. Maybe she wasn't ready to see her family's old cottage yet. The shock of Chichota's demise still reverberated through her.

"No, I don't think so. I mean, it needs some repairs, but it's not falling down. And like I said, the patrols try to keep an eye on it to prevent vandalism."

"The Appletons told me it was haunted. Why would they say that?"

He chuckled. "Did they now? Some people love to spread rumors."

"Especially Mrs. Appleton. But really, they said strange noises and lights inside the house have been seen. Have you heard about that?"

"Yes, I've heard the rumors." He laughed. "But, I'm sure there's a more reasonable explanation. After all, there *is* that old Indian burial mound on the property."

Lexie jerked her head to see his expression. She recalled the hill in the yard where they'd played 'King of the Mountain.' "I forgot about that. But surely you don't believe in that nonsense about Indian ghosts getting revenge, even though you and Robert tried to scare me with that old tale. But what about the noises and lights the Appletons mentioned?"

Russell shook his head. "Can't say. But we're almost there. You can see for yourself if Destiny has any ghosts."

Chapter 4

$\mathcal{T}$he yard and hedges along the crushed oyster shell driveway leading to the porte cochere were trimmed as they'd always been. But the oaks Lexie climbed as a child were now massive, towering over the house and reaching with their limbs in a protective embrace to keep the world out. Spanish moss draped from the branches and brushed the roof like long gray beards of old hermits.

Lexie scanned the cottage grounds alongside the Jekyll Island River then eyed Russell.

"Russell, if we fired the gardener, who's been taking care of the grounds?"

"Abner." Russell shrugged, his arms out to his sides. "After taking care of the property for thirty years, he insisted on keeping it up. Said it was a matter of pride in his work."

"But who paid him?" Lexie strode over to a camellia bush whose red flowers were disintegrating into a puddle on the ground beneath. She picked up one of the soft petals and held it to her nose, rubbing its silky texture with her thumb, then glanced back over her shoulder at Russell.

"Since he's on our crew, we've paid his salary. I've given him a little extra since he's doing us a favor keeping the place up."

"How strange." Lexie dropped the petal. "I must speak with him and thank him."

"Suit yourself." Russell nodded at the house. "Too bad he couldn't take care of the house too."

Lexie let her eyes roam over the aging cottage, once so welcoming, now depressing.

Scores of cedar shake shingles were missing from the roof while blistered gray paint peeled off the siding. The dingy white window frames around the dormers hung rotten from the ravages of southern humidity. As they drew closer to the house, she could see several broken windows on the top floor.

"Why would anyone break a window on the third floor?" Lexie

pointed to the third story where the family servants used to stay. "It wouldn't be an easy way to break in."

Russell shook his head. "Who knows why anyone vandalizes property? I suppose they think it's fun."

"How stupid." Lexie stomped up the steps to the sweeping veranda that wrapped around the house on three sides.

The wood floor groaned under the weight of their footsteps. Dark drapes covered the windows, hiding the interior from view. Lexie wrapped her arms around herself to suppress a sudden chill. Had the temperature just dropped?

"I do wish you'd let us air the place out for you first." Russell produced a key then grabbed the doorknob.

"No need. Especially since I'm not staying here." She stared at the door, holding her breath, wondering what would greet her inside.

Russell's forehead pinched with concern as he glanced at her over his shoulder. "Are you ready for this, Lexie?"

Lexie rubbed her upper arms and nodded. "Yes, of course. Let's get on with it."

Russell jiggled and jerked the key and knob with both hands before the lock gave way and relinquished its hold. Creaking hinges complained of years unused as Russell shoved open one side of the double doors.

Lexie hesitated before stepping inside, her eyes peering into the shadows within.

Russell touched her arm. "Wait. I'll get some light in here." He disappeared into the dusky room. Light creeped in as he went from window to window throwing back the heavy drapes. "All right. I believe you can see now," he called from across the room.

Musty air filled her nostrils as she entered the foyer opening into the parlor. Lexie covered her mouth with one hand, waved the air with the other, and coughed.

"You see, we should've opened the house before you came." Russell strode back to the front door and forced the other side free, pushing them both wide open. "There, that'll help. I'll try to open some of these windows."

She wanted to tell him not to bother, but she feared she'd suffocate without fresh air. The walls threatened to close in on her. Claustrophobia. She'd seen this among other patients at the hospital. Did she suffer from it too?

"Lexie, are you okay?" He approached her and put his hand on her shoulder, peering into her face. "We can come back later, give the house a chance to air."

She shook her head. She could do this. "No. Let's not leave just yet. I'd like to have a quick look around first."

"If you say so." He dropped his arm and motioned for her to go on.

As fresh air forced its way inside, Lexie let herself relax. Hordes of dust particles flickered in rays of light piercing the dirty windows. Her gaze followed the beams to the distorted shapes of sheet-covered furniture throughout the room. Squinting to force a memory of how the room used to look, she could see it—the sofa in front of the fireplace, Grandmother and Grandfather sitting there and talking. She shook her head. No. They were gone, like everyone else. She swallowed hard and bit back tears. Her grandparents would be so sad to see the condition of their beloved cottage.

She diverted her gaze to the fireplace and the mirror hanging above it, the surface marred with blackened spots where the silver had worn off, no longer able to look at the room in front of it. The rest of the walls were barren, showing pale squares where the family portraits were once displayed. The roses on the yellowed custom-made wallpaper appeared wilted and dying where the paper was still attached to the wall. Lexie cringed at the sight of cobwebs in every corner. Hopefully, the spiders had died too.

"Would you like to see any other rooms?"

Lexie jumped at the sound of his voice. She'd forgotten Russell was there, she'd gotten so lost in the past. She glanced over at him, noting the raised eyebrows as he watched her every move. Thank goodness he had come with her. She moved around the furniture, afraid to touch the dusty covers. The den contained more peculiar shapes created by the covered furniture. One piece, however, was not covered.

The antique secretary in the corner was not only exposed, it'd been violated. Every drawer had been opened and several dashed to the floor. The cracked beveled glass doors were open and the cubbyholes looked like they'd been smashed with a hammer. She ran over to the desk, picking up one of the drawers and holding it to her chest as tears filled her eyes. Russell rushed to her side.

"How could someone do such a thing?" She choked back a sob. "Why would anyone damage a piece of beautiful furniture like this?" This is where Grandmother sat writing her letters, where her mother had done the same, and where Lexie, the child, had drawn pictures. Grandfather used to tease them saying, "Every time I look at that secretary, there's a Smithfield woman sitting there." Lexie's heart cracked like the glass in the secretary doors.

Russell put his arm around her shoulder. "I'm so sorry, Lexie. I wish our patrols had noticed something amiss and been able to stop this destruction." He turned his head to view the rest of the room. "We don't know what damage there is to the rest of the house. Everything else is still covered."

He let go of Lexie and strode to one of the concealed shapes, jerking off the covering. The green velvet sofa showed no sign of damage. Russell walked through the room, ripping off covers and revealing furnishings that had long since seen light. Everything else appeared undisturbed, though. He turned and faced Lexie, arms outstretched with palms up.

"Nothing else appears to be damaged."

"But why would they attack this piece?"

"Maybe they were looking for something." Russell leaned over to examine the desk more closely.

Alarm shot through her. "What could they be looking for?" Vandalism was one thing, but searching her family's things was quite another.

Russell straightened, his hands on his hips. "Do you know if anyone, perhaps your father or grandfather, kept anything important in it?"

She shook her head. "Russell, I was twelve when we left. I've been gone ten years, so I don't remember a lot." She crossed her arms. "But do you think it makes sense for my father or grandfather to leave anything valuable here?"

He shrugged. "No, it doesn't. And if they did, it would have been kept in the safe."

Lexie whipped her head toward the hallway. "Russell, let's look at the safe."

There was no mystery about where the safe was located. Grandfather had been defiant about putting it inside its own locked closet. He didn't care who knew where it was, confident it couldn't be opened or moved by anyone but himself or Lexie's father.

"Let's see, I believe it's in the closet under the stairs. Is that right?"

Of course, Russell would have seen it in the past.

Lexie nodded and stepped into the dim hallway. Her eyes took a moment to focus and orient herself. The silence in the house unnerved her. Goose bumps traveled up her arm with the sensation of being watched. She glanced over her shoulder to see if Russell followed.

"I'm right here." Russell fell in step with her as they moved past the stairs. Lexie hesitated, glancing up. What did the upstairs look like now? She took a deep breath. One thing at a time.

Lexie squinted to see in the windowless space. A few feet past the stairs stood the door to the closet that held the safe. She stretched her hand out to the doorknob.

"Do you want me to open it?" Russell said.

"No, let me."

She grabbed the knob and turned. The door opened without protest, unlocked. She jumped back, expecting it to be locked. Recovering her composure, she stepped forward and jerked the door wide open. Inside, the safe's interior stood exposed, the door ajar.

The safe was completely empty. As it should be. But would they have left the safe open when they left and the closet door unlocked as well? Yet, if the safe was empty, it might as well be left open.

"Well, I don't see anything amiss here." Russell gestured to the safe.

"I guess not. But should the doors be locked?"

"Maybe, maybe not. Some folks leave them open so any would-be burglars don't have to tear things up to find out there's nothing there."

"I suppose you're right." Lexie stepped back, staring at the empty safe.

"Are you ready to look at the rest of the house?"

"No, I don't think so. Frankly, I want to get out of here and get some fresh air. Can we come back tomorrow?" Perhaps this trip would take longer than she expected. She'd seen enough for now and just couldn't abide staying in the cottage one more minute.

"Sure." Russell put his hand on her waist and led her back out to the foyer and the front door. "I have a meeting in the morning, but perhaps after that. Unless you want to come alone."

Lexie widened her eyes. Could she come back alone? She steeled herself. Of course she could. She was an adult now, not the little girl who left.

"Russell, you don't need to babysit me or change your schedule for me. Maybe I will come back by myself. I'm a big girl now, you know."

As they moved out onto the veranda, Russell faced her with a wide grin. "You don't have to tell me!"

Lexie's cheeks warmed. She gave him a little shove. "Stop it, Russell!"

He threw back his head and laughed. "All right. But I will have housekeeping get in here early tomorrow and clean the place up. I should've done it anyway, even though you didn't request it."

She didn't argue with him this time. It wouldn't hurt to get rid of the dust. At least she could breathe the next time she entered the house. As Russell turned to lock the door, Lexie gazed at Jekyll River behind the house.

"Let's take a walk in the yard. Do you mind?"

"No, of course not." They strolled around the veranda to the rear of the house that faced the water. Lexie pointed at the bay window.

"That was Grandmother's favorite part of the house. She made Grandfather build the breakfast room so she could look at the river and the marshes across the way."

The veranda ended, and they descended steps into the backyard then walked to the water's edge, startling a heron stalking fish nearby. It squawked its displeasure about being disturbed. Lexie couldn't shake the feeling that she was intruding in a place where she wasn't welcome. Her own family cottage shielded its privacy from her. She turned around and stared at the house. Framed by looming oaks and dripping moss, it held onto years of secrets. Lexie shuddered. What had once been so familiar now appeared mysterious. Why did she think the house looked back at her, telling her to go away and leave it alone?

Movement from the other side of the house caught her eye, and she glanced in that direction. Abner Jones stood in the shade, staring at her.

Chapter 5

Lexie grabbed Russell's arm. "Russell! That man. He's watching us!"

Russell followed her gaze and waved to the man. "Abner! How are you today?"

Flashing a glare at Russell, Lexie gritted her teeth. "What are you doing?"

"I'm speaking to Abner. Don't worry. I won't let him hurt you." He gave her an annoying wink as he motioned for the man to come.

The tall, lanky gardener ambled toward them, his eyes fixed on Lexie. A straw hat covered the top of his gray hair which matched his bushy gray mustache. As he approached, a memory flashed through her mind of herself as a little girl, holding a flower she'd picked off one of the bushes in the yard. The tall man stood over her, pointing his finger and scolding her for taking the flower. "Miss, you shouldn't do that. You go pickin' all the flowers off and they won't be any left in the yard to look at."

She had trembled at the reprimand turning her good intentions into a crime. "But I wanted to give it to my momma and make her happy," she said, with huge tears coursing down her cheeks.

"Your momma can buy all the flowers she wants from the club greenhouse. You just leave my flowers alone."

When the man stopped in front of them, Russell nodded and turned to Lexie.

"Abner, do you remember Miss Alexandra Smithfield?"

Rubbing his chin, the gardener looked her up and down. Lexie stiffened from the perusal. After a few uncomfortable moments, he nodded.

"You was that little girl? You all growed up now."

"She is indeed."

Lexie stifled the urge to kick Russell.

"Yes, that was me, Robert Smithfield's daughter. My grandfather built the cottage."

"Umm hmm. I knowed your grandfather real well. He hired me when I was just a boy."

Judging him to be in his fifties, that meant he'd worked for the family over thirty years.

"I understand you've been taking care of the property for us. That's very nice of you, considering … well, considering the circumstances." Heat rushed to Lexie's face as she stumbled to express herself.

"You mean since you fired me?" Abner Jones drew himself up and crossed his arms. "Hmmph!"

Lexie's stomach churned. "I'm sorry, you see, our accountant didn't think we needed a gardener anymore, especially since we haven't been here for years."

A bony finger pointed in her face. "Let me tell you something, young lady. I had a deal with your grandfather. He hired me to do a job, and he never fired me. So I'm still doing my job!"

Lexie jumped back and Russell stepped between her and Abner. "Abner, settle down. Miss Smithfield had nothing to do with the decision. I believe she was trying to thank you for your commitment."

Lexie peered around Russell to see the gardener's reaction. The man stared at Russell then shook his head. He turned and walked away, muttering to himself.

Russell faced her with a wistful smile. "Sorry, Lexie. Abner's manners are wanting."

Lexie stared after the retreating silhouette then glanced up at Russell. "I feel like such an outsider here. He acts like the house belongs to him and not me. And in a way, maybe it does. After all, he's the one who's stayed to take care of it."

"Abner knows he's not a club member. He's a bit set in his ways, but he's harmless."

"I'm sorry Grandfather isn't here to thank him." Lexie lowered her gaze. "I suppose Mr. Jones thinks a young woman like myself is not to be taken seriously. I'm just in his way."

Russell grabbed her shoulders, peering into her face. "Lexie, this is your cottage. You have every right to do what you wish with it. I just wish … well, you just do what you have to do, and don't worry about Abner, okay?"

"Okay, if you say so." They turned to walk away, but she stopped and faced Russell. "Russell, what do you wish?"

"Oh, I wish things didn't have to change, I guess." He let his arms drop to his side. "But they already have. Your family is one of the few remaining founding families of the club."

"Really? I didn't know that." Lexie recalled the waiter's words that morning. She didn't realize so many of the original members were gone.

They walked back toward the clubhouse while Lexie scanned the area beyond Destiny and the compound's ten-foot deer fence. Primitive woods still inhabited the area beyond—that part of the island which bordered a marsh. Grandfather knew their cottage would be more isolated than the others. It was his way of keeping the club's original intent of having a simple, rustic getaway from the throes of overbuilt civilization like their lives up north. As a child, the woods had always beckoned to her as a place of intrigue and mystery, but now they whispered dark secrets.

As if reading her thoughts, Russell spoke. "Remember when we used to hide in the woods?"

"Of course I do. You and Robert hid in there knowing I'd follow you. Then you'd jump out and scare me half to death!"

Russell chuckled. "We had fun hearing you scream."

Lexie gave his shoulder a shove. "You two were very mean, scaring a little girl like that."

"No harm done. You should've thanked us."

"Thank you, but why on earth?"

"Well, once we scared you, you ran back home. At least you didn't get hurt or in trouble by following us any further."

"Oh really? What kind of trouble would I have gotten into?"

"Oh, I don't know. Maybe you could've been bitten by a snake. Or a spider."

Lexie shivered. Thank God for small favors. "Maybe you're right. There were enough of those on the bike trails."

Russell stopped and turned to her. "Hey! That's a great idea."

"What is?"

"Let's go for a bike ride!"

"Now?"

"Let me check in at the clubhouse first and see if I'm needed. If not, we can go get the bikes. Would you like that?"

A bike ride on the island. What an inviting idea. "Yes, that sounds wonderful."

"Excellent!" Russell rubbed his hands together. "Don't worry. The trails aren't as wild as they used to be. We don't have wild boars running out of the brush anymore."

"Well, that's nice to know. I never did see those, but heard stories."

By now they had reached the Gould gymnasium on the left side of the road. Mr. Gould had built the indoor tennis facility complete with bowling alley before she was born, and her parents and grandparents had been guests there. She shook her head as she considered the huge building.

"Russell, does anyone use the Gould tennis courts anymore?"

"I think Frank's family might, but, for the most part, it's unused."

"What a shame to let it go to waste."

"I agree. But we have the club courts for other members to use. Our climate is mild enough to play on outdoor courts most the year anyway."

As they walked past Villa Marianna, the cottage named after Frank Gould's daughter Marianne, Lexie gazed up at the house's high square tower that overlooked the woods and club area. Once she and young Marianne had played in the tower, pretending to be princesses in a castle waiting for their knights to come rescue them.

"How old is Marianne now?"

Russell shrugged. "She's a teenager, but I'm not certain how old she is. I don't know if they're coming this year or not."

They passed Cherokee Cottage on their left, but Lexie barely noticed, still thinking about Marianne and what she must be like now, ten years older.

"Will you be coming to our church service this Sunday?"

Lexie stopped and looked at Russell. She followed his gaze and realized they were standing in front of Faith Chapel, the small rustic chapel built for club members. An involuntary shudder shook her, and she struggled with a desire to run away.

"No, I don't think so."

Russell cocked his head and studied her face. He seemed to be waiting for an explanation. What could she tell him? That she was afraid of the chapel, the place that haunted her mother? As a child, Lexie had been fascinated by the Gothic style chapel adorned with gargoyles. But her mother believed the ones inside the building, the grotesques, represented the six faces of death, and they had cursed the island and her family. Not that Lexie really believed that nonsense.

So why avoid the place? Had her mother's fears become hers too?

Chapter 6

She was a knockout. He hadn't expected that. He'd never thought that tomboy girl would turn out to be such a beautiful woman. Still feisty, though. It might take a little work for her to see things his way. Maybe the picnic would soften her up.

But those eyes. Those baby blues got his heart racing when she fixed them on him. They were enough to make him offer her the world. Ha. Like he had the world to offer. No, he wasn't one of the lucky ones born with money like all these folks around him. And now, with the economy shaky and the country at war, it wouldn't be long before this place shut down. Then what would he do?

His gaze dropped to his feet. "4F." That's what they called him. Couldn't be drafted with a lame foot. So he wouldn't end up killed like Robert, right? Russell shook his head. No, I'll get to stay behind with all the old men. What a hero.

He checked in at the front desk for his messages. A couple of phone calls and he should be free to take the afternoon off. A picnic on the beach with Lexie Smithfield. They're going on a bike ride! Who'd have thought?

He had one more call to make before he'd send for her.

Lexie plopped down on the bed. Why was she here? Old memories warred with her emotions, making her head spin. Destiny was so different now. Oh, it still looked pretty much the same on the outside, but inside it was lifeless and dead, like the family that occupied its walls.

But someone had been there, and it appeared as if they were looking for something. But what? Surely, anyone would know the family wouldn't leave valuables in a house after all this time.

And what about Russell? He didn't say anything about the telegram. Why had he wanted her to come? He certainly didn't act like someone who would send such an ominous-sounding telegram. Not with his carefree personality. The guy found everything humorous, with that constant smile on his face. The twinkle in his eye reminded her of how he teased her as a child. And he was still doing it! She clenched her teeth, stood up, and went to the wardrobe for her trousers.

As she unzipped her skirt and let it fall to the floor, a smile eased its way across her face. She could just see eyebrows lift at the sight of her in trousers. So what? If Katherine Hepburn could wear them, so could she. She pulled on the flared pants while her thoughts went back to Russell.

Had he always had dimples? She didn't remember him being so attractive. But that's not something you notice when you're twelve years old. And yet, now ... why, if she didn't know him so well, she might think he was good-looking. But she did know him. Or at least she used to know him. After ten years, maybe she really didn't. She'd changed a lot in ten years, and surely, he had too.

He probably had a girlfriend. But if he did, it seemed she would be jealous if he took other women on bike rides. Maybe she would be jealous of *other* women, but not his friend's little sister. There it was again. She had reverted back to her childhood. *Lexie, remember who you are.* Her grandmother used to tell her that. She always wondered what her grandmother meant. She asked once and was told "A Smithfield." Was that good or bad? She wasn't sure.

A tap on the door startled her and made her jump. A folded piece of paper slid under the threshold, stopping at her feet. She reached down, picked it up, and opened it. "Everything's ready. Meet you downstairs."

Lexie smiled and tucked the note into her pocket. She glanced at her reflection in the mirror and grabbed a scarf, folding it to make a headband, put it across her hair, and tied it underneath. That's the best she could do with her unruly curls. It was impossible for her to pin it up in side rolls, the popular style the girls at college wore. She stepped out into the hallway and locked the door behind her, just as the maid from the boat walked out of a room a few doors down. When their eyes met, the maid turned and hurried the opposite way.

"Wait!" Lexie dashed after her. "I need to talk to you."

The woman stopped, her back to Lexie, then turned around.

With her eyes cast down, she spoke in a soft voice. "Yes, miss."

"Are you the only housemaid on this hall?" Lexie tried to see the woman's expression.

"Mostly, but sometimes there's another maid. Is there a problem?"

Lexie studied the woman who seemed too meek to look up. "I'm not sure. While I was at breakfast this morning, my things were rearranged. Did you do that?"

"I'm sorry, ma'am, if the room's not to your liking. I'll try to do better next time."

"All right, well, thank you." The woman turned to go, but Lexie continued. "Aren't you the woman with the pretty little girl? Didn't we ride over together from Brunswick?"

The woman nodded. "Yes'm."

Lexie looked up and down the hallway. "Where is your little girl now?"

"She's over at the schoolhouse with the other children."

"Oh, of course. Well, she's a very pretty and sweet girl."

"Thank you, ma'am."

"You're welcome. Well, I won't keep you from your duties. Good day."

The woman nodded and walked away while Lexie tried not to stare after her. Something about her stirred a familiar chord. Had she worked there when Lexie came with her family? She'd ask Russell. There were several things they needed to discuss.

Russell! He was waiting for her. She raced down the stairs and spied him waiting outside, smoking a cigarette. As she approached, he dropped it and crushed it underfoot. Lexie didn't try to hide her dislike of the habit.

"I didn't know you smoked."

"Yes, afraid I've developed the habit. I take it you don't approve."

"No, I don't. I hate the smell and think it's foolish for people to put a burning object in their mouths and breathe the smoke. It can't be good for you."

Russell laughed aloud. "Well, if you put it that way, it does sound pretty foolish. Tell you what, I promise I won't smoke around you. Okay?"

She opened her mouth to tell him it wasn't a healthy habit away from her either, but she stopped herself. What business was it of hers what he did anyway?

Russell rested one elbow in the opposite hand, propping his chin on his knuckles as he eyed her up and down, an amused look on his face.

"What?" She set her hands on her hips and cocked her head. "Oh. It's the pants. I suppose the other club members don't wear them."

He shook his head. "Well, not the women." He chuckled. "I must say I'm not surprised, but I can't wait to hear the chatter."

"Well, you just enjoy it. I don't care to listen. Besides, plenty of women wear pants, especially the movie stars."

"Hate to tell you, but this isn't Hollywood. These members are trying to hang on to tradition as long as they can."

Lexie shrugged. "So I'm different. Women my age aren't as bound to tradition as they used to be."

"Lexie, dear, I don't think you've ever been bound by tradition."

Lexie rolled her eyes.

"Shall we go get our bikes?" Russell lifted a covered basket from the chair beside him. "Chef's got a nice meal prepared for us."

They walked around the corner of the building to the bike shop where two bikes were set out for them. Hers had a wire carrier in front, so he placed the picnic basket in it.

Russell motioned with his hand. "You go first, I'll follow."

"I'm not sure I remember the path."

"Just follow the signs to the bike trails and the beach."

Lexie took off, a bit self-conscious with Russell watching her. Soon though, she found a sign marking the Rockefeller Bicycle Path and turned off the main road through the woods. The temperature dropped as they entered the shade. Lexie pedaled all the harder, whether to warm up or to get beyond the sight of curious onlookers, she wasn't sure. Dense palmettoes filled in the space below the moss-hung oaks like a barricade to keep people from straying off the path. Above, the tree limbs laced together to form a canopy that closed out the sunlight. One wouldn't know the day was sunny outside the boundaries of the woods.

"Hey! What's your hurry?" Russell called out from behind. "I didn't know this was a race."

"What's the matter, Russell? You can't keep up?" Lexie turned her head so her voice carried his direction.

Russell's laughter sailed through the trees. "Still competing with the boys, huh?"

Lexie laughed over her shoulder. "And still winning!"

She sped on, losing him on the winding trail. Was he really that slow, or was she that fast? No matter. The exercise exhilarated her, and she embraced the freedom of the ride. She became a little girl again, riding with abandon, and no one could catch her.

A noise to her right drew her attention. Russell said there were no more boars, but something moved through the woods. Her heart pounded at the prospect of encountering a wild animal. She strained to see, taking her eyes from the path.

The bike thudded against an object, sending her flying. She screamed as she fell over, landing hard on the ground. Almost at once, Russell was beside her.

"Lexie! Are you hurt?"

She groaned from the ache in her side where she'd fallen on a large pine cone. Russell helped her sit up.

"What happened?" She looked around and saw her bicycle lying beside the path, the tire frame bent.

"Looks like you ran into that tree lying across the trail."

Lexie looked back and saw the young pine tree. Too bad she hadn't seen it in time to stop.

"I heard something. Over there." She pointed. "I tried to see what it was."

Russell scanned the forest. "I'm sorry, Lexie. We check the trails every day to make sure there's nothing like this in the way. I don't know how we didn't find this. There hasn't been enough wind lately to blow anything down."

"It's okay. I'll live. Can you help me up?"

"Are you sure?" Russell nodded toward the bike. "Looks like that's out of commission for awhile. Here. Ride mine and I'll walk."

He extended his hand and helped her up. She winced as she brushed off her clothes. There'd be some bruises for sure. "How much farther to the beach?"

"Not much." He leaned down, picked up the picnic basket, and gave her a rueful smile. "Well, our food's saved. Thank goodness, the latch held."

Of course, he found a way to joke about the situation. "I believe I'd rather walk the rest of the way too." Her body trembled from the fall, and she wasn't too eager to get back on a bike.

"You sure you're okay? Do you want to go to the infirmary and have a doctor check you out?"

"No. I'm fine. I can carry the basket." He shrugged and handed her the picnic hamper, then positioned himself between her and his bike.

Pointing toward the damaged bicycle, he said, "We'll leave that one here and send for it later."

Lexie drew herself up, inhaled a deep breath, and began to move alongside him, feeling her injuries with each step. She stole another glance over her shoulder at the tree across the trail, following it to its base in the woods. As far as she could tell, that tree didn't just fall, it had been cut down.

Chapter 7

$\mathcal{A}$ cool ocean breeze whipped Lexie's cheeks as she sat on the edge of a red-and-white checkered tablecloth spread out on the beach. She hugged her knees and closed her eyes, lifting her face to the sun's warmth, inhaling the salty air.

"These grapes are delicious! Here, try some." Russell stretched out his arm with a bunch of the red fruit.

She glanced at his hand and accepted the grapes, plucking one and popping it into her mouth. The burst of fresh fruit awakened her taste buds with its sweetness. A perfect setting with a handsome man, but this wasn't just any man. It was just Russell. Besides, she couldn't relax. There were too many questions invading her mind for it to be at peace. Who had ransacked the secretary in the cottage? Rummaged through her things in her room? And now the bike accident. Were these things connected?

"Russell, something happened in my room earlier today. I've been meaning to tell you about it."

The roar of the waves drowned out her voice, and Russell scooted closer on the tablecloth, pointing to his ear indicating he couldn't hear her. Her heart fluttered as he neared. She repeated her statement, and he raised his eyebrows.

"What happened, Lexie?"

"When I returned from breakfast, my things had been disturbed, both on top of the dresser and in the drawers."

"Was anything missing? "

"Not that I know of. I'm wearing the only valuables I brought."

He drew back and looked her over, a sly grin on his face.

"Seriously, Russell! Someone was in my room and handled my belongings!"

His features sobered. "My staff has been with us quite a while and pride themselves on their efficiency. These people are happy to have jobs. Maybe we have someone new. I'll check. Sorry about that, Lexie."

"I did speak to a maid in the hallway when I left the room."

"And?"

"She just apologized that the room wasn't satisfactory. She didn't really confess to doing it herself—said another maid could have done it."

"Hmmm. What did she look like?"

"About my height, average, thin with brown hair."

"Well, that describes a lot of people. Can you tell me anything else about her?"

"She looks like she used to be pretty when she was younger, but her face appears tired, like she's had her share of troubles. Of course, they all wear the same black dress with a white apron and cap." What was it that stood out? Her eyes. "You know her eyes were quite noticeable, that is, what I saw of them. She kept her head down like she was afraid to look at me. I guess you'd call them 'hazel.'"

Russell rubbed his chin and nodded. "Sounds like Stella."

Stella. That name rang a bell. "Has she been here long?"

"Ever since she was a teenager. Like most of our employees, she's been here a long time. That's why it doesn't make sense for her to bother your personal belongings. She knows better."

"Well, someone did. I didn't dream this up."

That smug grin again. "I never said you did, Lexie." He patted her hand. "I'll speak to housekeeping about it."

"Thank you. You know, Russell, I feel like I'm not welcome here."

He raised an eyebrow. "What do you mean? Of course you are."

"No, really. I've gotten the strangest reactions from people."

"You're talking about Abner, aren't you? Well, he's just a strange person."

Lexie stretched out her legs, wincing with the movement. She leaned over and massaged her calf.

"Your leg hurts? Would you like me to look at it?"

He gave her a little wink. She tried to ignore the flip-flop in her chest.

"No, thank you. It'll be all right. It's just sore, that's all." She looked up at him. "It's not just Abner. That maid—Stella—she seemed afraid to look at me, like she wanted to avoid me."

He laughed, his dimple deepening. "Probably just shy."

"Maybe." Remembering the boat captain, she said, "And that fellow that drove the club launch. He was very unfriendly—almost rude."

"Jack? He's Stella's husband. I admit he's kind of gruff. He's always had a chip on his shoulder."

"Well, it just seems to me that people aren't as friendly as they used to be." She brushed sand off her hands. "It doesn't matter. I won't be here long anyway."

"You keep saying that. So you came just to see the cottage?"

Lexie jerked her head toward him. "Well, yes. Isn't that what your telegram was about?"

He cocked his head. "My telegram? What telegram?"

"The one you sent me."

Russell leaned close to her face, his expression dead serious for a change. "Lexie, I didn't send you a telegram."

Chapter 8

$\mathcal{L}$exie drew back and stared at Russell, her mouth agape. She stammered for words.

"B … but you signed it."

"Did you say it was a telegram?"

"Yes."

"So I couldn't have signed it."

She shook her head. "But it had your name on it."

Russell laid his hand over hers. "Lexie, I promise you, I didn't send you a telegram."

She jerked her hand away. "Really? So how did you know I was coming? Why did you meet me at the dock when I arrived?"

"Lexie. It's my job to know which members are coming to the island. I review the reservations every day and discuss with the staff what preparations need to be made. So, when I saw you'd made a reservation for the twentieth of January, I knew you'd be coming on the club launch. That's why I was at the dock looking for you."

He must be telling the truth. Yet, someone had sent her a telegram and used his name.

"I don't understand. If it wasn't you, who was it? Why would someone pretend to be you?"

"Because you might not respond to an invitation from them? I don't know—what did the telegram say?"

"Destiny needs you. Please come right away."

"Destiny needs you?" Russell shook his head, his lips curving upward. "Rather cryptic."

Lexie frowned. "Why must you find everything so humorous? Here I am, in a place I never intended to be because I believed someone I knew wanted me to come!"

Russell sobered, tenderness softening his eyes. "Okay. Okay. I didn't mean to joke. I'm sorry, Lexie. The whole situation is just bizarre."

She blew out a breath and turned away from him, facing the sapphire water of the Atlantic. Why on earth was she here?

"So, if you didn't want me to come, I don't see why I need to stay. I've seen the house and know its condition. I'll just have our accountant draw up the papers to sell it."

Russell laid his hand on her arm as if to hold her in place. "Must you leave so soon? You're already here, so take a few days to relax."

"Ha! Relax, he says. That fall back there wasn't very relaxing."

"Let me make it up to you. Surely I can do something to make your time here more enjoyable. Or is there something back in New York you must return to? Or someone?" The last comment was accompanied by a wistful expression.

Lexie shook her head. No one waited for her back home, other than the staff at the hospital. She had taken a leave of absence, but expected to be back by the end of the month.

"I can afford a few more days here, if necessary."

"Necessary? All right then, I declare your enjoyment necessary to your health. But don't you want to stay to find out who sent the telegram?"

She did, but her gut feelings warned her to be careful. Still, she was curious about the strange events that had occurred since her arrival. The faces of people she had encountered paraded through her mind. Did one of them send the telegram? Based on the less than friendly reception she received, none of them seemed to want her here.

Cold water lapped her feet and she jumped, watching the stealthy wave recede back to the ocean.

"Tide's coming in." Russell stood and stretched, then leaned over to pull their things away from the encroaching water.

The wind picked up, sending a rush of cold air through Lexie's thin sweater. She hugged herself, rubbing her arms to get warm. "I think it's time to go," she said.

Russell glanced at her, nodded, and picked up the basket. Lexie took the tablecloth and shook the sand from it before folding it and placing it back in the basket. She brushed off her hands when she finished and turned to leave. Russell lifted the bike and joined her.

"Want to ride back?" He leaned the bike toward her.

She shook her head. "No, thank you."

"It's a long walk back."

Lexie's bruised leg throbbed, telling her the long walk would be painful.

"Well, we can't both ride the bike."

"Why not?"

"What?"

"Sure. You sit on the handlebars and I'll pedal. Remember when we used to race like that, with you sitting on Robert's handlebars?"

"But I was just a girl and much smaller."

"Oh, come on. Be a sport."

If there was one thing Lexie couldn't do, it was refuse a challenge.

"Promise me you won't run into any trees or anything."

Russell crossed his heart with his fingers then raised his hand as a pledge.

"I'll be very careful with you, m'dear. We'll take another path back."

"Well, okay. Hold the bike steady." Russell slipped the handle of the picnic basket over the handlebars and straddled the bike, bracing it while Lexie climbed up, using his shoulder for support.

"You can lean back on me if you'd be more comfortable."

The invitation was attractive, but she preferred to sit up and balance with her hands beside her on the handlebars.

"Okay, I'm ready."

"Keep those pants away from the spokes." Russell started pedaling over the hard-packed sand, and they were on their way.

"Good thing I wore pants, isn't it?" She spoke over her shoulder.

"Ha!" Russell laughed. "You didn't plan this, did you?"

"Of course I did. I planned to fall off the bike."

Russell might find the situation funny, but she didn't. What if someone did plan for her to fall? Maybe the tree was supposed to fall on her instead of just trip her. *Stop it!* She had to quit letting her imagination run wild. Accidents did happen, and she had no reason to believe someone was trying to hurt her. She gazed out at the ocean to their right. On the other side of this ocean, a war was being fought. There were more important things than falling off a bike. She noticed Russell hadn't turned off the hard-packed sandy beach yet.

"Russell, where is the other path?"

"Thought we'd go down to Driftwood Point then take the beach road back."

She started to protest but realized she had no place else to go, and no hurry to get there. They rode past part of the golf course that ran near the beach, but she didn't see any golfers out. She and Russell headed north for a while until the shore of Saint Simons Island came into view.

"Let's take a little break, stretch our legs." Russell stopped the bike and steadied it so she could climb down. "There's the lighthouse." He pointed across the water to the tall structure.

"Saint Simons. We used to go over there in the Vanderbilt yacht. Does a lighthouse keeper still live there? I heard some of the lighthouses are automatic now."

"Far as I know, there's still a keeper, but he's part of the Coast Guard. And it's electric. The keeper doesn't have to use kerosene to light it anymore. Just flip a switch." Russell mimicked the process with his finger.

"That must make his job easier. I always thought it would be such a lonely job."

"Could be, but he has the ghosts to keep him company."

Lexie shoved him. "Stop it. You don't believe that nonsense, do you?"

"Hey! You hurt me." He acted wounded. "I didn't make up those stories. There's supposed to be the ghost of the light keeper who got killed in a duel."

Lexie crossed her arms, staring at the tower across the water. "I remember that story. I might have even believed it when I was a child. But I don't believe those things anymore. Everything has an explanation." Just like the so-called ghosts at Destiny.

"Yeah, yeah. I don't believe in that stuff either."

"So I wonder if the light keeper gets bored if he doesn't have as much work to do now."

"Don't bet on it. He's part of the military now, so he has to protect our country from the enemy."

Lexie raised her eyebrows and looked up at him. "Enemy? Here?"

"Rumor has it the Germans have submarines off our coast. Those guys up there in the lighthouses are looking out for them."

"Surely the Germans wouldn't come this close to our shore!"

"I hope not, but I hear they've been spotted up north not far out."

"North? How far north?" Lexie pointed in that direction.

"From Cape Hatteras, North Carolina up to New York."

Lexie's heart trembled. Even though North Carolina was several hundred miles north, it was too close if German submarines had been seen there. She tossed her head. "Well, I just don't believe in rumors. And I don't believe they'd get that close to us here."

"Never can be too sure about those Nazis. Ghosts may not be real, but Nazis are."

Lexie was no longer comfortable standing on the beach. She shivered from the cold. Or was it from the threat of Nazis nearby?

"Can we go now? I've had enough of the beach today."

Russell chuckled, then arched an eyebrow. "Afraid the Germans will see you here on the beach?" His gaze scanned the ocean. "I don't see any out there. Don't worry, I'll protect you," he said with a wink.

"Honestly, Russell. I don't know when to believe you. I can't tell when you're joking and when you're serious. Did you just make that whole story up about German submarines?"

He sobered his expression. "No, Lexie, I did not make it up. I have friends in the Coast Guard that told me about them."

"So why hasn't it been in the news?" Lexie faced him, her hands on her hips.

Russell spread his hands. "He said the government doesn't want people to panic, much less tip off Hitler that he's giving us any room for concern."

"So the Coast Guard will get rid of them, won't they? At least we don't have to worry about them being on our soil."

Russell didn't answer as he continued gazing out at sea. The faraway look in his eye was unsettling, as was his change to a more serious mood. As she studied him, she had the impression she was seeing a different person, not the happy-go-lucky guy she'd spent the afternoon with.

"Russell?"

He faced her, a smile emerging. "Sorry, Lexie. Did you ask me something?"

She shook her head. "It wasn't important."

"Well, shall we continue our ride?"

"Sure. You up to it?" Lexie cocked her head at him.

"Ha! I barely noticed you were there!"

He held the bicycle while she climbed back on. As they left the beach and turned onto the beach road, the image of the lighthouse planted itself in her mind. She envisioned the keeper standing in the tower, scanning the horizon with his telescope, looking for submarines. At least he could spot the dangers out there and knew who his enemies were. In her life, though, it wasn't so easy.

She didn't know who her enemies were or even why she had any. Why would someone want her to come to the island? Why not approach her directly?

Whoever was behind this charade would be found out. She'd make sure of it, even if she had to stay long enough to uncover the truth herself.

Chapter 9

$\mathcal{R}$ussell watched the golden curls in front of him dance in the wind as he pedaled the bike. A telegram, huh? So that's what prompted her to show up on the island again. Wonder who sent it? Could it be Abner? The guy was pretty protective of the place. No. Abner wasn't the type to be mysterious. He was pretty upfront about things and didn't bother keeping his feelings to himself.

Whoever it was, though, Russell wanted to pat them on the back. He was glad she'd come so he could change her plans to sell Destiny before it was too late. He just needed to keep her here longer–one job he didn't mind.

Boy, was she adorable. When she stepped out in those flowing pants with that scarf tied around her goldilocks, he almost swallowed his cigarette. She had no idea how great she looked, and he didn't think she even cared. She was different—always had been. Not like the prima donnas that demanded attention. She got attention without even trying.

Russell steered the bike down the beach road toward the clubhouse passing other guests who laughed and pointed at the two of them. Well, this was one way to get attention. He hadn't planned the day to turn out quite like this, but he wasn't complaining. It wasn't every day he had the privilege of riding a beautiful woman around on his handlebars. He smiled and nodded at the curious onlookers. Wouldn't tongues wag tonight!

Speaking of tonight, maybe he could coax her into watching a movie. Wonder what they were showing? He hoped she wouldn't get tired of him, but it wouldn't surprise him if she did. What else did she have to do, though? Of course, it wouldn't take long for the other club members to invite her to their social events. The pretty new girl on the island would provide a welcome change to their groups. Floyd and his mother were already attempting to gain her attention. What red-blooded male wouldn't?

Soon as they got back, he would arrange for the cottage to get cleaned up. Maybe once she saw it in better shape, she'd reconsider her intentions. He shouldn't be too pushy though. It had to be her idea, not his.

They pulled up in front of the clubhouse, and he helped her down while onlookers watched, apparently amused at the sight of them.

"Feel like a movie tonight?" He offered her his most charming smile.

"A movie? There's a theater here?"

"Down at the tea house. We get the latest movie reels, you know, so maybe you haven't seen it already. I'll have to check and see what's playing."

"I doubt I've seen it, since I haven't seen any movies for a while. But I don't think so tonight, Russell. I'm pretty tired."

"From all this exercise?" He teased her, loving the reaction she gave him. Some things didn't change.

She frowned and pouted her lips. "No, maybe it's just the company."

"Ouch! Okay, okay. We can catch it tomorrow maybe."

"I'm going back to the cottage tomorrow, remember?" Her hands perched on her hips.

"I remember. I'm sending some people over to clean it before you go, so wait until after lunch, please."

"All right. I'll catch up on my reading in the morning."

She turned and walked up the stairs, favoring her right leg. She must've whacked it good when she fell.

"Sure you don't want to go to the infirmary and have that leg checked?"

"I'm sure. After a hot bath, it'll be better."

"I'll see you tomorrow." Russell straddled the bike, ready to ride it back to the bike shop. "I'll look for you in the dining room at lunch."

Lexie relaxed in the tub, letting the warm water massage her soreness, thankful one of the rooms with a private bath had been available. She studied the lump on her leg. That would be purple tomorrow, for sure. She reached out and touched it, wincing when her fingers felt the tender skin. Her side was sore too. How could she have been so careless? She replayed the accident in her mind. If Russell hadn't called to her, she wouldn't have turned her head and she would have seen the tree in time to stop. If Russell hadn't distracted her … he couldn't possibly have known about the tree, could he? She shook her head. What a ludicrous thought. Why would Russell want her to have an accident? She must put those suspicious ideas out of her mind and quit suspecting everyone she met.

A noise came from the adjoining room. She sat upright, her heart thumping. Did she hear the door open? She held her breath and hoped the pounding of her heart wouldn't be heard as she listened for another sound. A floorboard creaked, and she grabbed the towel lying on the edge of the tub. Was someone in her room again?

Her eyes wide, she glanced to the vanity where the delicate gold necklace lay. There weren't many things she owned that were valuable, but the gift from her father was special. It was a daily reminder of the affection they had for each other, and all she really had left of his love. But it was private, so she wore it tucked inside her clothes against her heart.

"Hello?" Lexie called out. "Anyone there?" Perhaps a maid would answer. On the other hand, a burglar may not.

She waited a few, painfully slow seconds, then called out again. "Hello?"

No answer. The water had chilled in the tub, and she shivered. Time to get out and face whoever it was. She stood and wrapped the towel around her. A knock sounded on the door from the hallway and she jumped. Her heart thumping in her ears, she stepped out of the tub. She tiptoed to the edge of the bathroom, snatching her bathrobe off the hook. She peeked outside the doorway, half-expecting to see another face looking back.

Another knock sounded at the door. After surveying the room and seeing no one else there, she exhaled. Throwing on her bathrobe, she shouted at the door.

"Who is it?"

"Room Service, ma'am."

Of course. She'd forgotten she ordered it. That must have been the noise she heard—someone at the door, not in her room. Goodness, she was jumpy.

"Please leave it outside the door."

"Yes, ma'am." Lexie noticed a hint of sadness in the waiter's tone at losing his tip.

She paused, giving him time to leave, then crossed the room, still searching for a sign of anything unusual. Opening the door, she glanced each way to make sure no one was in the hall, picked up the tray, and brought it in. The smell of roast duck, a house specialty, awakened her hunger as she placed the tray on the small table in her room.

One last glimpse around the room and she exhaled a sigh of relief. Assured she was alone, she bowed her head to bless her meal. As she recited her usual blessing, the irony struck her. Did she really believe God heard her rote prayer? If he did, would he listen to anything else she asked? She hoped he wasn't offended by her lack of church attendance. Even though she'd attended chapel at college with her classmates, she hadn't been in church since she graduated a year ago.

And now that she was here, he certainly didn't expect her to attend the island chapel. If he knew all things, then he'd know why she couldn't go. But if he really knew everything, there were a lot of questions she wished he'd answer.

For instance, who sent the telegram and why. Would they reveal themselves before she left? She hoped the truth wasn't as frightening as not knowing.

As she lifted a bite to her mouth, her eyes were distracted by a piece of paper poking out from beneath her plate. She lowered her fork to her plate and pulled the folded sheet out. Now what? Russell could certainly be persistent.

But when she unfolded it, she stared at the message. *We'd appreciate the favor of your company for breakfast tomorrow. See you at 9:00 in the main dining room.* This note was not signed by Russell though. It was signed by Floyd Appleton.

Chapter 10

Lexie steeled herself as she entered the dining room. The last thing she wanted to do was spend time with Floyd and his mother, but curiosity forced her to join them. Maybe they were the ones who sent the telegram, and they were ready to tell her why. Of course, it wasn't signed by them, and it was a strange thing to do, but Floyd and his mother were a bit on the strange side after all.

She spotted them near one of the windows where Mrs. Appleton waved with enthusiasm. As Lexie approached, Floyd stood and pulled out a chair for her.

"I'm so glad you could join us," Mrs. Appleton said, beaming like the Cheshire Cat.

"Thank you for inviting me."

"You look lovely, dear. Doesn't she, Floyd?" Mrs. Appleton bobbed her head and Floyd nodded.

"Yes, indeed. Lovely."

Lexie smiled, wondering if Floyd had an original thought.

"I truly believe young ladies look much nicer in skirts." The emphasis on the last word revealed the woman's knowledge of Lexie's pants the previous day. Fortunately for her, Lexie's pants were being cleaned after yesterday's spill. "Don't you agree, Floyd?"

Floyd nodded. What else would a puppet do?

"So you saw the cottage. How terrible that it's been neglected so long."

"Yes, I agree. But I was pleasantly surprised that the grounds looked so nice."

"Oh, you're right about that. It's a good thing your family kept the gardener."

Lexie nodded, unwilling to offer any explanation.

"You *are* planning to restore the cottage to its former beauty, of course."

Lexie hoped she could get the cottage repaired, but wasn't sure she'd have to in order to sell the house. Anyone who bought it would likely want to change it to suit themselves. She struggled with an answer that would satisfy the woman, but the waiter arrived to take their order and the conversation paused.

Eager to change the subject when the waiter left, Lexie faced Floyd and ventured a dialogue with him.

"What kind of business are you in, Floyd?"

"The family business—our chain of laundries, of course."

"Of course." Lexie would have been surprised if he said anything else.

Mrs. Appleton beamed her pleasure. "Floyd's doing a wonderful job running the cleaners."

Lexie was grateful when their food arrived and the conversation took a backseat to the meal. She had hoped to learn something from her time with the Appletons, but so far, it had been a lost cause. She would have enjoyed herself more back in her room reading a book. Maybe she could draw them out with a few more questions.

"I was surprised to see your note when I received my room service last night. How did you know I was eating in my room?" Lexie looked from Floyd to his mother for a hint of conspiracy.

"When we didn't see you at dinner, we inquired of the hostess, and she said you were dining in. Floyd asked them to put a note on your tray."

So much for revelation. She'd give it another try.

"Isn't it amazing that you recognized me after all this time? You know it's been ten years since I've been here." Once again, she studied their faces.

"It took me a while, but you really don't look all that different than you did when you were a child. Pretty as ever!" Mrs. Appleton affirmed with a nod.

So it wasn't them. They weren't likely candidates after all.

"Well, if you'll excuse me, I need to take care of some things." Lexie placed her napkin on the table and began to push her chair away.

To her surprise, Floyd leaped to his feet to help her. "May I escort you out?"

She nodded as he extended his hand for her to walk ahead. Once they stepped outside the dining room, he came alongside her.

"I wanted to ask you something privately."

She raised her eyebrows. "Yes?"

"Are you planning to sell Destiny or keep it?"

His directness caught her off-guard. "I plan to sell it."

"Do you mind if I ask why?"

Yes, she did mind, but she'd try to be polite. "As you know, I'm the only one left in my family, and I have no use for it."

"What if you marry and want your family to have a place to go for vacation?"

He was getting far too personal for her comfort. She bit her tongue to keep from telling him to mind his own business.

"I don't see that as a prospect in the foreseeable future."

"I see." He rubbed his pointed chin.

"When do you think you'll sell it?"

"Floyd, why are you so interested in what I do with Destiny?"

"Hmmm. It's crossed our … I mean, my mind that the cottage might be a good investment."

"So you're interested in purchasing it?" Why didn't he just come out and say so? "I'll inform my accountant, and he can contact you directly."

Floyd held up both hands to signal stop. "No, no." A sheepish grin crept onto his face. "I was thinking of another arrangement actually. We are both single, after all."

Lexie's stomach flipped, and her mouth gaped. He was actually talking about marrying her! If the idea weren't so repulsive, it'd be hilarious.

"Floyd Appleton!" She gave him a playful jab. "You're kidding me! You had me going there for a minute!"

"But … but, actually, Alexandra, I wasn't, I mean…"

"Ha-ha!" Lexie acted as if he'd just told a great joke. "Well, I'll think about it, Floyd! See you later!" Lexie hurried away, leaving poor Floyd still trying to explain himself. His mother had surely put him up to the task. She wouldn't be too happy with the response.

Lexie glanced out the window as she turned to go up the stairs. At the edge of the drive, she noticed a man and woman who appeared to be having a disagreement, based on the flailing of arms. She squinted to make out their faces, sensing something familiar about the couple. Recognition hit her as she realized it was the boat captain and the maid, the one Russell called Stella. While she watched, they parted company and the man stormed off toward the boathouse. It appeared that their marriage wasn't a happy one.

After a leisurely morning of reading, Lexie descended the stairs to meet Russell. She couldn't wait to tell him about her conversation with Floyd that morning. He'd get a good laugh out of that story. As she passed the front desk, the clerk called out to her.

"Miss Smithfield! I have a message for you."

Lexie paused, turned back to the desk, and took the envelope the clerk handed out to her. Surely it wasn't another invitation from Floyd. She couldn't tolerate spending more time with him or his mother. She opened the sealed envelope and pulled out a note.

Lexie, I have a meeting this afternoon I must attend. Sorry, I won't be able to go with you to the cottage. I've asked the maids to leave the house open for you though. Movie tonight? Russell.

Her heart sagged at the news. She sighed and shrugged her shoulders. Oh well. She didn't need his company anyway. Plus, now that the house had been cleaned, it would look much better. She started to the dining room for some lunch but changed her mind. If Floyd and his mother were in there, how would she avoid them? She wasn't that hungry anyway. She might as well go to the cottage now instead.

"Looks like we're going to have some rain."

Startled by the clerk's voice, Lexie glanced up to look out the window. The overcast sky appeared to grow darker by the minute.

"It does, doesn't it?"

"Ma'am, if you're going out, you better get your coat and umbrella. I 'spect it'll be getting colder too."

She nodded. "Thank you, I believe I will." So much for her plans—a nice, sunny afternoon stroll chatting with Russell … No. Much as she enjoyed his company, well, most of the time, soon she'd leave and head back to New York. No need to get more familiar. She had to admit, though, he was a nice distraction with his incorrigible sense of humor. Plus, it would be nice to have him along when she went back to the cottage. Regardless, he wasn't available and she was just procrastinating.

By the time she returned to the lobby wearing her coat, the rain blew in sheets across the lawn. Maybe she wouldn't walk after all. Outside under the portico, she approached the concierge. The gentleman nodded a greeting.

"Do you need a ride somewhere, ma'am?"

"Yes, please. I'd like to go to Destiny Cottage."

The man raised his eyebrows and looked her up and down. "Destiny, ma'am? I didn't know anyone was there."

"No one is, at least, no one is staying there. I'm Alexandra Smithfield. The cottage belonged to my family." Why didn't she just say it belonged to her? For some reason, it sounded more believable that it belonged to her family.

"Oh, excuse me, Miss Smithfield. I didn't recognize you."

Lexie gave a polite smile. "That makes us even. I don't recognize you, either."

The man's face turned scarlet. "William Sutton, ma'am. At your service." He gave a slight bow.

"Nice to meet you, Mr. Sutton." She glanced over at a black sedan parked nearby. "Is that car available?"

"Oh, yes ma'am! I'll drive you myself." He hurried to grab his umbrella before heading to the car and opening the back door for her. Then he ran around to the other side and got into the driver's seat. Starting the car, he shot her a glance in the rearview mirror. "Have you been here long, ma'am? I'm sorry. I didn't know you were here."

"Not long. Got in the night before last."

"I was off yesterday, so that explains it. You're staying at the clubhouse, ma'am?"

"Yes, I am."

He faced the road staring through the rain pelting the windshield, stealing an occasional glance at the mirror.

"Will you be staying with us all season?"

"No. My business here is brief." She had no desire to share her plans with this man.

As he pulled into the driveway of the house, Lexie peered out. *Hello Destiny. I'm back.* Would the house welcome her back?

Mr. Sullivan drove under the porte cochere and stopped in front of the steps, got out, and opened her door.

"Good thing you have this cover so you won't get wet." He extended his hand and helped her out. "Would you like me to wait for you, ma'am?"

"No, thank you. I don't know how long I'll be."

A low rumble shook the ground.

Mr. Sullivan gazed out at the rain. "Thunder. Most winter storms don't have thunder."

Lexie climbed the steps to the front door then looked back at the man. "Thank you, Mr. Sullivan."

"Should I come back later, say an hour or so?"

"No, that won't be necessary. I can walk back when I'm finished here." She lifted her umbrella to show him. "Perhaps the storm will stop before long."

Mr. Sullivan glanced back at the rain. "Doubt it. Those black clouds are coming this way. You be careful, ma'am." He tipped his hat and climbed back into the car.

As she watched the car leave, the sky lit up briefly, enough to show the man's face looking back at her. Seconds later, a loud boom followed, shaking the porch and rattling the windows. The gusty wind blew the rain sideways, invading the porch. A shiver raced down her spine. She needed to get out of the weather. She turned the doorknob, found it unlocked as Russell said in his note, and stepped inside.

Chapter 11

The smell of pine cleaner hit her first, masking the mustiness to some degree. A swift scan of the room assured her the maids had tried to restore some semblance of life to the vacant house. The covers had been removed from the furniture, revealing the familiar, but faded upholstery. The desk had been cleaned as well, with the damaged pieces stacked beside it. She shook her head, her stomach tightening with anger. What a shame that someone would damage such a lovely piece of furniture and her family's heirloom.

She moved past the sitting room to the dining room. Nothing amiss here. Nothing besides the aging wallpaper. Lightning flashed and rain blew against the house. Mr. Sullivan's prediction appeared to be correct about the storm. It might not end for some time. At least she was dry. Somewhere she heard dripping. There must be a leak upstairs. She entered the back wing off the dining room into the kitchen and pantry area.

Once a bustling hub of activity when the cook prepared breakfast for the whole family—empty and silent now. She could see the staff running around to get things ready. Breakfast was the one meal the family always ate in the cottage. Grandfather insisted they start their day together before they joined in any club activities. The only other time they used the kitchen was tea time. Often, Mother and Grandmother had guests for tea. Other times they took tea at the clubhouse as they did their other meals.

Lexie felt an occasional rush of cold air when a strong gust of wind whooshed against the house. A tapping noise accompanied each drafty breeze. What was that? She froze, scanning the room. Her gaze landed on the partially-open back door of the kitchen, which slapped the door frame in time with the wind. As she crossed the room to pull it closed, she stepped over puddles of water that had accumulated from the windblown rain. The maids should have been more careful.

After she closed the door tight, she turned around and walked back toward the dining room, passing the pantry door on one side and the door to the dumbwaiter on the other. So many memories that dumbwaiter held. She couldn't resist pulling up the sliding door to reveal the metal cage that had been used to transport the family luggage to the second floor. Plus a few playful children on occasion. The metal door creaked as she struggled to push it open, as if complaining of being disturbed after years of disuse. Lexie leaned in and looked around, tempted to climb in again. But it wouldn't be fun anymore.

Sighing, she forced the screeching door to close, turned, and passed back through the living areas, this time turning right into the hallway. She stood in front of the stairs, willing herself to go up. Somewhere in the house, the floor creaked. A shiver tingled her skin with the sense of being watched. Was someone else in the house? She stood motionless, waiting for another sound, but all she heard was the storm outside and the drip of water. She glanced up the stairs and gripped the bannister, convincing herself to take a step. It was her house and her responsibility to take care of it. She must find the leak and try to keep any more water from getting in. Perhaps the maids left a window open.

The boards groaned with each step as she climbed the stairs. A rueful smile worked its way across her face, remembering when those steps got her in trouble. Sounding like an alarm in her parents' room, the creaky steps made it impossible for her to sneak downstairs at night when she was supposed to be asleep. She'd resorted to climbing out her window instead, and could have been killed the day she fell. Thankfully, she'd fallen in a bed of pine needles that kept her from getting hurt. Grandmother said the angels stayed busy watching out for her. Were they still around, or was their protection limited to childhood?

She reached the landing at the top of the stairs and looked around. Lightning flashed, brightening the house for a few seconds. But the afternoon storm enveloped the house in premature darkness, making it difficult for her to see. Lexie groped the wall for a light switch hoping, by some chance, the electricity was on. But, of course, the light didn't come on. Too bad the house didn't still have the original gaslights. Sometimes progress wasn't an advantage.

Shadows danced along the walls like a ghostly ballet. The wind moaned in tune to the dancers' movements while tree limbs scraped the side of the house in rhythm. Lexie yelped when the house shuddered with the next crash of thunder. And to think, she used to like thunderstorms. But she'd never been alone in this empty, lifeless house during one before now.

Lexie fumbled her way through the dim light as she moved from room to room along the hall. The bedroom at the end of the hall facing the front yard had been her grandparents'. The largest bedroom, it now seemed the most empty, despite the furniture still present. Next to that room was her parents' room, then Robert's, then hers. The rest of the rooms in that wing were guest rooms. The servants' rooms were in the L across the other end of the hall over the kitchen. She eyed each of the family's rooms, reluctant to enter them lest she desecrate the memories of her loved ones.

Until she got to her room. Stepping into her old bedroom was like Alice walking through the looking glass into another world. The little-girl bed lacked its frilly pillows and ruffled bedspread, covered now with a sterile white sheet. The child-size wicker chair and table were void of the teddy bears and dolls that used to adorn them. Almost all semblance of the room to its former state was gone—missing, like the little girl who once inhabited it.

Lexie's eyes pooled with tears as she remembered the way the room used to be but was no more. If only she could go back in time to the days before all the bad things happened. But she couldn't. The past was gone, and she and the cottage were the only ones who had survived. What did the future hold for both of them? Would another family return life to the house? She thought of Floyd's suggestion that Lexie and her future husband, namely Floyd, perish the thought, live there. No, no matter whom she married, she didn't see herself staying in this house again. She didn't belong here anymore.

A crack of lightning jolted Lexie back to the present and the sound of dripping water again. She headed out of the room to find the source of the noise. As she moved down the hall, she followed the sound to one of the guest rooms where a glance at the window disclosed the cause. The window set inside one of the dormers leaked, water running down the length of the glass and dripping off the window sill onto the floor. Lexie looked around for some way to stop the leak or catch the water. Perhaps she'd find a bucket in the bathroom.

As she stepped out of the room, the creak of floorboards came from the servants' wing. She spun around and saw a shadow move along the wall. Her skin crawled as goose bumps sprouted.

She stared at the shadow, breathless, waiting. Someone must have come up the back stairs from the kitchen. But the longer she watched, the more she noticed how shadows from the tree limbs played against the wall. And the storm buffeting the house caused the noises she heard.

She was imagining things. No one was in that wing. She allowed herself to exhale.

As she returned her attention back to the leaking window, a noise came from the first floor below. The leak would have to wait. She tiptoed out the door and leaned over the railing and down the stairwell. She glimpsed a shadow move beneath, and this one wasn't from trees. Someone was down there. Her heart thumping against her ribs, she determined to find out who it was.

She eased down the stairs, hoping they wouldn't give her away. As she took a step, she bent down to peer between the railings but saw no one. She reached the bottom of the stairs and stood still, listening. Her gaze fell on the floor where wet footprints left a mark. They couldn't be hers, since she didn't get wet. They seemed to come from the direction of the kitchen. Her heart pounded as she followed them, her fear telling her to go the opposite way.

The footsteps went several directions when she reached the kitchen. Apparently, whoever it was came in through the back door. They must've gone back out the way they came. As she stood looking at the footprints, she heard a noise behind her. She wheeled around as a flash of lightning revealed Abner Jones standing in the shadows.

Chapter 12

"Oh!" Lexie gasped, her hands covering her mouth. "Mr. Jones! Wh … what are you doing here?"

Abner Jones took a step toward her, shrugging. "Got caught in the rain. Tried the door and it was open so I came in."

Lexie stepped back. Had he been following her around? The wet footprints throughout the house suggested it. She steadied herself, trying to control her shaking.

"I see. Well, you surprised me. I didn't expect to see you here."

"You don't mind if I come in out of the storm, do you? Or you want me to stay out in the rain?"

"Well, of course, I don't want you to be out in the storm." She leveled her gaze at him. "Did you know I was here?"

"Sure. Saw you roaming around."

"Why didn't you speak up and tell me you were here?"

He shrugged again. "Dunno." The man's blank indifference reminded her of someone she'd seen before.

Lexie glanced out the window and noticed the rain had slacked off. How could she get rid of this man? She wished Russell had come with her. Or even that the concierge had waited.

"Looks like the rain has almost stopped." She nodded toward the window. "We should be able to leave soon."

Abner made no effort to move. He just stared at her. She edged her way into the dining room, backing away as if she were trying to avoid a wild animal.

The front door hinge squealed as it opened. Lexie glanced to see why and noticed a man's silhouette standing in the doorway, his coat dripping rain.

"Lexie! Are you in here?"

Russell. She'd never been so happy to see someone. She rushed over to meet him.

"Russell! You came!"

He grabbed her shoulders and peered down at her. "Hey, steady girl. You okay?"

She lowered her voice. "Russell, Abner Jones sneaked into the house. He's back there, in the kitchen." She nodded toward the back of the house.

"He's in here?"

Lexie pointed back to the kitchen as Russell stalked through the house in that direction. She followed closely behind. When he got to the kitchen, he looked all around, then back at her.

"I don't see anyone. Abner! You in here?"

The man didn't materialize, and Russell turned to face Lexie with his eyebrow raised. "Are you sure you saw Abner? Maybe you just saw a shadow."

"No, Russell. He was here! Look!" She pointed to the puddles on the floor. "He tracked that water in when he came in through the back door."

"Well, he must be gone now. Abner! Abner!" Russell walked around in the kitchen, glancing around. He pulled the back door tight and locked it before returning to the dining room. Crossing his arms, he tilted his head at Lexie.

"You don't believe me, do you?" Lexie glared at him with her hands on her hips.

"I didn't say that. I just didn't see him."

"Russell, I'm not imagining things! He was here, in there." She pointed to the place where Abner Jones had stood. "He spoke to me."

"What did he say? Did he explain why he was in the house?"

"Why yes, he did. He said he saw the door open and came in out of the rain."

"Funny that he'd be close enough to know the door was open unless it was wide open. And I can't believe the maids would leave it like that."

"You see? That's what I find strange too. Do you think he followed me?"

"Mr. Simmons, the concierge, told me he drove you over."

"That's right."

"So Abner wouldn't have followed the car on foot."

"Why not? He probably knew I was going to Destiny."

"But I don't think he followed you. I believe he was already nearby."

Lexie recalled how Abner had hung around the house before. "Then he sure stays near here a lot. Doesn't he have someplace else to go?"

Russell laughed, his dimple adding to the amusement on his face. How could he be so annoying and look so charming at the same time?

"I suppose he could go back to the staff dormitory, but if he got caught out in that storm, I can't say as I blame him for seeking shelter."

Lexie shook her head. "Something just doesn't add up. And he acts so strange besides."

"All right, he's a little different. But still, you don't have to worry about him."

She remembered where she'd seen a man with the same dull expression—the hospital in Connecticut, where Mother had been.

"Russell, do you know if Abner has ever been hospitalized?"

"Sick?"

"Actually, I meant mental problems. Do you know if he ever had any psychiatric treatment?"

"Why do you ask?"

"His mannerisms remind me of a patient that was treated in the same hospital as Mother."

Russell's face sobered. "Oh." He glanced out the window. "Apparently, his relatives put him in a mental hospital after he came back from the last war. Said he wasn't 'normal.' But honestly, Lexie, Abner wouldn't hurt a fly. I really don't think you should be concerned about him."

"If you say so." After all her mother went through, she'd never want to unjustly accuse someone just because they were different.

"But I'll talk to him if it'll make you feel better. Tell him to keep his distance from you … and the house." Russell's smile returned as he pointed to the front door. "Storm's passed. Ready to get outta here?"

Lexie glanced out the windows and saw the afternoon sun peeking through the clouds.

"Sure."

They went outside to the car, and Russell opened the door for her as a brisk wind blew her hair into her eyes. "It's getting colder. How about a hot beverage?"

"That sounds wonderful." As they drove toward the clubhouse, they passed Abner Jones walking down the road. Russell brought the car to a halt beside the man.

"Russell, what are you doing?"

Lexie wanted to slide down below the dashboard. She had no desire to see this man again.

Russell hopped out of the car, leaving the door open and approached the yardman.

"Say, Abner! Need a word with you."

Abner stopped and waited for Russell to approach, eyeing Lexie in the car.

"Abner, were you in Destiny Cottage earlier?"

Abner looked to Lexie and back at Russell before nodding slowly.

"Mind telling me what you were doing there?" Russell stood, legs apart, his hands on his hips.

"Nope."

"Nope, what?"

"I don't mind."

Russell waited for Abner's answer while Lexie chewed on her hangnail. Abner peered over at her, then back at Russell.

"I went inside to get out of the rain."

"How'd you get in?"

"Back door was unlocked, so I walked in."

"Did you know Miss Smithfield was there?"

Abner nodded. "I saw her."

"Did you announce your presence to her?"

"Nope. No need to."

Lexie squirmed in the car seat. Couldn't they just leave?

"So, how did you know the back door was open?"

Lexie sat up a little, straining to hear the answer.

"Saw somebody else go in before."

"Oh, I see. I sent the maids over there to clean this morning."

Abner shook his head. "Weren't no maid. It was a man."

Lexie froze.

"A man? Was he there when you arrived?"

"Dunno. Maybe. I never seen him come back out."

"Did you recognize him?"

Lexie peered at the man from her side of the car, eager to hear the answer.

Abner shrugged. "Maybe, maybe not. Had on an overcoat and hat, so couldn't see much in the rain and all."

"Hmmm. Well, if you remember anything else about him, please let me know. Meanwhile, I need you to work over by the golf course tomorrow, okay?"

Abner nodded and ambled on. Russell returned to the car and closed the door. He put his hands on the steering wheel and looked at Lexie.

"You heard all that?"

She moved her head up and down. "Do you think he's telling the truth? Do you think he really saw another man?"

"Abner doesn't lie. In fact, sometimes he's too honest, blunt actually. I have no idea who he saw or why anybody else would be there, but I believe him."

Lexie hugged herself against a sudden chill, remembering.

"I think there *was* someone else there." She stared out the windshield. "I had the feeling I was being watched when I was upstairs, then I heard a noise coming from the servants' quarters. When I looked over there, I saw a shadow move, but I convinced myself it was caused by the tree limbs outside." She turned to face Russell as a thought occurred to her. "He must've come up the back stairs! Russell, who would be following me?"

Russell shook his head. "Maybe the same person who sent you the telegram."

Chapter 13

$\mathcal{W}$hat in blazes was going on? Russell focused on the road ahead, but his mind stayed on the pretty young woman beside him.

He was doing a lousy job of making her feel welcome. Well, he was doing all he could, but everything else was scaring her away. Seemed like somebody wanted to make her get rid of the cottage while he was trying to get her to keep it. But why lure her here with a telegram?

Surely Abner wouldn't harm her, but he was peculiar enough to scare some people. If he'd just quit turning up at the cottage when Lexie was there. He'd have to keep Abner assigned some place away from the cottage for a while.

But who was this other man Abner saw? He'd sure like to get his hands on him and find out what he was up to. Russell gripped the steering wheel as anger boiled inside his gut.

He pulled the car up to the clubhouse as a bellman opened the door for Lexie. Russell walked around and took her by the elbow. His foot ached as he led her up the stairs to the front door. It usually did in this kind of weather. As they reached the door, it opened and two well-dressed women engrossed in conversation walked out. When they saw Lexie, they stopped.

"Are you Alexandra Smithfield?" One of the ladies addressed her.

"Yes, I am."

Russell stepped forward. "Allow me to introduce Mrs. Jenkins. Mrs. Jenkins is president of our ladies' auxiliary. And this is Mrs. Lee."

"Very nice to meet you." Lexie extended her hand.

"Sweetheart, you met me many years ago, but I'm sure you don't remember. May I extend my condolences on the recent loss of your mother and your brother?"

Lexie nodded. "Thank you." No doubt Mrs. Appleton had been gossiping about her to everyone at the club.

The woman continued. "We'd love for you to join us at our meetings. We gather in the ladies' parlor once a week. Unfortunately, you just missed this week's meeting." She smiled warmly.

"Yes, please. We need some of you younger women to participate." Mrs. Lee nodded.

"Perhaps I will. That is, if I'm still here."

Mrs. Jenkins' eyebrows lifted. "Still here? Surely you're staying for the season?"

Russell could tell Lexie didn't feel like explaining herself again, so he jumped in. "Miss Smithfield has some business to take care of back home, so we might not have the pleasure of her company for long. If you ladies would please excuse us … "

The women exchanged curious glances, but before they could press her further, Russell placed his hand on Lexie's lower back and pushed her on through the doorway.

"Let's get rid of these coats and dry off." He helped Lexie out of hers. "Now, for that hot tea. Or would you prefer coffee?"

Lexie glanced toward the dining room but seemed reluctant to move. He sensed her need for privacy. "Say, I've got an idea. Let's go to my office. We can get warm and have a conversation without other guests hanging around."

She nodded and smiled. "Sounds great. And I'll take tea. Honey and extra lemon slices on the side."

"Yes, ma'am. At your service." Russell escorted her up the stairs to the fourth floor. They turned right at the top of the staircase and followed the hall around to the end, where he threw open the door to the tower room.

"I didn't realize your office was up here."

He took her coat and hung it along with his coat and hat on the Bentwood rack beside the door.

"Oh yes. I inherited the tower office. One of the perks of the job." He winked and waved his arm across the room. "Make yourself comfortable."

Russell picked up the phone on his desk and called the kitchen, ordering their tea and coffee.

Lexie eyed the large corner room with windows on two sides and a door leading to the balcony that wound around the clubhouse turret. From her vantage point, she could see the rooftops of all the cottages through the trees. She scanned the panorama before her, taking in the grand lawn in front of the clubhouse, the driveway, the wharf, and glimpsed the river beyond. If it wasn't so chilly, she'd go out on the balcony. As she turned around, she noted the tall ladder that led up into the turret. She'd love to see the view from up there. But not today.

"Excuse me. I'll be back in a jif." Russell strode to the door and pointed to a large leather sofa. "Have a seat."

As he left the room, she made her way to the sofa, taking off her hat and placing it on the coffee table in front. She rubbed her hands together, then her arms, to get some warmth. Her eyes scanned the comfortable office with its bookshelves on one wall, its generous mahogany desk, and executive chair. Russell had done all right for himself. A diploma hung on the wall behind the desk with a picture of his graduating class, she assumed. Guess he hadn't always stayed on the island.

She shuddered at the sight of the animal heads hanging on the opposite wall—deer and boar. She never had liked hunting, preferring the animals alive with their heads attached. Of course, she wouldn't want to cross paths with that hideous boar whose head was displayed. But after losing her father to hunting, she'd lost any inclination to take up the sport, even skeet-shooting.

Russell rushed in, closed the door behind him, and clapped his hands together.

"Now, our beverages should be here any moment. A nice, hot cup of coffee sounds good right now." His face broadened into a warm smile. "I take it you didn't want to go to the dining room and chance running into Floyd today."

She rolled her eyes. "Too late. I already have."

Russell took a seat at the other end of the sofa and turned to face her with a big grin, his arm resting along the back. "Yes? And what did dear Floyd have to say today? He was with his mum, I assume."

"Of course, until I left the table. But he followed me out, said he needed to talk to me about Destiny. He was very interested in what I was going to do with the cottage, and when I said I was planning to sell it, he intimated we might get married and keep it! Can you imagine?"

Russell roared with laughter. "His mother's always liked Destiny. I think she was jealous of your family for having it. You know, they don't have a cottage of their own. They've always stayed in the clubhouse. So I guess she thought she could marry you and Floyd off and get the cottage in return."

"Well, she thought wrong. I wouldn't marry Floyd Appleton if he was the last man on earth!"

"Ha. Poor Floyd. Maybe his mother will find some other woman for him."

"Seriously, Russell. I thought they might be behind the telegram, but it just doesn't seem like their style. Of course, they were very interested in the cottage…"

"Lexie, about today. Hey, I'm sorry I couldn't go with you. Business, you know."

"Of course. I got there fine. Mr. Sullivan, the concierge, took me."

"Yes, I know, but I was surprised he didn't stay and wait for you."

"He offered, but I told him not to."

"Bet you wish he had."

She sighed, then sat upright. "So someone knew I was going to the cottage or followed me. Wonder why?"

He shook his head. "Well, I guess they want to know what you're doing or going to do."

"Do you think it's the same person who got into the house and tore up the desk?"

A knock on the door and Russell answered. "Come in."

A young man entered carrying a silver tray with two silver pitchers, a sugar bowl, creamer, and china cups for each of them. A plate of lemon slices and a bowl of honey rested on a small plate alongside another plate of scones. The waiter placed the tray on the coffee table in front of them and handed them each a linen napkin. He poured hot tea from the small pitcher into one cup and handed it to Lexie.

Lexie took two lemon slices from the saucer the waiter held out to her. The young man's broad smile overtook his face as he beamed at Lexie. He offered her the honey and she helped herself, feeling the waiter's stare. Her face grew warm, and she avoided his eyes, wishing he'd look elsewhere or leave.

Lexie smiled at Russell over the plate of pastries on the tray. "Scones too?"

"A little bird told me you liked them." He gave her a wink and took the cup of coffee from the waiter. Turning his attention to the waiter, he said, "Walter, I hear you'll soon be leaving us for the army."

"Yes, sir. I'm reporting for duty in two weeks." The waiter snapped to attention and saluted.

Lexie did a double-take. Could this young man be old enough for the military? He looked so boyish.

"We'll miss you here, but wish you the best. We'll keep you in our prayers."

Did he say "prayers"? Lexie didn't realize Russell was so spiritual.

"Thank you, sir. I appreciate it. But we'll be back soon as we beat those Krauts!"

Russell stood and shook the waiter's hand. "You do that, Walter."

The young man gave Lexie another admiring glance before turning back to Russell. "Will that be all, sir?"

"Yes, that'll be all for now, Walter. Thank you."

The waiter bowed and left the room. Lexie stared after him for a few moments.

"He seems so young to be in the army."

"I'm sure he joined as soon as he was seventeen."

Lexie shook her head, then took a bite of a scone. "These are as delicious as ever."

"Good to hear that. We've tried to keep our specialties consistent, even with the changes in kitchen staff." Russell grabbed a scone and bit off a piece.

"I noticed that most of the staff isn't the same as it was when I was a little girl. But I do remember that waiter, Mr. Mason. He's always been here, hasn't he?"

"About twenty-five years. Thank God for the older employees, or we'd really be short-staffed."

Lexie raised her eyebrows. "This seems to be a desirable place to work."

"It is, or was. Before we got into the war. Now every able-bodied man like Walter is signing up for active duty. I heard they were lined up at the recruiting center in Atlanta."

Lexie nodded. "They were everywhere, from what I've read in the papers. Have you considered joining too?"

A pained expression crossed his face. He pointed to his foot. "They won't take me."

Her heart squeezed, and she regretted asking the question. "Oh, I'm sorry. What happened?"

"Stupid hunting accident. I tripped and the gun went off, taking a piece of my foot with it."

Lexie's stomach turned. "Oh. I didn't realize. Thank God, it wasn't worse."

"Yes, thank God indeed."

Her face warmed and she grasped for a change in topic.

"Russell, you said Abner Jones was placed in a mental hospital after the first war. How did he get out?"

"Your grandfather. He vouched for him, said the war did strange things to people."

"Really? No wonder he's so indebted to Grandfather."

Russell slapped his knee. "You know, I just realized why Abner went inside the cottage."

"Why?"

"Thunder. Abner hates loud noises—they call it 'shell-shock'. I bet he went inside to get away from the thunder."

"Oh dear. Poor man." Lexie studied her hands in her lap, suddenly feeling sorry for him. "I saw people like that in the hospital."

Russell's forehead creased with concern. "It's a shame about your mother, Lexie. She was always a beautiful woman."

"Yes, she was—used to be. But she was never the same after Father died."

"I remember how hard she took it when your little brother died."

Lexie's heart wrenched. He was right. Mother never recovered from Kenneth's drowning, then Father's accident. Tears filled her eyes, and she wiped them with her napkin.

"Hey, why don't we do something fun?"

Lexie glanced up, amazed at how fast the man could regain his cheerful attitude. Wouldn't it be nice to have that ability?

"How'd you like to take on the club billiard champion?" Russell stuck his chest out like a proud peacock.

"You?" Lexie laughed, covering her mouth. "That shouldn't be too hard."

"Oh yeah? You don't know what you're up against."

"All right. You're on!"

As she stood from the couch, Lexie smoothed her skirt. Maybe her pants were ready now. She'd stop by the laundry and get them first. She scanned the room, nodding at the animal heads.

"Did you kill all those?"

"Not all of them. Actually, Robert got the buck."

Lexie gazed up at the massive deer head with its large rack of antlers. "Why did he leave it here, in your office?"

"Your mother wouldn't allow it at the cottage, so he told me to keep it to remind me what a good shot he was." Russell crossed his arms, smiling.

"Who shot the boar?" She pointed at the creature and grimaced.

"I did. Ugly, isn't it?"

She nodded. There was a variety of other animals—pheasant, wild turkeys, even a large fish mounted on the wall. She stared at them while Russell got her coat. Some pictures of groups of men with their trophies accompanied the animals on the wall. One of them caught her attention, and she drew closer to study it.

"Russell, that's you, Robert, and Father, isn't it?"

Russell joined her to look at the picture. "Yes, that's right."

The men posed with their rifles beside them, a couple of deer lying on the ground in front.

She studied the picture. "Who are the other men?"

"That's Edwin and Frank Gould." He jabbed his finger at each of the men standing to the left of her father.

"Who's that man?" Lexie pointed to another man standing in the background.

"Oh, that's Jack Barnes."

"The boat captain?" She faced Russell frowning. "I wasn't aware that he was a friend of yours and Robert's."

"His father was the game warden, so he assisted us on a lot of hunts. Now that hunting's not popular, he drives the launch for us."

"He sure has changed. I thought he was much older than you and Robert. He's certainly aged since this photograph was taken."

"Life has been pretty rough for him." He held up her coat for her to put on. "Are you ready for some billiards?"

She took the coat and draped it over her arm. "I want to change clothes first. Meet you in the billiards room in thirty minutes. It's in the annex, isn't it?"

"Actually, between the main clubhouse and the annex. You'll find it."

"I'm sure I will."

As she went down to her room, the picture in Russell's office remained planted in her mind. For some reason, it made her feel uneasy. Was it the expressions on their faces? Her heart lurched. Was this picture taken the day her father was killed?

Chapter 14

Glancing over his shoulder to make sure Lexie wasn't around, Russell crushed out his cigarette. He needn't get her all worked up over his smoking. She had enough concerns already. Good thing she couldn't read his mind. The way she looked at him with those big blues made him think she was trying. That was okay. He'd been keeping secrets for years for a lot of folks, so he'd stay mum. But she was curious. And smart.

He blew on his hands and rubbed them together before putting them in his coat pockets. Best be getting into the billiards room before she did. Just as he reached the door, Stella rushed past. He stepped into her path to intercept her.

"Stella! Can I have a word with you, please?"

She halted before jerking her head to face him. "What do you want?"

He ignored the lack of respect in her voice. She always acted as though she was better than he was, better than any of the staff. Back when she was younger and prettier, the men of the club used to flirt with her and she got snooty. She'd been a head-turner, sassy too, so she'd gotten big tips from the wealthy club members. But those years were gone, along with her youthful charms, replaced with bitterness and sarcasm. Poor Jack. She made his life miserable trying to please her. The good thing was she kept her mouth shut around the guests these days, so they thought she was just shy.

"Say, did you help clean Destiny Cottage this morning?"

She huffed a short breath of frosty air. "I tried, but that place was a wreck. Needs a going-over again."

"So, who else worked with you? I asked for several housemaids to work on it before Miss Smithfield went back in today."

A sneer contorted her face. "Louise and Jane and me, that's all. We needed more help, but that was all they said could be spared. Of course, the three of us got behind on our own work to make sure *Miss* Smithfield was taken care of."

"Stella." He wanted to reprimand her for her attitude toward Lexie but changed his mind. That was one battle he wouldn't win.

"So why do you want to know? Did *Miss* Smithfield have a complaint?" She crossed her arms.

"No, not really. However, the back door was open, and it rained inside some."

"You told us to leave the house unlocked. The wind must've blown it open. That's not my fault."

"I didn't say it was, Stella." He shook his head. "Was anyone else there besides you three?"

She glared at him. "I told you it was just us." Then, she nodded and pointed in the air like she just remembered something. "Yeah, that crazy old coot was hanging around there, like always, doing something in the yard."

"I assume you're referring to Abner."

"Who else?" She twirled her finger beside her ear motioning craziness. "Anyway, why do you want to know?"

He shrugged his shoulders. "Just curious." Forcing a smile, he said, "That's all. And thank you for your hard work getting the cottage clean."

"Hmmph!" She spun and hurried back to the clubhouse, passing Lexie on the way. He noticed how she slowed her steps when she neared Lexie and took on her humble persona. He exhaled a deep sigh. If he didn't care about her family and didn't need her, she might have been dismissed already. But she was a hard worker and he had to keep her.

Lexie recognized the maid as they passed and gave her a smile. However, Stella, if she remembered her name correctly, averted her eyes and walked on. The woman acted like Lexie had a contagious disease.

Up ahead, Russell stood waiting with a big grin on his face. As she walked up, he opened the door and gestured with a sweep of his hand for her to enter.

"Are you sure you know how to play this game?" Russell gave her that quick wink that made her heart flutter. She wished he wouldn't do that. It was so distracting.

"Russell, I bet I know this game as well as you do. After all, we did have a billiards table in our home in New York."

"I'm sure you did. Did Robert ever play with you?"

"Of course. And I must warn you, I beat *him* too."

Russell drew back. "No! Well, I see I have a challenge. How 'bout we make a wager on the game?"

"Wager?" Lexie's face began to warm. She didn't have money to throw away on a billiards game. "I don't play for money."

"Ha-ha!" He threw back his head, laughing. "No money required."

"Then what?" Maybe she'd gotten herself into more than she wanted.

"Movie and popcorn. If you win, you treat me to a movie and popcorn."

"That doesn't sound right. And what if you win?"

"I'll treat you to a movie and popcorn."

"You're impossible!"

They took off their overcoats and hung them by the fireplace. Lexie placed her hat and gloves on a small table nearby. Russell removed his jacket as well, adjusted his suspenders and tucked his tie inside his shirt before choosing his stick. Lexie chose hers while Russell racked the balls.

He glanced up at her. "Would you like to break or do you want me to?"

"Oh, please help yourself. It might be the last time you hit the balls." A familiar thrill of competition energized her.

Russell raised an eyebrow, leaned over the table and sent the balls spinning in all directions with his break. None of the balls fell in a pocket, though, and he twisted his lip in disappointment.

"Your choice." He motioned to the balls, stepped away from the table, and leaned on his cue stick.

"Solids." Lexie sighted a red ball, took aim, and sank it with the white cue ball. She gave him a wry smile and strolled around the table before choosing her next target, the yellow ball. She banked it off one side before it headed for the corner pocket.

"So you're lucky. Big deal." Russell taunted from the other side of the table.

"I assure you, luck has nothing to do with it." Lexie re-chalked her cue stick, eyeing him over the top of it.

Her next shot bounced off the edge of the pocket before going in. She couldn't resist the grin that claimed her face. Should she tell him she'd belonged to a billiards club in college? The next shot missed the pocket, so she moved aside to let Russell approach.

"Your turn, or do you want to concede now?"

"Not on your life! Step back, now. I don't want anyone to get hurt." He motioned for her to move farther away.

She burst out laughing. He could be quite entertaining. Soon the game was over with Lexie the winner. Russell asked for a rematch, so they played again, but this time he won.

"Shall we play a tie-breaker or would you like to call it even?"

"Even is fine for now," she said.

"Let's have a seat over there and give it a rest." Russell pointed to two large armchairs in the corner. When they sat down, he nodded to the decanter on the coffee table before them. "Would you like a cordial?"

Lexie shook her head, but Russell poured himself a small glass of the amber liquid. Her father's attraction to alcohol had killed any desire she might have had for it. She blamed liquor for the change in her father from a happy, carefree family man to an irritable person no one wanted to be around. Others attributed the cause to the stock market crash when he lost a fortune, driving him to drink for consolation. Other men had reacted the same way, but they weren't her father.

Russell lifted his glass to her. "To a pretty good billiards player." He took a sip before resting his elbow on the armrest.

"Pretty good? We're even, remember?"

"For now, that is." He eyed her pants and chuckled. "I see you're wearing your trousers again."

Lexie crossed her legs and reached down to straighten a cuff on the full pants leg. "Of course. They're much warmer than skirts."

The radio in the room played a Benny Goodman tune, reminding her of Robert and how much he liked to dance. Her heart twisted as tears pooled in the corners of her eyes. Oh, how she wished he were there with them. Wouldn't it have been grand if the three of them could have played billiards together? The music ended and an ad for war bonds came on.

"Are you going to buy some of those?" Russell motioned to the radio with his glass.

"Sure." If her accountant said she could afford to. "I'd like to do something to help."

"You might want to go to one of the ladies' club meetings then. I hear they're working on various ways to support the cause. Of course, a lot of our members contribute financially to the war anyway."

She wasn't surprised to hear that. Her grandfather had helped support the Great War out of his own pocket. However, she'd have to find another way to help.

"I suppose it wouldn't hurt to go to one of the meetings. I just don't know how long I'll be here."

"So what will you do when you go back home?"

She fingered the pearls at her neck. "I hope to return to what I was doing before." At his raised eyebrows, she continued. "I worked in a hospital."

"Is that right? Never pictured you as a nurse."

"I'm not a nurse. And it wasn't an ordinary hospital. It was the one where Mother was, a hospital for people with mental problems."

Russell's face lost the casual smile. "So, if you're not a nurse, what do you do there?"

"I'm a doctor's assistant. I want to learn more about mental illness. I don't think the treatment we give mental patients is the best we can do. There's so much more to it than what we've thought for centuries. The doctor I work with has some different ideas about treatment."

"That's very brave of you, Lexie. And commendable."

"Brave? How so?"

"Well, I mean, with your mother's problems and everything, well, I'm just surprised you'd want to be around that sort of thing anymore."

"It's not that I *want* to, Russell. It's more of a *need* to." She looked away. "It's hard to explain. I don't suppose you'd understand."

He leaned forward and placed his hand on her knee. The shock of his touch sent a warm current through her. "I'd like to understand, though. I admire you for what you're doing." He sat back. "At least you know what you want to do."

This serious side of him took her by surprise. "You don't?"

"I'm not sure I have a choice. I just took over my father's duties when he retired, since I seemed to be the *obvious* choice. Looks like I'll always be here."

A pang of sympathy touched Lexie's heart. It hadn't occurred to her that he might prefer to be somewhere else.

"You went away to college, didn't you?" She remembered the diploma hanging in his office.

"Sure. Studied business and came right back to help Dad, like a good son." He made a face and laughed as the familiar jovial attitude returned. "Ready for that tie-breaker?" He stood and reached for her hand.

She smiled and allowed him to pull her to her feet. As Glenn

Miller's band played "Chattanooga Choo Choo" in the background, they commenced another game of billiards. During a particularly tricky shot, Lexie had to position her body at an odd angle to make the shot, and Russell teased her.

"You've got great form!"

She made her shot, twirled around, and threatened him with the cue stick. Laughing and cutting up with Russell lifted the somber mood that circumstances tried to impose. The game drew to a tie with one ball each left on the table. Russell attempted to show off and make a fancy banked shot, but the ball didn't go in. When Lexie took her turn, she stretched out to reach the cue ball. As she did, her gold necklace fell out of her blouse. She sank her shot and jumped up with an exultant smile.

"I won!" She resisted the urge to leap into his arms for a hug. Instead, she crossed her arms and gave him a nod. "Again. Guess I'm the real winner."

Russell lifted his hands in surrender before fixing his gaze on the locket. "Nice necklace. I didn't notice it before. Somebody special give that to you?"

Lexie's hand flew to her neck, and she fingered the filigree heart. "You might say that."

"I see." Was that a look of disappointment on his face? "Well, I'm not surprised you have a boyfriend."

"Boyfriend?" Lexie tilted her head at him. "Oh, no. My father gave this to me for my twelfth birthday."

As relief washed over his face, he reached out and touched the key hanging beside the heart.

"You keep the locket locked?"

She felt the key, touching his fingers in the process. "No. Father told me it was the key to his heart. It doesn't even fit the locket." Her eyes misted over as she recalled the day he gave her the necklace, the look of love in his eyes. It was the last gift she ever received from him. She lifted the necklace and dropped it back inside her blouse.

Russell put his arm around her shoulder and gave her a squeeze. "That's real sweet, Lexie." He turned her around to face him. "Are you ready?"

"For what?" She felt a tremor of anticipation.

"The movie!"

"The movie?" She exhaled. For a moment, she thought he was going to kiss her, "But I won."

"That's right. So *you* get to treat *me*, remember?" He checked the clock on the mantle. "It starts in two hours, so we have time for dinner first. Do you need anything from your room?"

"No, but … something about this doesn't seem right. You got your way no matter who won."

"Are you backing out of our deal?" Russell drew back and acted wounded.

"No, I'll go, but next time, I make the wager."

"Swell! Long as there's a next time, I'm not worried."

What was she saying—"next time"? And yet, the idea wasn't all that unpleasant. Spending time with Russell made everything else that had happened more bearable. But he couldn't make the problems go away.

Chapter 15

As Lexie stepped out of the car at the club's beach teahouse, a gust of cold wind blew off the ocean and peppered her with sand. Russell draped his arm around her shoulders, a welcome gesture against the chilly air. They hustled inside the building where chairs were lined up in rows before the projector screen.

The place wasn't packed, due to the cold weather, so Lexie got a good look at the other people present. Most of them were staff members enjoying some time off, surprising her that they had been given the privilege of sharing a movie with the club members. She scanned the crowd for a familiar face, recognizing a few of the waiters and bellmen. There were some obvious couples, reminding Lexie that it was a Saturday date night.

"So what's playing?" Lexie asked Russell.

A voice beside her spoke up. "*The Maltese Falcon.*"

Lexie jerked her head and saw the young waiter Walter standing nearby. His grin revealed sparkling white teeth as his eyes met hers. Was he flirting with her? Her cheeks warmed under his scrutiny.

"Evening, Walter." Russell nodded to the waiter, grabbed Lexie's arm and led her to two empty chairs. "I do believe young Walter is smitten with you," he whispered in her ear as he took her coat. "I'll go get us some popcorn."

Lexie offered him a twisted smile before he dashed off to the refreshment table. She kept her gloves on and rubbed her cold hands together as she waited for Russell to return, meanwhile avoiding eye contact with Walter. She certainly didn't want to invite his attention. Soon, Russell came back holding a bowl of popcorn and handed it to her.

"Thank you." She closed her eyes and inhaled the aroma before lifting her gaze to Russell. "I didn't realize the staff mingled with the members."

"Things have changed, haven't they? War has a way of unifying us."

He nodded toward a group of young men across the room. "Many of these guys will be going off to fight soon."

Lexie followed his gaze, seeing Walter standing among them.

"What kind of soda would you like? Coca-Cola? Root beer?"

"Root beer sounds good." She smiled up at Russell, pleased by his eager effort to make sure she enjoyed the evening.

"Be right back."

Russell scurried off again, and Lexie watched the room fill up in the meantime. Could any of these people be responsible for sending her the telegram? She folded her arms across her chest and shivered. Did anyone here follow her to the cottage? If so, why? She glanced over at the refreshment table and saw Russell laughing with a young woman. Lexie pursed her lips and her stomach tightened.

How silly the girl looked, throwing herself at Russell that way! Could she be more obvious about her intentions, cocking her head from side to side? Lexie tried not to stare but couldn't help noticing the way Russell returned the woman's attention. She was rather attractive, but bobs that short were no longer in style ... Maybe she was Russell's girlfriend. Lexie shook her head and looked the other way. It was no concern of hers anyway, so why should she care?

"Is this seat taken?"

Lexie jumped, her thoughts interrupted by a familiar voice. She glanced up to see Walter waiting by the chair next to her. She gave him a polite smile. "No, I don't believe it is. Have a seat. I'll save this one for Russell." She pointed to the other empty seat beside her. Better than sitting totally alone and standing out like a sore thumb.

"Terrific!" Walter plopped down, his smile running from ear to ear. He indicated a sign posted on the wall. "You going to the dance?"

"Dance?" Lexie's gaze traveled to the poster announcing a Sweetheart Dance for Valentine's Day.

"Sure! It'll be loads of fun! if I were still going to be here, I'd love to swing you around a few times!"

Lexie's face warmed, and she shook her head. "It sounds like fun. But I don't expect to be here in February."

Walter drew back and studied her face. "You don't say. You're not staying for the whole season?" He nudged her with his elbow. "You're not joining the army, too, are you?"

She knew he was kidding, but wanted to come back with, "Why not?" Instead, she just smiled. "I have business to attend to back home."

"Well, if you change your mind, I'm sure there's some fellas here that'd love to give you a spin."

Lexie glanced around the room, wondering what fellas that might be. None of them really attracted her, yet the very thought of dancing excited her. She looked over at Russell, still engaged in conversation with the bob. Was he a good dancer? Or did his foot hinder him? It certainly didn't get in the way of anything else he did. Like flirting. No doubt that woman he was talking with would love to dance with him.

The lights went out and the sound of the projector came from the back of the room. Russell slid into the chair beside her just as the image appeared on the screen in front of them.

"Sorry. Here's your root beer." He handed her the cold glass bottle.

Lexie waited for an explanation, then chastised herself for expecting one. Why did he have to give her an excuse?

"Thank you," she whispered and tried to appear nonchalant, focusing ahead. Out of the corner of her eye, she noticed someone slip into the room late, but she couldn't see who it was.

"The Eyes and Ears of the World" newsreel played first, as it always did these days. A booming voice announced how successful "our" soldiers were in battle, showing pictures of men in uniform marching down a road, climbing out of ditches. Planes took off from an airfield somewhere before the picture changed to an aerial view of a battleship, followed by a close-up of sailors with broad grins. For a second, she searched the faces for Robert's until it hit her with gut-wrenching reality that he was dead. Her eyes filled up and overflowed, streaming down her cheek.

Russell reached and placed his hand over hers. He must know how she felt because he felt it too. A selfish thought crossed her mind when she realized he couldn't be in the military. He wouldn't have to leave, get hurt … She squeezed her eyes shut so she didn't have to watch the rest of the news clip and exhaled a sigh of relief when the movie's theme music began to play.

Soon she was caught up in the melodrama with all its intrigue and mystery. Everyone in the movie acted suspiciously, and it was difficult to know the trustworthy characters from the dishonest ones. Sort of like her own life. She shivered and glanced around her, sensing that she was being watched again. Humphrey Bogart's character was besieged with people who wanted a statue he had—the Maltese Falcon. She sympathized with him as he was drawn into a conflict over the object.

The idea resonated with her.

Did she have something someone else wanted? Her heart raced. If so, what could it be?

The movie ended, the lights came up, and people took their time departing, taking the opportunity to stretch and visit with friends. Russell retrieved their coats while she waited, studying the folks around her. A man shoved past her toward the door with his head down, not speaking to anyone on his way. He certainly appeared to be in a hurry.

Just before he went out the door, he glanced back over his shoulder, making eye contact with her. She froze. It was the boat captain Jack. Was he looking at her or had she just imagined it?

As if she needed to be, the movie must have made her extra-suspicious. When Russell returned with their coats, she told him about seeing the man.

"Why do you think he was here alone?"

"Guess Stella stayed home with their little girl. He probably just wanted to get out."

Of course. Why not? He had every right to be there, maybe even more than Lexie did.

"He doesn't seem to like me."

"Why do you say that?" Russell cocked his head. "He doesn't even know you."

"I know, but he just gives me such hateful looks."

Russell put his hand on Lexie's shoulder and peered into her eyes. "Lexie, I know you've got questions, but you've got to quit thinking everyone is out to get you." He smiled with tenderness in his eyes. "And you don't need to worry about Jack. He's just not a happy guy, and I'm sure it has nothing to do with you." He helped her with her coat and ushered her back to the car. She shivered in the damp cold, her breath emitting frosty clouds.

As they rode back to the clubhouse, Lexie stared out the car window into the dark night, replaying scenes from the movie in her mind.

"Thanks for coming with me tonight, Lexie." Russell's voice startled her back to the present. "I hope you enjoyed the movie, even if it wasn't a very cheerful one. Next time, we'll watch a movie that's not so serious, I promise. Maybe one with Bob Hope or Jack Benny."

Lexie faced him. "You can get whatever you want? Even with the war?"

"Oh, I can't get the newest movies—they go to the troops. But I can still get my hands on some pretty recent ones." He glanced over at her and laughed. "It helps to have a member who owns a chain of theatres."

She stared at his profile as he drove, admiring his pleasant, chiseled features. He didn't seem to let anything get in his way when he wanted something. And he must be the most upbeat guy she'd ever known. How did he manage that, with all the depressing things going on in the world?

"Have you reconsidered going to the chapel tomorrow? Service starts at 11:00."

Lexie stiffened at the suggestion. Not this again.

"No, but thanks for asking. I think I'll just relax, maybe visit the horses. I brought my riding habit, hoping to get a ride in while I'm here. I haven't done that for a long time."

"I'd love to go with you after church, but if you prefer to go alone, I'll arrange it with the head groom."

"Don't go to any trouble. I'd like to get out before noon, and I'm sure you'll still be in church. But I can call for a horse myself or just walk over to the stables..."

"Actually, I'll have to take care of it. The staff usually takes off Sunday morning to go to their church, so the stable hands need to get the horse ready before they leave."

"Oh. I didn't think of that. I didn't mean to put anyone out. In fact, I can wait."

He held up his hand. "It won't be a problem. What time do you want to go? I'll make a call first thing in the morning before church."

"How about ten?" As long as she was nowhere near the chapel during the service. Someone else might try to convince her to attend, and she wasn't ready to set foot inside that place again. And maybe never would be.

Chapter 16

Sunday morning's cool air made for a brisk walk, but the bright sunshine and exercise were invigorating. As Lexie hurried past the chapel, she heard a piano being played. The service shouldn't begin for at least another hour, so the music surprised her. She fought an urge to stop and listen, try to recognize the melody of the hymn. But she turned away and let the music fade as she continued toward the stables. After she strode past the tennis courts, she reached the dormitories where many of the employees lived. A few of the men, dressed in their Sunday-best suits and hats, strolled around and chatted with each other. They nodded as she walked by but gave her questioning looks.

When she finally reached the horse barn at the end of the road, a friendly stable hand by the name of George met her holding the reins of a gorgeous palomino.

"Good morning, Miss Smithfield. Mr. Russell called and tole me to git you a horse saddled up. Need any 'hep gittin' on her?" The stocky Negro man with graying hair grinned at her.

"No, thank you. I can manage." Lexie placed her foot in the stirrup and threw her other leg over, wiggling to get comfortable in the saddle.

"All right. You enjoy your ride. Angel here's a real sweet girl. She won't give you no trouble."

Lexie noted the man's starched white shirt, unusual attire for working in a stable. "Thank you for meeting me this morning. I hope I didn't interfere with your plans."

"No, ma'am. I'll be goin' to church now and spen' the res' of the day there, so no harm done." He waved good-bye over his head as he walked away. After taking a few steps, he stopped and turned around. "You jus' put her back in that first stall there when you git back." He motioned to a trough beside the barn. "Let her drink some water first if she wants it, if you don' mind. I'll take care of the res' later."

"Will do. Enjoy your day!" Lexie watched the man's back as he sauntered away, whistling a tune. Leaning over, she patted the horse's neck. "Angel, huh? What a coincidence on a Sunday. Well, Angel, I hope you plan to watch out for me. You might have your work cut out for you, though, the way things have been going."

Lexie nudged the horse with her heels, and the animal responded with a slow gait. She guided the horse down the beach road, enjoying the quiet and solitude. Would she be the only person not in church today? Well, if so, she would have her own service out in nature, enjoying God's creation. Surely He wouldn't fault her for that. She didn't have to be in the chapel to appreciate the natural beauty of the island. The melody of the hymn she'd heard played through her mind. The tune was familiar, but remote, like a memory of a long-past event. Not able to get the melody out of her head, she found herself humming the tune.

A cool breeze ruffled the curls around her head as she trotted down the crushed shell road. The brilliant winter sun peeked through the moss-laden oaks, dappling her path in light and shadow. Days like these were what brought the first millionaires to the island to get away from the frigid cold in the northern states. Southern winters were so erratic, starting out chilly in the morning, then changing to pleasant spring temperatures in the afternoon. How could such a lovely place be cursed?

Had Mother ever appreciated its beauty?

Deep down inside, Lexie recalled days from her earliest childhood when Mother was happy and family outings here were enjoyable. Yes, there had been lovely days on the island at one time. Lexie caught glimpses of the Atlantic through the trees to her right. The water was so still, more like a lake than an ocean. Tranquil. Something Mother had not been, growing more and more troubled.

Lexie wanted to reach out and embrace the serenity of the moment, keep it for the next time her world was rattled. But how could she be peaceful with so many unanswered questions? Somebody wanted her here, but she didn't know who or why. If they wanted something from her, why didn't they present themselves and ask for it? The sight of the ransacked antique secretary flashed through her mind. Whatever they had been searching for must be important. And if they didn't find it, were they following her around, hoping she might lead them to it?

Her temporary tranquility vanished as she glanced around her, watching for signs of another person's presence. There were no other horses out today, so someone following by foot would have a hard time keeping up with her, but she urged Angel to a faster gait anyway. And there were no cars either, at least not out this way. She shook her head. She was just being silly. No one knew where she was. No one except Russell, and he said he'd probably be at church by now. Surely he was honest with her.

She continued heading to the northern tip of the island, where she and Russell had ridden together on the bike. A smile crossed her face and she chuckled to herself. What fun that had been, riding on the handlebars! She could just picture the two of them flying down the beach in tandem. Angel seemed to know where Lexie wanted to go as she trotted onto the beach. At the water's edge they stopped, and Lexie gazed out on the calm sea, barely lapping the shore.

Squinting against the bright sunlight, she shielded her eyes and scanned from east to west, stopping to gaze at the town of St. Simons across the way to the north. The white lighthouse tower glistened as if the structure itself could radiate light. On such a beautiful day, it was hard to believe there was a war going on in the world, even harder to believe there was an enemy threat close to their own shores. And yet, didn't the people living at Pearl Harbor think the same thing the day they were attacked? She shuddered, and the horse nickered. Did it sense her fear? She'd heard animals could do that.

She stroked the horse's neck. "You don't see any enemies out there, do you?"

Angel answered with a whinny, and Lexie laughed.

"You know, you're a pretty good conversationalist. You might even understand me better than anyone else."

At that remark, the horse snorted.

"Ha! Okay, maybe that's too much to ask of anyone, even you." She pulled on the reins and turned the horse the opposite direction. "Let's go down the beach, shall we?"

The horse nodded and proceeded along the hard-packed sand. Once again, Lexie relaxed with the rhythm of the horse's gait and slow, steady swishing of the incoming waves. A lone white pelican soared over the gray-blue water, its eye fixed on an object below. He swooped and plunged in, surfacing with a fish he maneuvered into position. Then stretching out his neck, he gulped his dinner down.

Other than the bird, the vacant, pristine beach showed no sign of life, and Lexie imagined the scene must've looked the same to the first explorers to the new world. They, too, must've found the beaches empty. Little did they know they were being watched by native Indians hiding in the woods.

Lexie jerked her head toward the trees. The Indians were long gone, so who watched the shores now? She remembered Russell mentioning the club guards that were supposed to keep intruders out of the compound and off the island. A distant memory of the guards patrolling the beach on horseback came to her.

"Hi, little girl. What are you doing out here?" The man on the tall black horse gazed down at her.

"Will you take me for a ride on your horsey?" She extended her arms hoping he'd pick her up.

"Sure. I'll take you for a ride. Where's your mother?"

"Over there." Lexie pointed behind her.

"All right. We'll ride over there and see her." He leaned over and lifted her up to the saddle, putting her in front of him with his arms encircling her as he held the reins. She was so high above the ground.

The panic on Mother's face was not the greeting she expected when the guard rode up with Lexie.

"Lexie! What are you doing?"

"I wanted to ride on the horsey!"

The man lowered Lexie to her father's arms. "Thank you," her father *said before the man tipped his hat and rode off.*

"Lexie, you are never to ride on one of those animals again! Why, you could have fallen off and broken your neck!"

Tears clouded Lexie's vision as she re-lived the crush of disappointment she'd experienced from her mother's words. She wiped her eyes with the back of her gloved hand. Mother's reaction had only deepened Lexie's desire to ride again, but she had to wait until she went away to college to fulfill that desire. And so far, she hadn't fallen off and broken her neck.

She glanced around her. No beach patrol was in sight. In fact, she hadn't seen them since she'd been on the island.

As Angel plodded along the shore, Lexie studied the sand, looking for seashells and admiring interesting pieces of driftwood. How curious that sun-bleached dead trees could be such works of art. As she rounded the bend, she glanced up and saw a lone figure standing some distance away. The man appeared to be gazing out at the ocean, holding an object in his hands. She stared at the person, trying to figure out what he was doing. Maybe he was one of the guards.

Binoculars. That's what he held. The man looked familiar. Just as she realized who it was, he turned and looked straight at her. She pulled up the reins, stopping the horse, and looked directly at Abner Jones.

Chapter 17

Russell stood up from the piano bench and straightened, stretching his muscles. After sitting on the hard seat for two hours, he was stiff. He'd been so engrossed in the sermon, though, he hadn't even thought about being uncomfortable. Of course, it didn't help that he'd come in an hour early to practice. Even though he could play most of the hymns blindfolded, he still liked to warm up beforehand. To be honest, playing hymns before anyone else came to the chapel was comforting and helped him get into the right attitude for worship.

A few of the congregants made their way over and thanked him for playing.

"We're so blessed to have someone with your talent playing for us."

He nodded and smiled in return. "Guess those piano lessons were worthwhile." Not to mention that minor in music at college. At the time, he'd entertained the notion of playing professionally. Father's heart attack put an end to those plans, though. The club members had agreed with his father's recommendation that Russell was the best qualified to take over the position of club superintendent. So maybe God had a different plan, and playing music in His house of worship was the purpose for Russell's talent. Fame and fortune would have to wait a while longer, if ever.

He shook Reverend Wright's hand and thanked him for his message.

"Will you be able to preach for us all season?" Sometimes finding ministers to come to the island was difficult, especially those with their own congregations.

"I'll do my best. I told Mrs. Prentice I would definitely commit for January and maybe for February, too, if I can work it out."

"We appreciate your willingness to come. I understand you'll be joining some of the ladies at the club for lunch?"

"Yes, they've been nice enough to invite me. Since the missus passed away, I enjoy the opportunity for a nice meal when I can get it."

"You're welcome to join us any time as our guest." Russell patted the reverend on the back as they walked down the aisle to the front door. "Mr. Sullivan will take you back to the launch when you're ready to leave."

The reverend nodded, put on his hat and coat, and walked out the door and down the steps where a cluster of women waited, their hats bobbing in unison as the man approached. Russell smiled and waved, whether anyone noticed or not. Then he walked back in and closed the piano before turning off the lights. Sunlight illuminated the Tiffany stained glass window at the rear of the chapel, sending rainbows throughout the room. He loved the feel of the small chapel, the sacred quiet now that he was alone.

He crossed his arms and stood before the stained glass, commissioned as a memorial window for a former club president. The scene depicting King David on his throne reminded him of the sermon. It was about Joshua, who became the leader of the Israelites when Moses, the great prophet, died. God told Joshua three times to be strong and courageous. Joshua must've felt the same way Russell did when he took over his father's position. Maybe David felt the same way following the footsteps of King Saul. Sometimes it was hard to follow someone who'd been in charge a long time. Wonder if Lexie felt that way about taking over the family responsibilities after Robert died?

Lovely Lexie. Why didn't she want to come to church? Her family used to be regular attendees—they'd sat in the fourth pew on the left. If his memory served him right, though, Lexie's mother and father had become less frequent worshippers, and Lexie attended with only her grandparents. He and Robert sat in the back pew, making jokes about everyone else in the sanctuary. Robert said his mother didn't like the carved animal heads that adorned the end of the rafters. The grotesques, part of the building's Gothic architecture, frightened her. Russell shook his head. What nonsense. But fear took many forms and prevented many people from thinking clearly. How well he knew that.

He checked his watch, noting the time was half past twelve. His stomach growled, reminding him it was lunchtime, but he had an urge to saddle up and find Lexie. He had no idea where she'd gone; however, she was bound to be on a main trail. What would she think about him showing up uninvited? He chuckled to himself. When did he need an invitation to go horseback riding? The stables were his to enjoy as much as anyone else. He glanced down at his suit. This wouldn't do— he'd certainly look ridiculous riding up in this attire. Better hurry and change if he hoped to catch her before she came back, whenever that was.

There was no point in turning around and riding away like some scared ninny. She would just continue on her course and act polite, like a mature adult. Her stomach tightened. She straightened in the saddle and nudged Angel forward.

"Good morning, Mr. Jones."

He grunted and turned back to the sea, raising the binoculars.

She made an effort at conversation. "See anything interesting out there?" Maybe the man was a nature lover.

"Germans."

Lexie's heart stopped.

"Germans? You can see them?"

He shook his head. "Not yet, but I know they're out there. I can always sniff out a German."

Apparently, the man suffered paranoia from his years in the war. Didn't Russell say the German submarines had been spotted farther north? Maybe he was delusional and saw Germans everywhere. She hoped he didn't think she was one.

"Oh, you mean across the Atlantic. I thought you meant right out there." She pointed to the water while Angel snorted and shook her head.

He lowered the binoculars and looked back at her. "They're closer than you think."

Now he was just getting creepy again. She struggled for something else to say.

"If that's the case, I'm certain our military will make sure they stay away." If there were any of Hitler's ships coming close to this country, the U.S. government would keep them from getting too close. Wouldn't they? The war was being fought over there, not here.

Mr. Jones looked up and down the beach before fixing his gaze on her. "Where's our army? Do you see any here?"

She opened her mouth to speak but shut it. Uneasiness made her glance around. He was right. There really wasn't anyone on the island that could protect them from a foreign invasion. Did Abner Jones think he could hold off an invasion by himself? Maybe he did.

"Well, thank you for watching out for the island, Mr. Jones." She had to get away from this man. As she nudged the horse to move again, Abner Jones reached out and grabbed the halter, the horse neighing at the abrupt gesture. Lexie gasped, and her heart raced. The man drew close to the saddle and peered up into her eyes.

"You should watch out, too, Miss Smithfield. You never can tell when an enemy will pop up."

Her breath caught. What should she do?

His attention diverted to something behind her, and the approaching beat of hooves on the beach made her turn to look too. Russell galloped toward them on a gleaming chestnut stallion.

As he neared, he called out. "Hello! There you are, Lexie. I hope I didn't keep you waiting long."

Abner Jones dropped his hand from the halter. Lexie exhaled relief but stared at Russell, confused. Was she supposed to meet him? Russell drew alongside, between her and Abner.

"Abner. I see you're out patrolling the beach. I'm sure Miss Smithfield appreciates the fact that you're looking out for the enemy, don't you?" Russell glanced at Lexie and winked.

"Why, yes, of course. It is a great relief."

"Keep up the good work, Abner." Russell nodded down at the man, turned back to Lexie. "Are you ready to see the other end of the island?"

"Sure. I've been waiting for you." Well, maybe that wasn't quite true, but she sure was happy someone had shown up. Frankly, she couldn't think of anyone else she'd rather see at that moment.

They urged their horses forward, Russell looking over his shoulder to tell Abner good-bye. But the man had resumed his lookout position, binoculars held high and seemed not to notice, much less care about, their departure. They trotted out of Abner Jones' sightline, Russell leading the way.

Lexie called out to Russell above the sound of the waves. "Russell! Stop!"

He pulled his horse to a halt, and he twisted in his saddle to watch her catch up. His broad, cheerful smile warmed her heart in a way she wasn't used to.

"Am I going too fast for you?"

"What? No. I just want to talk to you. I didn't remember that we were meeting today, for one thing."

"You don't? Well, maybe because we weren't—not officially, anyway."

Lexie cocked her head. "So why did you say that?"

"Oh, I don't know. Guess I couldn't think of anything else to say at the moment. Got his attention though."

"Thank goodness you showed up. That man scares me! And I think he scared my horse too." She patted Angel on the neck.

"Angel? Oh, she knows him. Just doesn't like to have her halter grabbed like that." He gave her a wide grin. "I'm glad you're happy to see me."

Lexie blushed. She gave him a twisted smile as she tried to keep focused on her questions.

"Is Mr. Jones really guarding the beach? You said…"

"Well, he thinks he is, so what harm is there? He's still serving his country."

"He warned me, Russell. Told me to be careful. Was he talking about Germans or something else?"

Russell shrugged. "Who knows?"

"Maybe he was warning me about himself."

"Oh, I doubt it. Like I said before, he's harmless, just different."

"Russell, he told me the Germans were close by. You said they were way north of here, like North Carolina or further." She studied his face.

"We don't know exactly where they are. But they could go up and down the whole Atlantic seaboard, for all we know."

"Well, maybe we really *do* need someone to guard the beach. Someone besides Mr. Jones."

"We have somebody. The Coast Guard keeps a man out here walking the beach, looking out for anything suspicious."

Lexie looked around, scanning the distance for a sign of anyone. "Where?"

"Probably at the other end now. The guard rotates men. They come over from the base on the mainland."

"Well, that's good to know. It makes me feel safer, and I'm sure you're glad to have them here to protect the club members."

Russell laughed and shook his head.

"What's so funny?"

"Don't know how much protection one lonely man walking the beach is against a submarine, but I guess that's better than nothing."

So much for feeling safer.

Chapter 18

Russell turned his horse away from the beach to the trail through the woods. Lexie followed suit, casting an anxious glance up at the trees, just in case one decided to fall.

The narrow path didn't allow them to ride side-by-side, so Lexie was happy to let Russell take the lead should anything unexpected occur.

Lexie studied Russell's silhouette from behind. He sat straight and tall, quite comfortable in the saddle. He probably rode often, since it was so convenient. Unlike her, especially after Father died. Mother had become so overprotective—afraid to let Lexie out of her sight lest something bad happen to her as well.

College had given Lexie freedom to do what she wanted—as long as she came home every weekend to check in and assure Mother she was all right. Strange that her mother wanted to take care of her daughter's well-being when she couldn't even take care of her own. In the end, it was the reverse, with daughter taking care of mother, especially after Robert joined the navy.

Now she had the independence she'd yearned for, but was she capable of taking care of herself? Watching Russell lead the way, she realized he was taking care of her. At least he seemed to be. He always showed up at the right time—right when she needed him. How did he manage that? It was almost as if he knew she'd need help.

The smell of fresh-cut pine wafted through the air. Lexie inhaled the fragrance, which grew stronger as they moved along. She glanced through the trees to her left and saw more daylight, indicating a clearing. With alarm, she noticed a large area of tree stumps and fallen trees. She called out to Russell up ahead.

"Russell! Why are all those trees cut down?"

He stopped his horse and turned it in the direction of the clearing. She pulled up beside him and pointed.

"Timbering. We contracted with a lumber company to sell some of the trees on the island."

"But why? I thought everything would be kept natural."

Russell gave her a sad smile and lifted his shoulders. "Money. The club needed more revenue."

She shook her head in disbelief. "There was no other way?"

"We've considered a number of ideas to increase the club's income— golf tournaments, tennis tournaments, and so on, but it hasn't been enough." He nodded toward the cut trees. "This has been the most lucrative idea yet."

She remembered her conversation with Mr. Mason, the waiter, about the club lowering the dues to attract newcomers.

"I understand some of the original members no longer belong to the club. Weren't they replaced by new ones?"

Russell's dimples revealed themselves in the smile he gave her. "Some were, but it seems our country's running out of millionaires. Your grandfather's generation is almost gone, and along with them, the wealth they brought to the island."

Why did she feel guilty? It wasn't her fault the family money was gone and she needed to sell the cottage. Yet, for some reason, she wanted to help. After all, her grandfather was one of the founding members of the club. What would happen if all the founding families left the island? What would happen to Russell? He'd spent his life here.

"I'm sorry, Russell. I had no idea."

"So you see why we'd like you to keep Destiny?"

She nodded, but could she tell him she couldn't even afford the taxes on the property?

"I'll give it some thought." Not that thinking about it would solve her problem, much less provide the funds.

They rode on past the island dairy where fat cows grazed in the fields. Beyond the dairy, the path led past the ruins of Horton House, its tabby walls keeping secrets of the earliest settlers on the island. Russell paused beside the old structure and waited for her to pull alongside.

"Remember when we used to play here?" Russell's grin hinted mischief.

"Of course I do." Lexie scanned the area. "I pretended it was my castle."

"And Robert and I were the Indians attacking the castle."

"Indians didn't attack castles."

"*We* did." Russell laughed as he turned his horse back to the trail. He pointed to his right. "And the ghosts were over there."

Lexie followed his gaze. She shuddered when she saw the fence surrounding the old cemetery where the island's first inhabitants were buried. "That was always a creepy place. I never liked going there," she said.

"Just old tombstones. Actually, I've always found it interesting to read the epitaphs."

"Really? I never read them. Besides, Mother would have killed me if she'd known I ventured this far from the compound."

"Would you like to take a look now?"

Lexie flashed a frown at him. "No, thank you. Let them rest in peace."

Russell laughed again, nudged his heels into the stallion, and the horse began to trot. Lexie followed suit, and they proceeded along the trail back to the stables. When they reached the building, Russell dismounted then helped her down. A rich bass voice greeted them from inside singing, "Great is thy faithfulness! Great is thy faithfulness!" George appeared in the doorway of the stables.

"Y'all have a nice ride?" The man's grin covered his face. "Nice day for it."

"Yes, we did, George. It's a beautiful day for a horseback ride."

"Yes, sir. This is the day the Lord has made."

George took the reins of the horses, patting each one of them on their necks. "Did Angel behave for you, Miss Smithfield?"

"Yes, she did. Well, she was an angel."

George laughed as he turned to lead the horses to the stalls. He resumed his singing as he walked. "Great is thy faithfulness!"

Lexie glanced at Russell, who beamed his familiar smile.

"What a beautiful voice he has."

"He sure does. He preaches at the servants' church."

Lexie looked back at the stables. "He does? How did he have time to meet me this morning?"

"Ha-ha! Well, the service goes on quite a while because they spend so much time singing and praising God before the sermon starts. They probably didn't even miss him."

"He certainly seems happy, like he doesn't have a care in the world."

"You might be surprised. He's had his troubles, but he keeps a positive attitude."

Troubles? She'd like to know how he stayed so happy.

As Lexie and Russell strolled away from the stables, she recalled hearing music from the chapel earlier that morning.

"Russell, I thought you said the church service at Faith Chapel didn't start until eleven."

"That's right. Why?"

"Well, as I walked to the stables this morning, I heard a piano when I passed the chapel."

"I'm sure you did. The pianist was probably practicing, warming up."

"The melody was lovely and stayed in my mind. Have you ever had that happen?"

"All the time. Do you remember it? Maybe if you could hum a few bars, I might recognize the tune."

"No, I'm afraid I lost it when I encountered Abner Jones. But I would know it if I heard it again."

"Well, if you'll come to service next Sunday, you might hear it again."

Lexie bit her lip, trying to come up with another excuse.

"All right, I won't pressure you. But you were missed."

She raised her eyebrow and crossed her arms. "Missed? By whom?"

"Oh, a few of the ladies inquired about you. And I also saw Floyd and his mother watching the door so they could pounce on you when you entered."

"Wonderful. And you were giving me reasons *not* to attend?"

Russell chuckled, his dimple appearing. "Perhaps I should try another tactic?"

"Like give up?"

"Never."

Lexie was grateful for the long walk back to the clubhouse and the chance to talk with Russell. His relaxed way of making everything look better, even fun, lifted the burden she carried. She had to trust him. She had no one else. As they passed the dormitories, Russell nodded and waved at the servants milling around on their day off. Of course, he knew everyone's names, their positions, and their family history, which he explained to her along the way. Why did everyone seem so much friendlier now than when she walked by them that morning?

"Howard, how's that leg doing? Better rest it up and not rush it. We need you back healthy." Russell addressed a man whose knee had a large bandage around it.

"Darlene, how's that grandbaby? Will we be seeing her soon?" The woman on her porch smiled and nodded.

"Soon as they bring him over for a visit, Mr. Russell."

"Ernest, any word from your son yet?" Russell explained to Lexie that the man's son was in the army overseas somewhere.

Lexie studied Russell. Was he really that nice?

"What?" He turned toward her with a grin and a twinkle in his eye. "What are you looking at?"

"I'm just amazed that you know everybody's business."

Again laughter accompanied his response. "Lexie, I've known these people all my life, and it's a small community. Everybody knows everybody's business."

"But all the servants don't live here, do they?"

"No, some live in Brunswick and come over daily. Many live in the dorms just for the season, but there are a few cabins on Red Row that were built a long time ago. Those families live here year-round."

Lexie stopped. "Well, if everybody knows everybody's business, they should know who's been hanging around Destiny, shouldn't they?"

"If it's someone who lives here, yes. But you know Destiny is on the other side of the island from the servants' quarters, so they don't see it all the time."

She nodded and continued walking before stopping again. "Russell, I've been doing a lot of thinking. When I watched the movie the other night about all those people trying to get their hands on the Maltese Falcon, it made me wonder if someone's trying to get something I have, or they think I have. I just don't know what it could be."

"That would explain a few things, but we don't know who or what."

"Not yet. But I want to find out. Tomorrow, I want to go back to the cottage and see if I can figure out what it might be. Plus I haven't been to the third-floor servants' rooms."

"You think there would be anything valuable in the servants' rooms?"

"Not really, but it might trigger a memory."

"Are you sure you want to go back after last time?"

"Yes, I do. But I would like for you to go with me, if you can spare the time."

Russell's grin covered his face. "My dear Lexie, I'll find the time. Come by my office after breakfast, and I'll let you know when I can leave."

"Terrific." This time, she'd be ready to face whatever or whoever she found. The memory of someone's shadow triggered a chill. "Do you know what the weather will be like tomorrow?"

As if he read her mind, he said, "No thunderstorms."

She breathed a sigh of relief. Thank goodness, there'd be no storms, at least not the weather-type.

Chapter 19

$\mathcal{L}$exie enjoyed the privacy of being first in the dining room the next morning. She had discovered that if she went to breakfast as soon as service began, no one else would be there and she wouldn't have to run into other people, such as Floyd and his mother.

The aroma of fresh-brewed coffee mingled with the smell of bacon frying, waking Lexie's senses. Shafts of morning sunlight pierced the windows, promising a lovely winter's day. Today would be a good day to face the cottage. This time, she'd be ready for any surprises.

Or so she told herself. Today Russell would go with her again. Not that she needed his company, but he was beginning to be a habit. A smile eased across her face at the thought. There could be worse habits. She'd expected to be completely alone on the island, but Russell had prevented that from happening. She appreciated his protection. But what did she need protection from here? Or who?

Lexie fiddled with her pearls while hearing the murmur of the staff as they readied the room for incoming guests. Each time the kitchen door opened, the volume of noise rose with the rattle of pans and dishes. Lexie looked over her shoulder and saw Mr. Mason coming her way.

"Good morning, Miss Smithfield. The usual?"

"Good morning, Mr. Mason. Yes, please."

"Lovely day today, ma'am." The waiter took her napkin, shook it, and handed it to her. "Will you be going to Destiny this morning?"

Lexie retorted, "Why do you ask that?"

The waiter frowned. "No reason, ma'am. I heard you were here to check on your family cottage. I didn't mean to intrude on your personal affairs."

Lexie cringed with remorse. She had to stop suspecting everyone. "I'm sorry, Mr. Mason. Yes, I am going to the cottage."

"Yes, ma'am. Excuse me while I get your tea and scones." He bowed and turned.

As the old gentleman walked away, Lexie scolded herself. How could she possibly question the motives of kind Mr. Mason? He had probably heard about the condition of the cottage from the housekeeping staff.

When he returned with her breakfast, she touched his hand and peered up at his face. "Mr. Mason, I apologize for my abrupt response earlier. I don't know what came over me."

The gentleman smiled and nodded. "No need to apologize ma'am."

"Thank you. What time do most of the other guests arrive for breakfast?"

"I don't know when all the guests arrive, but the Appletons usually come in around nine." He gave her a knowing look.

A quick glance at her watch told her she still had time to enjoy herself before they appeared. Mr. Mason was a very attentive man, and it was clear he was on her side.

She smiled a thank you, and he left her to her meal. After breakfast, she'd go to Russell's office, and they'd go to the cottage together. He told her he usually started work about seven-thirty, so he'd be there before nine. Other people began to trickle into the dining room, among them the ladies she had met before. They acknowledged her with nods and smiles across the room. Lexie hurried, just in case one of them wanted to talk with her.

When she finished eating, she rose from the table and made her way across the room, weaving between tables. As she passed by one, someone grabbed her hand. She halted and glanced down, noting an elderly lady holding onto her.

"Helen? Why Helen, I haven't seen you in so long! Where have you been?"

Lexie sucked in a breath, and she stared at the woman. An elderly gentleman seated beside the woman leaned over to her. "Gladys, that's not Helen."

"It's not?" The lady scrutinized Lexie up and down. "Why, she looks like Helen."

"Helen was my mother. I'm Alexandra Smithfield, her daughter."

A confused look crossed the woman's face. "Well, you're just like her."

Lexie forced a polite smile and eased her hand out of the woman's grasp. "Please excuse me." She hurried out the door.

No. She was not like her mother. She would *not* let that happen.

Two uniformed men passed Lexie in the hallway as she exited the dining room. Their dark blue suits were similar to Robert's Navy uniform. She watched them as they took the stairs, the somber expression on their faces denoting a serious visit. Since Lexie was headed the same direction, she ended up following them. She stopped at her floor as they continued up the stairs. But curiosity got the better of her, so she waited a moment, then crept up the stairs to the fourth floor. When she heard Russell's door close, she halted.

No doubt this was not a good time to see Russell. She should go elsewhere and come back later. But the sound of voices drifting into the hallway piqued her curiosity. Although the men closed the door behind them, it had not latched and reopened a crack. Lexie recognized Russell's voice and another man's—Mr. Prentice. She really shouldn't stand out there and listen.

However, she couldn't will her feet to move and found herself straining to hear. When she heard "submarine" and "torpedoed," her attention was riveted to the conversation. Her heart raced as she ventured a step closer. "Off the coast of North Carolina" jolted her attention. The voices lowered, preventing her from hearing more. As she turned to leave, the word "president" rang from the room. Murmuring followed, then the scraping of chairs, signaling her that the men were about to leave.

She spun around and rushed down the hall, trying to keep her footsteps quiet. As she turned the corner, she heard the men come out the door behind her, saying their good-byes.

She hurried down the stairs and, when she reached the lobby, strode over to an armchair beside the fireplace. Lexie plopped down and grabbed a copy of *Life* magazine from the table adjacent, waiting for the officials to leave. A few moments later, they strode past her, speaking in low tones while she peered over the top of the magazine she pretended to read.

When they went through the doors and left the building, she closed the magazine and put it back on the table. She couldn't wait to find out what the men's visit was about, so she hurried back upstairs to Russell's office. But through the partially closed door, she heard the voices of Russell and Mr. Prentice. So Russell was still in a meeting. She puffed out a breath. How long would he be tied up? Should she wait here for him?

"Looks like we might have to cancel the tennis tournament. First the golf tournament, now the tennis … don't know how we'll raise enough revenue this year."

"Bernon, shouldn't our concern be about the safety of our members? I know we need the money, but U-boats this close seems to me a bigger priority."

"I know what the officers said, but really, do you expect the Germans to shoot at our beaches? I can see the harm to ships, but why would they bother with our little island?"

"Because 'our' little island has some of the world's wealthiest Americans, that why. They told us the president is concerned."

Lexie's heart dropped. German submarines were that close? So Abner wasn't so crazy after all. Maybe he really had seen them.

Before she had a chance to react, the door to Russell's office opened and Mr. Prentice came out. His frown disappeared when he saw her, and he assumed a relaxed expression.

"Good Morning, Miss Smithfield. How are you today?"

Lexie fought to keep from blushing. "I'm fine, thank you. I was on my way to meet Russell." As if she needed to explain her presence and appear innocent of eavesdropping.

"You're going back to the cottage today?"

Did everyone know her business?

He smiled and answered her unasked question. "Russell told me he was going back over there with you this morning."

Russell stepped out of his office, shrugging on his jacket. A grin spread across his face when he saw her. "I thought I heard your voice out here, Lexie."

Her heart surprised her by doing a little dance when he appeared. "Hi, Russell. I hope I'm not interrupting you." She hoped her expression didn't give away her guilt.

"Not at all." He gestured toward Mr. Prentice. "We were just getting finished."

"Well, I'm off." Mr. Prentice gave Russell a mock salute. "Miss Smithfield, I'm still waiting for that game of tennis. The weather is nice enough today if you're interested in hitting a few balls later."

Lexie offered a shy smile. "Perhaps I'll take you up on it sometime, but I don't know if it'll be today."

"Whenever you're ready, I am." He spun on his heels and headed down the hall.

"Are you all set to go to the cottage?" Russell looked down at her as she watched Mr. Prentice stride away.

"Yes, if you are."

"Let's walk, shall we?" Russell stepped beside her and gestured for her to proceed. "We need to do our patriotic duty to conserve gas."

"Of course. I'd prefer it, actually." Perhaps walking was more difficult for him, though, with his foot injury. As they moved along the hall, she glanced at his foot, then his face for any sign of discomfort. "Does it hurt?"

He looked at her, followed her eyes to his foot, and smiled. "Not usually. When it's cold and damp, though, it reminds me it's there."

"I suppose winter isn't your favorite time of year."

"Oh, there are trade-offs, though."

"Such as?" She tilted her head.

"Since winter is our busy season here, there's a lot to do to keep me distracted from my foot."

"Oh, I didn't think of that." Her heart winced thinking of his pain. "I'm sorry, Russell."

"Sorry? For what?"

"I'm sorry about your foot. However, you'd never know it bothered you at all, much less interfered with your ability to do anything."

"It doesn't, for most things. Just military service." He gave her a wistful smile. "So looks like I'll be staying here, protecting the home front."

Should she let him know she overheard anything? "And you think the home front needs protecting?"

He didn't answer while they exited the building but took a deep breath of fresh air outside and smiled. "Terrific day for a stroll. Shall we?" He extended his elbow for her to grasp.

Lexie accepted and turned her attention to the cloudless azure sky. It was evident Russell wanted to change the subject, so she didn't pressure him for more information. But sooner or later, she'd get the truth out of him. Besides, if the news was so serious, wouldn't they be sharing it with the other people on the island? Why would they keep such things secret?

Lexie was beginning to believe there were too many secrets on the island, including those that involved her. She promised herself she'd discover the truth and trust Russell to help her. Unless he was too busy keeping his own secrets.

Chapter 20

Lexie looked happy for a change, her smile fixed on her face as they strolled together. Maybe it was the nice weather. But she even seemed happy to see him. Or did he imagine that because he wanted to believe it? The more time they spent together, the stronger his feelings were for her, but he had little hope they'd be reciprocated. She was out of his league, and he needed to remember that. Besides, she'd be gone soon, away from the island and probably out of his life. Unless she kept the cottage and came back next season. But even if she did, she might bring a new husband with her.

It was going to be hard to keep his feelings under control though. The way her blonde curls danced as she strolled alongside enchanted him. Especially so today, when she didn't seem to have a care in the world. If only that were true. Just 500 miles to the north, an American tanker was torpedoed by a German U-boat during the night. There were no survivors. The guys from the Coast Guard told him and Prentice to keep it under wraps for now. If word got out, people on the coast might panic. So how was he supposed to keep everyone on the island safe when he couldn't tell them what was going on in their own backyard?

The Coast Guard told him they'd increase the beach patrols. Guess that meant sending two guys instead of one. He'd have to solicit extra help from some of his own employees. And yet, he was supposed to do that without arousing suspicion. Sometimes he and Prentice didn't see things the same way. If the members really were in danger, why not tell them and let them leave if they wanted to? But the club president wanted to keep them there for as long as possible and get more of their money. Sure, they needed the money, but at what risk?

Right after lunch, he'd get on it and round up some guys to serve guard duty. For now, though, the feisty woman next to him had his attention. And that of everyone else, based on the heads that turned as they walked by. The smack of balls hitting each other caused them to glance over at the people lawn bowling. At least this tournament wouldn't be cancelled, since it was so close.

"Looks like they're practicing for the tournament this weekend," he said.

An elderly gentleman in white pants and shirt sporting a beret rolled his ball on the grass.

"I didn't realize there was a tournament." Her eyes grew big as saucers and her mouth fell open. "Is that Floyd?"

Russell grinned and nodded as the human scarecrow took his turn. "Yep. Sure is. He hopes to win the Cup this year."

"I never knew him to play a sport!"

Russell noted the other players, most of whom were twice Floyd's age.

"He keeps trying to beat out Mr. Gibbs, who wins every year. But Gibbs is getting pretty old and might not be as steady this year."

Lexie covered her mouth and giggled, her blue eyes sparkling with delight.

"We better move on so you won't distract him from his game." Russell took her arm and led her away, his heart melting at her smile.

"Do you play?" Lexie glanced up as she walked beside him.

"I can, but it's not my favorite sport. I prefer golf when I get a chance. Do you play golf?" Of course she did, as competitive as she was.

"Yes. I played in college and a little since, but I haven't had much time to play anything since I got out of school."

He drew back and studied her. "Why not?" As he watched her expression turn solemn, he regretted his question.

"I've spent most my time at the hospital where Mother was."

Did she need to work for the money or did she just want to? It wouldn't be polite to ask her, but he was curious. Robert had mentioned the finances being tight, but were things that bad? Still, the girl had moxie. Poor kid—having to deal with her crazy mother all these years. Yet she still wanted to work around folks like that. It took a special kind of person for that kind of work. She was special, all right.

"Oh, I see. I didn't realize you spent so much time there. No time for fun?"

"Not really."

"So, what are you planning to do? Be a doctor?" He chuckled at the thought of the cute blonde as a doctor.

She stopped and faced him, hands on her hips. "Maybe. Why not? Don't you think I could be?"

What a look of determination she had. He put his hand on her shoulder and gazed into blue eyes that matched the sky. "Lexie, I believe you can be anything you want to be."

Her face turned rose-red, adding a pretty blush to her cheeks. She turned away from him and quickened her pace. He hadn't meant to embarrass her, but she was so cute when she got flustered. Time to change the subject.

"So what are we going to do at the cottage today?"

"I want to go to the third floor, the servants' quarters. Plus, I'd like to get a good look at the whole place in good light and make a list of what needs to be repaired. Oh, shoot! I forgot to bring something to take notes on."

He pulled a tablet out of his inside jacket pocket and held it up. "Like this?"

Her face lit up with a wide grin. "Gee, thanks. What would I do without you?"

"Always looking out for you, you see." Once again, he watched her cheeks turn pink. He really was looking out for her, but his reasons were partly selfish, to be honest. He wanted to convince her to keep the cottage, but there might be some people who'd convince her otherwise. Keeping her in sight would prevent her from listening to them. But he had to admit, he enjoyed this part of his job.

He was like having another big brother around. Sort of. On the other hand, the way her heart fluttered when he smiled at her, his green eyes sparkling, was not a typical reaction to a brother. Lexie couldn't get over how much time had altered their rapport. And his appearance. He was a dapper dresser, his suit and tie impeccable, his hat at just the right angle. She always did admire a man who knew how to dress. His limp was barely noticeable.

She couldn't shake the image of Floyd Appleton bowling and wanted to laugh out loud. Maybe he wasn't the most athletic man she knew, but she had to admit she was glad to see him outside and away from his mother. No doubt she was watching him from a rocking chair on the veranda. And if she were, she also saw Lexie walk by with Russell. Lexie quickly glanced over her shoulder.

"What's wrong?" Russell looked back to follow her gaze.

"Oh, nothing. Just wondered if anyone was following us."

"Don't see anybody. Why would anyone follow us?"

"I don't know. Guess I'm just a little jumpy."

Russell placed his hand on her arm and patted it. "Hey, remember I'm here. Who's gonna bother you with me around, eh?" He held up his arm as if showing off a muscle. Although his jacket covered his arm, Lexie had seen him without it and noticed how strong he looked.

She crossed her hands over her heart. "Ooh, my hero!"

Russell laughed aloud and nodded. "That's right. Ready to save a damsel in distress."

Lexie laughed, too, and gave him a little shove. "You shouldn't overestimate yourself, Russell."

As they neared the cottage, Lexie noted how far away from the others it was and how close to the woods and marsh. Grandfather's quest for privacy had resulted in isolating the cottage from the rest of the club. It would be easy for someone to get into the house without being noticed. The sound of a motor drew Lexie's attention to Jekyll River behind the house where the men from the Coast Guard puttered past after leaving the island dock. Someone could get to the cottage from the water too.

Lexie turned to Russell, whose attention was on the departing boat as well.

"What were those men doing here?" Might as well come right out and ask.

His expression was more serious than normal as he faced her, but he tried to mask it with a smile. She could tell he was worried, even if he wanted her to think he wasn't.

"They come by occasionally to check on things. Remember, I told you they keep a patrol on the beach?"

"Russell, I think you're not telling me everything. Please, tell me what's going on."

He studied her face a few seconds, his eyes penetrating as if he could see through her. A warm tingle worked its way through her body. What was he thinking?

Sighing, he blew out a breath. "All right. I'll level with you, but please keep it under wraps."

"I promise I won't tell anyone else." She crossed her heart with her fingers. Besides, she had no one else to tell.

"They came to tell us that a ship was torpedoed off the coast of North Carolina—sunk by a German submarine."

Her eyes widened. "When?"

"During the night."

"And the Coast Guard thinks that might happen here?"

"It's pretty shallow near our coast. But yes, they could be in the deeper water out there."

"So what should we do? What did they say?"

Russell glanced away. "They think we should end the season here early. Meanwhile, they will increase their guard duty and asked us to keep an eye out as well."

"But they don't want anyone to know?"

He focused on her face again. "No. The government doesn't want people to panic, just be on the lookout."

"For what? Submarines? Do they think submarines might come in here?" She pointed to the river. "There?"

"I suppose anything is possible. However, I think they'd be seen from the beach side before they got to this side of the island."

"I can't imagine a submarine there in the river."

"No, I don't think they'd bring a submarine back here. It'd be more likely that they'd launch a raft with a few men that could come into shallow waters."

"Russell! Destiny is the first cottage they'd come to. Nobody would see if they came ashore behind the cottage!"

Russell grabbed her shoulders and peered into her face. "Lexie, calm down. Nobody's going to come ashore back here. They'd be seen before they got this far. Besides, I think they'd prefer to sink tankers and hurt our oil supply. That's what was sunk last night. See, I shouldn't have told you about it and gotten you upset."

Lexie took a deep breath and exhaled slowly. "No, I'm glad you told me, Russell. So what will you do about the club members? Will you tell them the season's been shortened?"

"I'm not sure yet how Mr. Prentice will handle it. He's already cancelled the golf tournament in March just because so many golfers have joined the war effort, and it just doesn't seem right to have a major golf tournament during the war. We may still have the tennis tournament, but make it a club tournament instead of a major tournament. I'm sure he'd like you to play in it."

"I don't know, Russell. I still don't know how long I'm staying."

"If it's up to me, I'd keep you here as long as possible."

Lexie's heart lurched. She cocked her head and stared at him.

"Why?"

"To keep you out of trouble, of course." The familiar grin appeared, and he winked at her. "Robert would want me to watch out for his kid sister."

So that was it. She was still just Robert's kid sister. Some things never changed. Why did she think he meant anything else? She gave him a crooked smile.

"So does that mean you're not going to let me out of your sight? Shouldn't you be watching out for Germans instead?"

Russell laughed as they approached the door to the cottage. He withdrew a key from his pocket and unlocked the door.

"Never fear. I can do both at once. From now on, you go everywhere with me. No more horseback riding on the beach alone."

Lexie's mind flashed back to her horseback ride on the beach where she came upon Abner Jones looking for Germans. Maybe he wasn't so crazy after all. Or maybe he knew something no one else did.

Chapter 21

L exie entered the cottage with Russell close behind. Everything looked the same as before, but brighter without the storm. The musty smell still permeated the air, despite the maids' attempts to clean the house. Must be the old wallpaper, sadly in need of replacing.

She pointed to a stain running from the corner of the ceiling down the side of the wall. "There must be another leak. There's one upstairs too."

Russell glanced over and nodded, taking out the pad and making a note.

There were so many things she would do if she was going to stay here again—buy new furniture and curtains, add pictures, replace the mirror over the fireplace—but she wasn't here to renovate the cottage, just repair it so someone else could make the other changes. It would never be the way it used to be, no matter what she did to it. She squeezed her eyes shut to hush the voices from the past that whispered memories. The past was gone, and she needed to leave it behind.

She rounded the corner and stepped into the kitchen, remembering the last time she'd been there and found Abner Jones inside. An involuntary shudder shook her shoulders.

"Are you okay?" Russell watched her cautiously tread around the room. He walked over to the back door and turned the knob. It opened without hesitation. "Hmmm. Looks like the latch is pulled loose. I know I latched it last time, but the wood is worn. I'll have someone from maintenance check on it." He made another note.

Lexie paused in front of the dumbwaiter.

"Want to climb in and play hide-and-seek?" Russell pulled the creaky horizontal steel door open to reveal the mesh metal cage inside.

"No, I don't think so. Not sure I would fit now anyway."

He eyed her up and down. "Sure you could. You're taller, but still small enough to fold yourself up to fit."

She shook her head. "It wouldn't be fun anymore, just uncomfortable."

"I suppose you're right. Hard to believe we all used to fit in there, isn't it?"

Lexie remembered how they used to take turns hiding. She couldn't imagine tall Russell in there now.

"Let's go upstairs." Lexie led the way, anxious to leave the kitchen. She scanned the rooms, then the hall, looking for anything unusual.

The stairs groaned with their weight as she and Russell climbed up. At the top, Lexie surveyed the open landing before proceeding to each room. As she entered her mother and father's bedroom, she had the urge to open the dresser drawers. When she did, she gasped.

Russell ran over to her. "What is it?"

She pointed to the drawers. "They're all broken. The bottoms have been broken out." She turned to Russell. "Why? Why would someone do this?"

He shook his head. "All I can figure is that someone thought something might be hidden in the drawers or under them." He rubbed his chin. "You didn't open these last time you were here?"

"No, why?"

"I wonder if the damage would have been noticed by the maids. If so, no one mentioned it to me."

"Let's check the other drawers, Russell."

They went from room to room, checking drawers. Every one of them had been damaged.

"Somebody's certainly trying to find something," Lexie said.

"Sure appears that way." Russell squatted down and examined one of the dressers.

"I wish I knew what they were looking for."

Russell looked up at her. "Apparently, whoever it is thinks you know."

"Why would you say that?"

"Because they wanted you to come here and find it for them, lead them to it." He pulled himself up as he focused on her face.

Lexie's hands flew to her mouth, her heart thumping. "How do you know that?"

"They sent you a telegram so you'd come."

"So they must be following me ... or watching me." Lexie whispered the words as she glanced around, trembling.

Russell put his arms around her and pulled her close. "It's okay. We'll get to the bottom of this."

She felt the tears forming but forced them back. She couldn't fall apart and make Russell think she was helpless. But his arms strengthened her and his commitment reinforced her resolve. Much as she wanted to collapse, she fought for control. She pushed back and raised her eyes to peer up at him. "I'll be all right. Thank you for being here."

"Looks like you're stuck with me now." The warmth of his smile radiated through her. "Are you ready to go?"

She shook her head. "No. I wanted to go to the third floor, too, remember?"

"That's right." He nodded. "I almost forgot there was a third floor. I think Robert and I only went up there a few times to hide."

They passed by the room that had the leaky window and Lexie pointed it out while Russell jotted down a note. The only stairs to the third floor were around the corner in the servants' quarters. The children's nannies stayed in the second-floor quarters so they could be near the children. The other servants were on the third floor, which was only accessible by the back staircase which came up from the kitchen.

As Lexie and Russell climbed the stairs, Lexie sensed that someone had been there recently. She sniffed the air, which wasn't as musty as other parts of the house, a sign that the doors had been opened recently, allowing fresh air to flow through. They climbed the creaky, narrow stairs to the top then stepped out into a small hallway with doors on either side. Lexie and Russell peeked in each of the six small bedrooms, which were much smaller than Lexie remembered with a single bed, tiny table, and short dresser taking up most of the space in each.

Lexie halted in front of one of them and pointed to the window. "That's the one I saw from outside that looks like someone threw a rock at it."

"That or they shot a gun at it."

Lexie drew back and looked up at him. "A gun?"

"Those are fairly small holes, and it's a pretty far distance to throw a rock that high."

"Oh my. Someone could've been hurt if they'd been standing by the window."

"Maybe. But they'd have to be standing close to it, since the bullets would go straight up." He glanced at the ceiling. "See?" He reached up and pulled a bullet from the ceiling. "But Lexie, no one's been here, so no one's been shot. It was just a stupid prank."

Lexie scanned the room, trying to figure out what bothered her. A whiff of cigarette smoke invaded her nostrils.

"Russell! Someone's been in here recently."

"Sure they have. The maids probably came up here to clean."

"That was several days ago. But I smell cigarette smoke, like someone smoked in here not long ago."

He looked at her askance. "I don't smell anything."

"Of course you don't because you smoke too." Lexie faced him with her hands on her hips. "I know you smoke when I'm not around to see you. I can smell it on your clothes, your breath."

"I confess. I still have the habit. Are you saying I was in here?"

Lexie shook her head. "No, of course not. But someone has been here recently and smoked in this room."

"The maids know better than to smoke inside while they're cleaning."

"Maybe it wasn't a maid." She studied the floor as she walked around the small room.

"What are you looking for?"

"A cigarette butt, ashes, anything."

"Do you think someone would put that on the floor?"

She looked up at him and cocked her head. "Maybe not, but I bet there's some around here somewhere."

Her eyes traveled to the window pierced by holes. "Out there. I bet we'll find a cigarette butt outside below the window." She turned and ran out the door.

"Hey, wait for me!" Russell yelled behind her.

She ran to the servant staircase door, opened it, and ran down the steps. The cigarette smell was even stronger in the stairwell, confirming her suspicion. She ran out the back door and around to the lawn below the third-floor window. Russell joined her, and together, they studied the grass and ground below the shrubs by the house.

"Russell, does Abner smoke?" Lexie kept her head down as she asked.

"Probably. Everybody smokes."

She stopped to glare at him. "I don't."

"All right. Everybody *else* smokes. But honestly Lexie, as fastidious as Abner is about the lawn, I don't think he'd litter it with cigarette butts. What if this 'smoker' put out the cigarette, then put it in his pocket?"

She hadn't thought of that. But they didn't see any sign of cigarettes, so maybe that's exactly what happened.

"Of course, it could've been one of the maids when they were here."

"Maybe, but they haven't been here in a couple of days, and the odor was recent, like even today."

After scrutinizing the ground, they still found no sign of cigarettes. She was about to give up when a glint from the top of the bushes caught her eye. She reached across a shrub and grabbed an object stuck between two leaves.

It was a cigarette butt, a silver stripe around the filter revealing its location. She held it up for Russell to see. He took the item from her, turning it around to examine.

"Looks new," he said. "So someone's been in the house recently and they smoke. What does that mean?"

Lexie put her finger to her chin. "They must have been looking out the window." She spun around and ran to the back door, with Russell following. She ran up the stairs to the third floor and back to the bedroom with the broken window. She crossed the room and gazed out, no longer looking at the window, but beyond. When Russell caught up with her, he was breathless.

"Look." Lexie pointed out the window.

"Look at what?"

"What can you see from here?"

"The yard, the trees, the river."

"That's right. Russell, this is the only room on the third floor that has a view of the river!"

"Are you sure?"

"Yes! The thought crossed my mind when we looked at the other rooms that they had no view because they looked straight into the trees. But this room is between the trees, so there's a good view of the water."

He gave her a quizzical expression. "So somebody came up here to look at the water?"

"I think so. Maybe he expected someone, someone who was coming up the river."

"So why not wait for them at the boat dock?"

Lexie's heart stilled. "Maybe they weren't going to the dock. Maybe they were coming ashore here. Russell, do you think someone on the island is working with the Germans and is helping them get on our island?"

Chapter 22

Russell wanted to tell her the idea was absurd, but he couldn't discount the remote possibility. Should he mention it to the Coast Guard? What if it was nothing, just a maid throwing a cigarette out the window? He'd look pretty ridiculous if that's all it was. Still, he had to calm Lexie down and not let her imagination get carried away.

"Lexie, I sincerely doubt Germans would want to invade the island. What good would it do since they'd still have to get to the mainland?"

Her widened eyes told him she still worried about the scenario she'd proposed.

"I don't know, Russell. Maybe use the island as a base to signal their subs? It's a pretty big island and there aren't many of us here."

He shook his head. What she didn't know was that President Roosevelt was already concerned about the wealthy club members on the island, many of whom were his friends.

"If it'll make you feel better, we'll have our guards patrol the river bank too. But we know most of the people here pretty well and know they're on our side, not our enemy's."

Her shoulders relaxed. "Okay. Maybe I am jumping to conclusions."

"I need to get back to the clubhouse. Are you ready to go?"

She nodded, and they started walking back.

"I'll get the window fixed right away." At least he could do that much. Perhaps if he took care of the repairs quickly, Lexie wouldn't be so spooked about the cottage. Still, he couldn't make sense of the situation. Maybe she had blown things out of proportion, but these days, he had to be more alert to any possibility. Was there a chance someone on the island was aiding the enemy? If so, who?

"Thank you." Lexie's face was set with determination. She thought she was on to something, and he could tell she was eager to find out what it was.

"Lexie, I just don't see a connection between damaged drawers and a person looking out the third-floor window."

"I don't either, Russell. I've been wracking my brain trying to figure out what's going on. I suppose there's a chance neither has anything to do with the other."

As they approached the clubhouse, Lexie glanced over at the lawn bowlers again. Floyd was still there, watching another man take his turn as smoke curled up from the cigarette in his hand.

"So Floyd smokes too." Lexie nodded in Floyd's direction.

"Do you see a man out here that doesn't?"

He watched her scan the group, frowning as she shook her head. "No. I guess you're right. Most men smoke."

"Looks like you haven't narrowed down your list of suspects."

"No, but there's only one man I've seen around the cottage." She leveled her gaze at him.

"Abner." Why did she insist on pointing the finger at the old yardman?

"Yes, Abner," she said, crossing her arms. " You don't think he's the one, though, do you?"

"No, I don't. Abner watches over the property. He wouldn't damage it."

"Hey, Alexandra!"

They paused and turned to see Floyd striding across the lawn toward them.

"Alexandra, I had hoped to see you today." Floyd glanced at Russell. "Hello, Russell." If that was a hint for him to leave, Russell wasn't taking it.

Russell nodded. "Floyd." Besides, Lexie would kill him if he abandoned her to Floyd.

Floyd moved around to Lexie's side in an effort to speak with her privately. Russell planted himself firmly, curious to see what the old boy was up to.

"Are you busy for lunch? Moth … I mean, I'd love for you to join us."

Lexie gave Russell a pleading look as if begging him to give her an excuse. He sneaked her a wink and watched her face fire up.

"Sorry, Floyd, old chap." Russell grabbed Lexie's elbow. "*Alexandra* already has plans for lunch." He pulled her toward the clubhouse while she looked over her shoulder at Floyd and gave him an apologetic smile.

When they were out of earshot, Lexie said, "Thanks, Russell. I owe you one."

"And don't you forget it." As they entered the dining room, the

Maurice sisters waved them over.

Russell waved back and escorted Lexie over to the table where the women welcomed with warm smiles.

"Hello, ladies. Welcome back. Did you arrive this morning?" The Maurice sisters were among Russell's favorite club members and were always very cordial.

"Yes, we did. And it's so nice to see Hollybourne again." Margaret Maurice beamed.

"Who is this young lady, Russell?" Marian Maurice tilted her head, studying Lexie.

"Excuse my manners, please. This is Alexandra Smithfield. I'm sure you remember her family."

The two sisters exchanged glances before turning back to Lexie. "My goodness, you must be the little girl. Well, of course, not a little girl anymore!" Margaret looked Lexie up and down.

"Please join us," Marian said. "We want to hear all about you." The woman gestured to a chair across the table. "You, too, Russell."

Lexie glanced at Russell, who nodded. "Thank you."

Russell pulled out her chair, then sat beside her. "I'm afraid I can't stay long, ladies, but I do want to catch up with you. You're both looking well."

"Oh, Russell, you're such a gentleman and a delight for these old eyes." Margaret batted her eyelashes at him.

The conversation revolved around the Maurice sisters and their visits around the country to various relatives and friends. Russell enjoyed the sisters from Pennsylvania and looked forward to their return to the island each season. Lexie's shoulders relaxed, a good sign she was comfortable with the sisters.

"I have a wonderful idea, Peg," Marian spoke to her sister, using Margaret's nickname, and turned to Lexie. "Alexandra, do you play bridge?"

"Why, yes, I've played before, but…" Russell watched Lexie search for an excuse.

"Of course, Marian." Peg turned to Lexie. "Dear, we need a fourth for bridge. Our sister Emily won't be here until next month. Would you please join us for bridge and tea?"

Russell kept quiet, watching Lexie's response. He wouldn't offer any reason for her to get out of this invitation. What harm could come from spending time with the sisters? At least she'd be safe with them.

"When do you play?"

"Every Tuesday afternoon, so tomorrow. All right? Come to Hollybourne at 3:00. Oh, what fun! It's been so long since we've had a Smithfield join us. Your mother and grandmother were wonderful bridge players and we so enjoyed their company."

"Thank you. I look forward to it," Lexie said, surprising Russell.

"Well, if you ladies will excuse me, I need to get back to my office."

"I'm afraid I must go too." Lexie laid her napkin down and Russell stood to pull her chair. "See you ladies tomorrow."

They walked out of the dining room where Russell paused before going back to his office.

"Lexie, I'm pleased that you accepted their invitation. They're very nice ladies."

"I'm not sure why I did. I remember going to Hollybourne with my mother and grandmother when I was a little girl and enjoyed acting like a grown-up having tea with the other ladies. I guess I just want to know what it feels like to actually participate as an adult."

"You won't regret that decision, I'm sure." Russell looked at his watch. "I must get to work now. I'll have someone get started on the repairs at Destiny."

They parted company, and Russell hurried up the stairs to his office. He made a list of available men for guard duty and arranged a schedule for each man to follow. He'd tell George to have the horses ready for each shift. The Coast Guard used foot patrols, but since the club had horses, it would be much more efficient to use them, plus it wouldn't tire out his men too much so they could perform their other duties.

He bowed his head and sighed. *Lord, give me wisdom in handling Lexie and her situation. Show me the truth—what's real and what's not, and help me help her deal with it.* As he lifted his head, the word "truth" hovered over him. Did God want him to tell Lexie the truth about her father? About the accident? But what about his promise to Robert? He shook his head. He just couldn't justify breaking his promise when it had nothing to do with the present.

He pushed back from his desk and stood, looking out the tower window. The panorama gave him a view across the great lawn to the trees and a glimpse of the boat dock behind them. He followed the river north to the mouth where it emptied into the Saint Simons Sound. He could just barely make out the rooftop of Destiny through the old oak trees that enclosed it. No, it didn't seem realistic for the Germans to enter the Sound to get to the back side of the island. Surely someone in the St. Simons lighthouse would spot them if they passed the north end of Jekyll.

It didn't seem probable, but it wasn't impossible either. At one time, he might've scoffed at the idea that German submarines could torpedo American ships so close to the United States coast, but he now knew the possibility existed. The men who were on the tanker that sank knew the grim reality. Poor guys.

Hard as it was for Mr. Prentice to accept, the war hovered at their doorstep. It just didn't seem right for the club to carry on business as usual while men like Robert were dying for their country. What gave the islanders the right to be so frivolous during such a serious time?

Russell shook his head and picked up the guard schedule from his desk. He would take one of the shifts himself. Maybe he wasn't fit for the military, but he could do his part to protect the people on the island. He grabbed his hat and coat before heading out the door. First, he planned to visit the stables, talk to George, and get him to spread the word about tomorrow's meeting with the men. Before he went home, though, he wanted to stop by the chapel. He and God needed to spend some time together, and he did his best communicating with the piano.

Chapter 23

$\mathcal{L}$exie strolled down Old Plantation Road to the Maurice cottage, Hollybourne. As the house came into view, Lexie noticed the difference between it and the other cottages as the only cottage built of tabby— native shells and sand. Why weren't any of the others made out of the same material? It must be pretty sturdy, based on the ruins of the 18th century Horton House.

Many years ago, she had ridden up the circular driveway bordered by manicured hedges with her mother and grandmother. The house still looked the same, but the palm trees in the yard were much bigger than she recalled. They had grown, as had she.

"Now mind your manners, Alexandra. Act like a little lady," *Grandmother had said in an effort to restrain her granddaughter from* *her tomboy tendencies.*

"Lexie will behave, won't you dear?" Mother had given her a warning *glance.*

"Yes, ma'am." The highlight of the visit was the wonderful treats the *Maurice family chef prepared for the ladies, and Lexie could control* *herself long enough to enjoy them. Of course, learning the game of bridge* *presented a new challenge, and Lexie had looked forward to beating her* *brother as soon as she mastered the game.*

As Lexie lifted her gloved hand to tap on the leaded glass doors, a servant opened them, admitting her to the main foyer.

"Come in, dear." Peg Maurice rushed forward to greet Lexie. "We're in the parlor." Peg gestured to her left as Lexie entered where she saw another woman seated next to Marian Maurice. The older sister introduced Lexie to Mrs. Josephine Prentice, the wife of the club president.

"My husband tells me you played tennis in college," Mrs. Prentice said.

"Yes, I played at Vassar." Lexie squirmed in her chair, uncomfortable knowing they'd discussed her.

"I really do hope you'll play in our tournament. With the war going on, we won't be able to get the celebrities we normally get, but we could use some good players to raise the level of the competition."

"Do you play, Mrs. Prentice?"

"I do. Bernon and I enjoy playing doubles with other couples. Perhaps there's a young man here that could play as your partner."

Lexie thought of Russell, remembering his limp. She didn't know if he could play or not.

Marian placed her hand on Lexie's arm. "Dear, we were so sorry to hear about the death of your mother. Had she been ill long?"

How could Lexie answer that? She didn't know exactly when Mother became ill, mentally ill, but it had been a long time. She nodded in lieu of words.

After a brief, but uncomfortable, silence, Peg spoke up.

"I'm pleased that you've continued to have the grounds taken care of at Destiny. I hate to see the cottages get overrun like some have." The other ladies' heads bobbed in agreement.

She couldn't take the credit since Abner Jones was responsible for its upkeep. If it had been up to her family, there would be no gardener keeping the lawn. Before she had a chance to answer, however, Peg continued.

"Abner does a good job. He helps our gardener sometimes too. He's a fixture around here, like Charlie Hill, our driver."

"When I was a little girl, I was afraid of him," Lexie said. To be honest, he still scared her.

"Abner's a little odd. Some people think he's rude. But he wasn't always that way. The Great War changed him," Marian said.

"Did you know him before?"

"Not well. But he seemed to be a typical teenage boy, happy-go-lucky like most his age." Marian smiled as she shuffled the cards before handing them to her sister.

"Sister, remember how good-looking he was?" Peg's eyes twinkled.

"Now, Peg. But I must admit he was a handsome young man."

"I remember when he started working for your grandfather, Alexandra." Peg nodded as she began dealing the cards out.

"Is it true that his family committed him to a mental hospital after the war?" Lexie found it hard to believe what Russell had told her.

The ladies exchanged glances as they peered over the tops of their cards. Finally, Marian sighed and nodded. "Yes, unfortunately, it is true.

I suppose they didn't understand the change in his behavior after the war and didn't know what else to do."

"It just doesn't seem fair to treat a returning soldier like he's mentally ill. Couldn't there have been another way to help him?" Lexie's stomach tensed with anguish.

"He wasn't the only soldier that ended up in a mental ward. Lord only knows what those men had to see, much less do, during the war. It must be a terrible thing to live with," Peg added.

"But thank God for your grandfather." Marian pointed a finger at Lexie. "When he found out what happened to Abner, he moved mountains to get the man out."

Lexie studied her cards but didn't really see them. She looked up at the sisters. "That's what Russell told me. I wonder why he went out of his way to help Mr. Jones."

"Abner saved his life!" Peg glanced up at Lexie. "You didn't know that?"

"No, no one ever mentioned it, or if they did, I was too young to understand. How did he save my grandfather's life?"

"Your grandfather was Abner's commanding officer in the army. During a battle in France, your grandfather was knocked unconscious. The enemy was advancing and he would have been killed, but Abner risked his own life to pick your grandfather up and carry him back to safety."

Lexie thought of the picture of her grandfather in uniform that used to hang on the wall in the cottage.

"I had no idea. So Grandfather paid him back. No wonder."

"It was the decent thing to do. Your grandfather was an honorable man. Everyone respected him," said Peg.

"One sure thing about Abner is his loyalty. He never forgot the debt he owed your grandfather," Marian added.

Lexie knew her grandfather garnered respect wherever he went. Now she knew one of the reasons. She wished she'd known him better, but he died when she was only eight years old.

Now, she also had an elevated opinion of Abner Jones. He had done an honorable thing as well, sacrificing his own safety for her grandfather. Surely, he deserved respect, too, regardless of his behavior.

When the bridge game ended, the ladies enjoyed tea and pastries from the Maurice's own kitchen. Unlike most of the cottages, theirs had a fully-quipped kitchen capable of producing meals for large gatherings. The Maurice family always brought their own chef with them to accommodate the many social functions they hosted.

Marian looked at the clock on the mantel. "It's four o'clock, ladies. Time for a ride!"

Lexie glanced from one sister to the other. Were they leaving?

"Come on, dear." Peg took Lexie's arm and led her to the front door where the maid handed them their hats, coats, and gloves. "Charlie's waiting for us. As Papa would say, 'It's time to roll.'"

The ladies exited the house and went down the stone steps where a horse-drawn carriage waited. The Negro driver tipped his hat and beamed as he assisted the ladies to step up onto a stone pedestal built especially for the purpose of aiding their climb into the carriage.

"Good afternoon, ladies."

"Good afternoon, Charlie. This is Alexandra Smithfield—remember the Smithfields?"

"I do." He nodded to Lexie. "Welcome back to the island, Miss Smithfield."

"Thank you." She settled into the seat opposite the sisters and next to Mrs. Prentice.

"Mr. Hill—Charlie—has been our family driver since we first started coming to the island. We're so lucky we have him to keep our tradition of afternoon rides."

Charlie climbed into the driver's seat and clucked to the horses. For the next hour, the ladies enjoyed a leisurely ride. The peaceful tour of the island relaxed Lexie and lifted her heart, filling her with a connection to happier times there. Perhaps things weren't as ominous as she'd thought. Maybe she was blowing things out of proportion. And maybe Abner was just a misunderstood, unfortunate man who had dealt with the ravages of war.

As they passed Faith Chapel, Lexie shrank back against the seat. She cast a glance at the small gothic-style church building, its terra cotta gargoyles leering down from the base of the steeple. The ugly heads were as menacing as ever.

"Ah, one of my favorite places!" Marian Maurice smiled as she swept her hand toward the chapel. "I've always loved our quaint little chapel."

Charlie pulled the horses to a stop while the sisters discussed the building. Lexie held her breath, waiting for him to move on. The sisters were in no hurry, however.

"Mother was so fond of the chapel, wasn't she, Marian?" said Peg.

"Oh, yes, she made sure we had plenty of guest ministers while we were here."

Lexie listened with rapt attention to the sisters, surprised to hear the chapel discussed with such admiration.

"Remember Emily's wedding there? I don't believe anyone else has been married there."

"No, they haven't—not that I know of," said Mrs. Prentice. "Guess they prefer the large lavish weddings in the major churches up north."

"Well, I don't think they could be any better than Emily's. Such a lovely, cozy ceremony, wouldn't you say?" Marian asked her sister. "Lovely" and "cozy" were not words Lexie would use to describe the chapel. And to think someone got married there! She wondered if their marriage had been cursed.

The sisters chatted while Lexie observed what a close relationship they had. She envied them, never having had a sister of her own. Neither of them had ever married, and they didn't seem the worse for it. Instead, they had a zest for life and an eagerness to share it with others. They reminded her of Russell and his upbeat attitude. If only she could share it too.

Through the partially open doors of the chapel, a piano played notes of a hymn. Lexie's ears strained to hear the tune—the same one she'd heard before.

"I love that hymn, don't you?" Peg asked the question to no one in particular.

Marian and Mrs. Prentice nodded in agreement.

"One of my favorites," said Marian.

Lexie hated to show her ignorance, but she had to know the name of the hymn.

"What is the name of that hymn?" She tried to ask as if she'd forgotten it instead of not being familiar with it.

In unison the ladies replied, "It is Well with My Soul."

"I like the melody." Lexie really did, even if it did emanate from the chapel. Were there words to the hymn? The title intrigued her, and she wanted to know the rest of it. How could she find out without entering the chapel?

The carriage started again, the road eventually running parallel to the beach. The afternoon sun began to make its descent, changing the color of the sky to shades of pink and orange as it peeked through the clouds. The ladies oohed and aahed at the magnificent display.

"Sometimes God just outdoes himself, doesn't he?" Peg said. "I'd love to capture this scene in a painting."

While they watched the sun sink, a lone rider appeared on horseback. He trotted along the beach, gazing out at the ocean, binoculars hanging around his neck.

"Who is that?" Marian said.

"He's part of the beach patrol," Mrs. Prentice replied.

The sisters jerked their heads to face her, their eyes wide.

"Beach patrol?" Peg said.

"Yes, the Coast Guard has increased their patrol and we've increased ours as well."

"Is there a threat to us?"

"Probably not. They just want us to help spot German submarines. Frankly, I think it's too shallow for a submarine around here," Mrs. Prentice continued.

"I agree," Peg asserted with a nod of her head. "I can't imagine a submarine being close to us."

A loud boom shook the ground and the ladies jumped.

The horse whinnied and pawed the earth.

The women all looked at each other, their eyes wide. Lexie glanced at the rider and saw him stop and focus on the distance with his binoculars. Was that smoke on the horizon?

"We better get back," Charlie said. "It's gettin' late, gonna be dark soon."

"Charlie, do you know what that noise was?" Marian looked up at the driver as he urged the horses on.

"No, ma'am."

"Have you heard anything like that before?"

"No, ma'am."

Lexie's heart pounded while she stared at the spot on the horizon where she thought she saw a trail of black smoke. What happened? She couldn't wait to get back and ask Russell. Did the rest of the people on the island feel the jolt? So much for a peaceful day. She knew it couldn't last.

Chapter 24

"Let's turn on the radio when we get back to the cottage. If anything has happened this close to our shore, I'm sure it'll be on the news." Marian fixed her gaze across the carriage at her sister, emphasizing her statement with a firm nod of her head.

"Of course, you're right, Sister. You know how they interrupt programs with important messages." Peg nodded back her affirmation.

"I'll speak to Bernon about it. He would be the first to know if anything happened so near to us." Mrs. Prentice offered the others the most immediate solution.

"Oh, yes, please do. I know if anything is important enough for us to concern ourselves with, he'll let us know," Marian said.

Lexie watched Charlie Hill to see his reaction. Although she could only see the back of him from her place in the carriage, she thought she detected tension in his body and tightness in his jaw. What did he think about the incident? If he was frightened, he did a good job hiding it. She applauded his calm demeanor, despite the anxiety emanating from the ladies.

As soon as they returned, Lexie would make a beeline to find Russell. Had anyone else on the island heard the noise or just those near the beach? When the carriage neared the chapel, Russell came out the door and hurried down the steps. Another man walked beside him, carrying on an animated conversation. Russell strode briskly toward the clubhouse, not bothering to look in the direction of the carriage as he crossed the street.

Lexie started to call out to him but resisted, not wanting to call attention to herself, much less interrupt his discussion. His face was set with a serious determination she hadn't seen before as he marched away. What a dramatic difference to the easy-going, jovial person she had come to know. She no longer needed to question whether he could be serious. If the occasion warranted it, indeed he could be. But what was the occasion?

When Charlie drew the carriage up in front of Hollybourne, the ladies breathed a collective sigh of relief.

"It's so good to be home." Marian turned to their driver, who had come around to help the ladies out. "Thank you, Charlie."

"Yes, ma'am."

"Would you like to come in a while, listen to the radio with us?" Peg addressed Lexie as she stepped down from the carriage.

"No, thank you. I need to get back to the clubhouse. But thank you both so much for a wonderful afternoon."

"It was our pleasure, dear. We would love to get to know you better. Why, it almost felt like old times having a Smithfield here again."

Lexie smiled and nodded. Indeed, the afternoon spent with the sisters had almost been like good old times that weren't yet tainted by tragedy. Almost.

"Yes, we so enjoy having people here at our home, don't we Peg?"

Peg nodded and clasped Lexie's hand. "You're welcome to our home anytime, Alexandra."

As Lexie walked back to the clubhouse, the sisters stayed on her mind. They were so close, so happy here on the island. Why, they even called Hollybourne their home. Destiny certainly wasn't home for Lexie—not the safe, comfortable place the sisters enjoyed. Even her home in New York lacked a homey atmosphere. No, living with Mother before going off to college, before Mother went to live at the hospital, was anything but. And the best times at Destiny existed only in her mind.

Her chest tightened with yearning. A place to call home and someone to share it with seemed like a distant goal, out of her reach. She didn't know where or when she'd find her home, but she knew one thing—it would be in her future, not in her past.

When she got back to the clubhouse, she stopped at the front desk and asked the clerk if he knew where Russell was. The older gentleman glanced up the stairs.

"I believe he's in a meeting, miss. I can give him a message when he gets out, if you wish."

Her eyes traveled to the grandfather clock in the hallway. Just past six o'clock, rather late for a meeting.

"No, thank you. I'll just wait."

"Meeting might take a while. I'm sure he wouldn't want to keep you waiting."

He must've known what the meeting was about, guarding Russell like a watchdog. She hadn't been deterred from Russell's office before. She might as well go up to her room and wait.

"Of course. I'll just speak to him later."

She turned and walked to the staircase, but as she placed her hand on the banister, she heard voices above her at the next landing. She peered up the stairwell and glimpsed two women seated in the alcove beside the stairs. Oh, no. Not Mrs. Appleton again. There would be no way to get past her. If only there were another set of stairs. A memory of Stella the maid exiting the hall at the opposite end came to mind.

As she strolled away from the staircase, she gave the clerk a nonchalant wave and smiled, heading toward the front door.

Once outside, Lexie looked toward the river where the sun was slipping below the horizon. Men and women chatted as they passed her on the way to the dining room to join those already inside. With the absence of sunlight, the temperature had dropped, and the moist chill of southern winters returned. Lexie turned away from the front of the building and hurried along the sidewalk in the opposite direction. When she reached the far end of the building, she moved around to the side, searching for the outside staircase the employees used.

The dim twilight disappeared into darkness where no other lights illuminated the area. Lexie found herself treading in the damp grass, staying close to the shrubbery as she searched for the stairs. An eerie sense of solitude played with Lexie's imagination, taunting her with fears of isolation. Everyone else was inside the clubhouse where it was warm. She was the only one outside. Alone. In the dark.

Maybe she should abandon her idea. But when she saw the staircase on the end of the building, she sighed relief and hurried toward it. As she reached the steps, she grabbed the handrail and took a step up.

The bushes rustled nearby and she paused, her breath stuck in her throat. What was that noise? She took another step, then heard movement behind her. Someone was there.

"What you doin' out here by yourself?"

Lexie jumped at the deep voice so near. She knew that voice. She slowly turned around and faced Abner Jones standing at the foot of the stairs, blocking her retreat. She could barely make out his face in the darkness, but there was no doubt it was him.

A battle of emotions erupted inside her. Part of her wanted to run. Or scream. Or both. "Abner is harmless," Russell had said. Was he right?

She hoped so.

"One sure thing about Abner is his loyalty," Marian Maurice had affirmed.

Those people had no fear of the man, so why should she? And if he was truly loyal to her grandfather, why would he want harm to come to her, the granddaughter? *Okay, Lexie, here's your chance to treat the man with respect, not like a strange animal the way many mentally disturbed people are treated.* Wasn't that what she believed?

Lexie took a deep breath, then exhaled slowly.

"Mr. Jones, you startled me. I just thought I'd go up to my room this way for a change." Did that sound as ridiculous to him as it did to her?

"Young ladies like you shouldn't be out here by theirselves at night."

"Yes, well, I was just going up the stairs."

He stepped closer and lowered his voice.

"It's dangerous out here."

"Thank you for your concern, but I think everyone here is friendly."

"You don't understan'. There's enemies around."

A chill ran through Lexie. "Enemies? You mean Nazis?"

Did he nod his head? It was hard to tell in the dark.

"Germans. And spies."

Spies? Did he know who they were?

"Oh! Well, thank you for keeping an eye out for them."

The chilly air penetrated Lexie's clothes, and she began to shiver. She had to get inside—to get warm and to end this conversation. She turned to continue up the stairs, wondering what he would say or do next. As an idea came to her, she stopped and spun around. Somehow, she summoned the strength to do what she had to do.

She stepped back down to where Abner Jones still stood.

"Mr. Jones, I understand you saved my grandfather's life."

"That's what he told people. I just did my duty."

"Well, I want to thank you. If you hadn't saved him, I wouldn't have known him."

She extended her gloved hand.

For a few moments, no one moved. Then slowly, Abner Jones lifted his hand and allowed her to shake it before he dropped it back down by his side. Then he raised it again and moved it across his face. Did she hear him sniff? The moon peeked out from the clouds and glistened off the trail of tears that ran down the weathered face.

Lexie's heart squeezed with compassion for the poor old man.

After a weighty silence, he cleared his throat.

"Miss Smithfield, you're a lot like your grandpa."

Lexie fought back her own tears. No one had ever told her that. And no one could have paid her a higher compliment.

"Thank you, Mr. Jones. That means a lot to me." She smiled at the man, hoping he could see her face in the moonlight. "Well, good night." She turned once again to go up the stairs.

"Miss Smithfield?"

She paused and looked back over her shoulder.

"Yes?"

"Be careful."

"I will."

He was not a threat to her anymore. So who was?

Chapter 25

When Lexie reached the back door to the second floor, she gripped the doorknob, anxious to get inside. But before she went in, she had an idea. What if she went all the way to the top where Russell's office was?

She reached the fourth-floor landing, winded from the long climb and freezing from the cold. She pulled open the door and stepped into the hallway, hoping no one would see her enter from the servants' stairs. She tiptoed down the hall, passing some of the staff bedrooms. Other rooms had the doors open and inside them, Lexie noticed stacks of trunks and suitcases where the luggage was stored for the season.

At the opposite end of the hall, voices rose and fell, telling Lexie the meeting was still in progress. From the sound, she guessed several people were involved. She couldn't very well stand in the hallway listening, but she needed to know when the meeting ended. As she considered her options, she heard footsteps tramping down the wood floors in her direction.

She ducked into one of the open storage rooms and hid behind a huge trunk, her heart racing.

The steps passed her and continued until she heard a door close down the hall. She listened for more noise, and hearing none, stepped from her hiding place and into the corridor, right into the path of the boat captain. His eyes widened in surprise, then narrowed as his perpetual frown returned.

Lexie searched for an explanation. "I was just looking for my bag … I believe I left a scarf in it."

He harrumphed before mumbling, "Excuse me," as he walked past her toward the stairway at the end.

The voices coming from the direction of Russell's office grew louder, indicating the door had opened and people were leaving the meeting. She scurried down the main staircase to the third floor, a more logical place for her to be—on a guest room level. If she timed it just right, she could pretend she was going up while the others were coming down.

Sure enough, several male staff members passed her. When the young waiter Walter saw her, a smile lit up his face.

"Good evening, Miss Smithfield! How are you today?"

His youthful enthusiasm made Lexie feel so much older than the few years' difference between them. He didn't seem to have a care in the world, his attitude as yet unspoiled by the realities of life. And yet, soon he would be exposed to the harshest truths of war. She remembered Russell's promise to pray for the young man and wanted to do the same, if she only knew how. God would listen to Russell's prayers—he was the faithful churchgoer. But God would probably be offended if she asked him for anything.

She could at least offer a smile. "Very well, thank you, Walter. Do you know where I might find Mr. Thompson?"

"Sure. He's coming downstairs behind me." He glanced up over his shoulder before trotting down the stairs.

Lexie followed his gaze and saw Russell turn the corner of the staircase above. Upon seeing her, the lines in his face relaxed and his welcome smile appeared along with his endearing dimple.

"Good evening, Lexie. Fancy meeting you here." He winked, and her face warmed.

She pursed her lips and tried to act nonchalant. "Russell, I hoped I might run into you."

He cocked his head and raised an eyebrow. "Is that so? What a nice surprise."

Once again, heat rushed to her neck and face. "I need to talk to you about something that happened today—actually, a couple of things that happened today."

He came alongside her and placed his hand on the small of her back. With the other hand, he gestured down the steps. "Have you had dinner yet?"

"No, I haven't."

"So will you join me? I'm famished, and we can talk in the dining room."

"But … can we? I'd like our conversation to be kept private."

He cast a sidelong glance at her. "I'll request a table at the back of the dining room." He checked his watch. "Most of the early diners should be gone by now, including the Appletons."

How nice to know he appreciated her need for privacy.

"Good." She nodded and headed into the dining room, grateful to have his company.

Waiters cleared dishes from the half-empty dining room when they entered. They walked all the way back to the rear corner of the room where she took a seat with her back to the rest of the patrons. The dim candlelight glowed golden, soothing Lexie with its gentle embrace.

As Russell placed his napkin in his lap, he said, "So did you enjoy your outing with the Maurice sisters?"

She nodded, waiting until their server took their order before responding.

"Quite enjoyable. They're very nice ladies and made me feel very comfortable."

"Good. I thought you'd enjoy being with them. Did you have a fourth?"

"Yes, Mrs. Prentice."

"Of course. She's a good bridge player." With a twinkle in his eye, he added, "Did you win?"

"No. My bridge game is a bit rusty."

"No doubt the rust will wear off with a little practice, then the ladies better look out."

"Russell, please. I don't want to talk to you about bridge."

His face sobered. "I'm sorry, what else did you want to discuss?"

"After tea, we went out for a carriage ride."

"Good old Charlie Hill."

"Yes, well, we stopped at the beach for a while. We saw a man out there patrolling—someone I didn't recognize."

She studied Russell's reaction, but his blank expression revealed nothing, so she continued.

"While we were there, we heard, and actually felt, a large boom. The man on the beach fixed his binoculars out to sea. I looked, too, and thought I saw a trail of smoke in the distance. Did you hear it? Do you know what it was?"

He examined his fork before answering.

"No on both counts. I did not hear it, and I don't know what it was."

"But you heard about it, didn't you? Do you think it could have been a German submarine? What if they torpedoed one of our ships?"

Russell remained unusually quiet, as if contemplating her question. The muffled sound of voices at other tables blended with the tinkling of silver and crystal while Lexie waited for his answer. When he didn't respond, she persisted.

"Russell, you must know something about this. Please tell me."

He looked up at her with an expression so grave it frightened her.

"I did hear about it. The patrol reported what they heard and saw. We called the Coast Guard, but they haven't confirmed an attack."

"But it could have been."

"Yes, it could have been." He leaned toward her and lowered his voice. "But Lexie, if that's the case, it happened miles off our shore— maybe ten or fifteen miles at least. If the German submarines are out there, they're not firing at the land, they're firing at other ships."

"And that doesn't affect us?"

"Not directly, no"

The waiter arrived at their table holding a tray aloft with their meals. Lexie held her tongue until he'd placed their food in front of them. Russell thanked him and the waiter excused himself.

As soon as he was out of earshot, Lexie faced Russell again. "So you're not going to tell anybody about it? What about those of us who heard and felt it?"

"I can't tell what I don't know, and there's no need to upset people without proof. I'm sure the Coast Guard will tell us if anything significant happened. I promise I'll let you know what I find out."

Lexie stared into his green eyes, so intense as he studied her. She had to believe him. Who else could she trust? She pushed her food around and took a few nibbles of her salad. An image of Abner Jones' face in the moonlight came to her mind.

"You know, Russell, I'm not afraid of Abner Jones anymore."

He glanced up at her and lifted his eyebrows as he took a bite of steak. "Did something happen to change your mind about him?"

"Yes, the Maurice sisters told me why Grandfather was so indebted to him, why he got Abner out of the mental hospital. Apparently, when they were in the war, Abner saved Grandfather's life."

"You didn't know that? I thought you did."

"No, well at least I don't remember if I heard about it as a child."

"And that made your opinion of Abner change?"

"I think so. I saw him earlier tonight." She stopped. How could she tell him what happened without revealing her trip up the servants' stairs? She fingered her pearl necklace while trying to figure out how to explain her meeting with Abner.

"Where?"

"Outside. On the lawn."

"And?"

"Well, at first he spooked me like he usually does. He has an unsettling habit of appearing unexpectedly."

"And you thought he followed you, right?"

"I did suspect him of that. In fact, maybe he has been following me. But I think his motive is good." She leaned forward, glancing each way. "I think he's trying to protect me."

Russell sat back in his chair, resting his hands on the edge of the table. "Could be, now that you mention it."

"I believe that part of his gratitude to my grandfather is taking care of me, the granddaughter. He just acts odd, but I don't think he can help it."

Russell's smile eased across his face. "I told you he's harmless. I'm glad you've decided not to concern yourself with him anymore."

"But that still doesn't explain someone else at the cottage, or the telegram. You don't think Abner sent the telegram, do you?"

"No. I doubt Abner has ever sent a telegram."

"Someone wanted me here badly enough to send that telegram. But who? Why?"

Russell shook his head. "Got me. Maybe we'll never know."

He paused while the waiter refilled their water glasses and checked on them. When the server left, he continued.

"By the way, I put in the work order for your repairs. I expect they'll start tomorrow or the next day."

"Thank you. I almost wish I could do more, like put up new wallpaper. That old paper looks terrible."

"Just say the word, and I'll have it done."

"No. I don't suppose that's a necessary repair. Perhaps the next owner will want to choose their own wallpaper."

She had to keep the costs down, and new wallpaper would only add to it. But her heart wrenched at the prospect of turning the cottage over to someone else. Funny that she hadn't felt that way before she came back to the island. But now that she'd seen the house, she almost felt sorry for it and wanted to return it to its former condition. Maybe what she really wanted was to return to a time when life was happier and less complicated, when the house was filled with family and activity.

But she couldn't do that. She had no family to fill it with anymore. Her eyes grew moist, and she dabbed them with her napkin. At least the Maurice sisters had each other. Despite the fact that many of their family members had died, they continued to come to their cottage and relive happier days from when they were there before. No, Lexie couldn't see herself in that picture, a lonely woman rambling through a big old house by herself.

"What's wrong?" Russell's hand covered hers, surprising her with both the gesture and the heat that radiated up her arm and into her body. His eyes gazed into her own, conveying a sense of genuine care and concern. Maybe there was something else, too, something more. Had she imagined his feelings for her or hoped for them? The candlelit atmosphere must have deluded her into thinking these things. But, she didn't move her hand, afraid to break the spell.

"I'm not sure, Russell. When I came here, I had one thing in mind— to check on the cottage and get it ready to sell. But now that I'm here, part of me wants to stay, or maybe I just want to go back to the way things used to be."

"With Robert and the rest of your family here."

Tears rolled down her face. "Yes."

"Sometimes I'd like for things to be the way they were, too; when I was a kid and had no worries. But we have to grow up sometime, don't we?" His smile warmed her inside out.

"Why is it when we're children, we want to be grown-up?"

"Because we don't know what grown-ups have to deal with. We just want all the power they have." His hand continued to stroke hers as if it was a natural thing for him to do. "Lexie, what you said about part of you wanting to stay—do you have to get back to work right away?"

"No, I don't have to. I left after Mother died, and the hospital doesn't expect me back until I've handled all her affairs."

"Then, you can stay a while longer?"

"I suppose so. Plus I really want to get some questions answered."

Russell leaned back and laughed, releasing her hand. "That's my girl!"

Lexie laughed, too, happy and content to share the moment with Russell.

When she saw Russell furrow his brow, she followed his gaze behind her to one of the waiters standing across the dining room in the doorway, trying to get his attention.

He pushed back, stood, and tossed his napkin on the table. "Please excuse me, Lexie. I need to see about this." He came around the table, pausing beside her. "I'm sorry. I hate to leave you. I've really enjoyed our time together this evening."

"Me, too," she said. He lifted her hand and kissed the back of it with a flair of melodrama.

She giggled and watched him walk to the doorway where he spoke with a man before they both hurried away. She scanned the dining room and noticed the other tables were now empty, and she was alone. Or was she? A tingle on the back of her neck signaled that she was being watched. She spun around in time to see the door to the kitchen swing shut. It must have been their waiter. When the door opened again, two servers came out carrying trays of silverware which they took to the empty tables and began to reset the place settings.

They acted like she was invisible as they passed by, so engrossed in their own conversation. She left her table and meandered through the room on her way out.

"So who you gonna ask to the Valentine's dance?" One of the waiters walked around the tables, placing the spoons on the right of the plates.

"Probably Shirley. What about you?" The other waiter added forks to the opposite side of the plates.

"Well, if we still have it, Polly. But I'm not so sure there'll be a dance, what with all the German subs out there."

"Do you really believe there's German subs that close to us? I think it's just a rumor."

"You know what Thompson said—we might close early this year because of them."

"Well, I intend to keep on living until they tell us to leave. Life's too short to live with fear. And God help me, I won't."

The words hit Lexie square between the eyes. Indeed. Life was too short—at least it was for Robert. But he hadn't lived with fear. And neither would she. Would God help her too?

Chapter 26

"Where is he?" Russell asked the server as they strode outside.

"Over there." The man pointed to another fellow smoking a cigarette, just beyond the circle of light from the clubhouse. The red glow extended from his hand like a red flashlight.

Russell marched over to the man. "John, I hear you saw something tonight."

The man tossed his cigarette to the ground, then crushed it with his shoe. "Yes, sir. You told us to come find you if we seen anything."

"That's correct. So what did you see?"

"Looked like a small boat, maybe a raft." John extended his arms out to demonstrate the length.

"Where was it? Could you see anyone on it?" Russell set his hands on his hips.

"Looked like it was floating over toward St. Simons. Far as I could tell, there was four, maybe five people in it."

"Could you tell what they looked like? See any uniforms?"

"No, sir, it was pretty dark. If the moon hadn't been so bright, I wouldn't a seen 'em."

"Thank you, John. As usual, don't discuss this with anyone else. I'll notify the Coast Guard."

John nodded, turned, and walked away.

Russell spun on his heel and stalked back inside, hoping he wouldn't run into Lexie. Much as he'd like to see her, he couldn't waste any time making the call to the Coast Guard. He paused at the front desk and addressed the clerk.

"Please call Mr. Prentice and ask him to come to my office—right away. Thank you."

Russell climbed the stairs to the fourth floor and turned to his right at the top, heading to his office. Bernon would have to be there when he made the call. While he waited for him, he gazed outside the windows of the room to the night sky. The full moon had risen and illuminated the grounds below. He opened the door to the balcony and stepped outside, letting the brisk winter air cool him from his hike up the stairs.

Lexie's face appeared before him, gazing at him in the candlelight at dinner. The atmosphere at the table hinged on being romantic, at least for him. Had she felt it too? There had been moments when he thought so, but he wasn't sure. What he wouldn't give to have her beside him right now, his arm around her in the moonlight. He heard Bernon enter the office and close the door behind him. Russell turned around to go back inside, shaking his head. What made him think someone like her would ever be attracted to someone like him?

"Russell, what's going on? Did something happen?"

"John, one of our lookouts, saw a boat or a raft out in the water tonight. He said it was drifting toward St. Simons."

"Ours or theirs?"

Russell shrugged and lifted his hands. "He couldn't tell—it was too dark. But he did see several people in it."

"We better call the Coast Guard, don't you think?"

"Yes, I was about to." He pointed to a chair and Bernon sat. Russell lifted the phone receiver and asked the operator to connect him as he sat down across from the club president.

When he finished speaking with the man in charge at the Coast Guard office, he hung up the phone.

"Seems like the Germans torpedoed a tanker this afternoon, about 15 miles off the coast. They got a mayday signal from the tanker."

Bernon slammed his hand on the desk. "Blast it! Any survivors?"

"They picked up a few in a lifeboat but don't know if there were any more. The raft could be another lifeboat, or it could be from the German submarine. They're going to check it out and let us know." Russell raked his hair with his fingers.

"Maybe someone at the lighthouse saw something."

"They saw the explosion from the tanker."

"Good Lord." Bernon ran his finger inside his shirt collar as if it was too tight. "I can't believe this is happening so close to home. Should we mention it to anyone?"

Russell shook his head. "They told me they still want us to keep it under wraps."

Bernon stood to leave. "Well, I guess there's nothing we can do until we hear from them tomorrow."

"No, we just sit tight."

Bernon waved. "Good night. See you in the morning."

"Night, Bernon."

As the door closed, Russell stood and stared out the window into the darkness. He had an urge to go up into the tower to look through the telescope, so he climbed up the wooden ladder into the glass turret. He could barely make out any lights across the sound to Brunswick. The moonlight shone a path across the water, revealing nothing amiss. As he looked toward the water, he thought he saw the flicker of light in the trees around Destiny. He aimed the telescope down at her house and focused the lens. He saw it again—a light inside the cottage, and it was moving from room to room.

Russell watched, straining to see more, but he was too far away. Something was going on in that house. He'd have to go check it out himself.

He climbed back down the ladder, hurried out of his office, and down the steps to the front door, hoping no one would approach him before he could leave the clubhouse. He passed the desk clerk who opened his mouth to speak, but Russell waved him off. Whatever it was could wait.

His foot ached as he ran down the front steps of the clubhouse. He blew out a breath and pushed ahead, wondering what he would do if he surprised the intruder. He should've grabbed a gun from the gun case in the event the other guy was armed. If he could just see who it was, if it was someone he knew, they could apprehend them later. If not, he didn't know what he'd do.

He trotted down the dark road, illuminated only by moonlight where the trees allowed. Russell's balance wasn't the greatest with his bum foot, and the shadows hid any obstacles that might be in his path. *Lord, please don't let me trip and fall down.* Before the accident, he'd been one of the fastest on the school track team. But that was a long time ago. Ten years ago, to be exact.

As the cottage came into view, he slowed, breathing hard. Boy, was he out of shape. He had to catch his breath lest his heavy panting alert the intruder to his presence. Stepping behind a shrub, he kept his eye on the upstairs windows. A golden glow drew his attention to the room at the front of the house—Lexie's grandparents' bedroom.

Russell stared at the window, hoping to catch a glimpse of the person in the room. A silhouette passed in front of the window, and Russell thought he recognized something familiar. The man wore a hat, but so did most men. Russell's stomach tightened. What if there was more than one person?

Russell's heart pounded as he recovered from his jog and waited for another glance. The light moved away from the window and the house reclaimed its nocturnal disguise. Russell edged closer to the house, hoping to detect someone leaving the building. It was unlikely that an intruder would use the front door, so he crept around the rear, hiding in the shadows.

When he reached the back of the house, he glanced toward the river, half-expecting to see a boat along the bank, loaded with a bunch of Germans. What would he do then? He breathed a sigh of relief to see the riverbank empty. Just as he stepped toward the cottage, he heard movement nearby. Russell froze, wondering if a gun was pointed at him.

"Who's there?" Russell whispered, summoning all the bravado he could.

A gruff voice mumbled, "Abner Jones."

Russell spun around and saw the tall, stooped man emerge from the shadow.

"What are you doing here, Abner?" Russell kept his voice low, in case someone else was within earshot.

"Watching."

"Watching what?"

"The house."

Russell started to ask why but realized Abner might have seen the light inside too. While they stood there, the screen door off the kitchen banged shut. Leaving Abner alone, Russell rushed around to the other side of the house, hoping to catch a glimpse of whoever went out. But as he rounded the corner of the house, there was no sign of anyone else. If Abner hadn't delayed him, Russell might've seen the intruder. His temper rose, ready to lash out at the old man. But when Abner appeared at his side, he drew in a breath and blew it out to calm himself.

"Abner, I'm sure you have a good reason to be here."

No response.

"Abner, would you please tell me why you were watching the house?"

"Want to see who's trespassing."

"And did you see who it was?"

"Nope. Some man."

"Someone we know? Or a stranger?"

"Not sure. Could be somebody who works here though."

"Do you have any idea who it might be?" Russell's patience wore thin.

"Could be a German spy."

"Why do you say that?" Russell stuck his hands on his hips and glared at the man.

Abner shrugged his shoulders. "'Cause they're around here."

Russell was getting nowhere. Had the man seen anyone or was he just hallucinating?

"Okay, Abner. Tell you what. You keep an eye on the house and let me know right away if you see anyone. If you don't know them, at least give me a description. All right?"

Abner nodded. "That Miss Smithfield. She's nice. Like her grandpa."

Russell's mouth fell open. Was this Abner talking?

"I agree, Abner. She is very nice." He recalled what Lexie told him. "And she spoke well of you too." He had an idea. "Miss Smithfield would very much like to know who's been in her cottage. Do you think you can help her find out?"

Abner nodded his head. "When I get through at the golf course, I'll come over here."

"Never mind the golf course. I'll have you put back on the grounds crew this side of the island."

Another nod.

"Tomorrow, there will be some people coming to work on the house, fix some things. But they're okay—I'm sending them." At least he thought they were okay. He wasn't sure about anybody anymore.

Chapter 27

The morning staff greeted Lexie as they hurried into the dining room to start their shifts. She had arrived even earlier than usual but assured Mr. Mason she didn't mind sitting alone in the empty dining room while the kitchen prepared for breakfast. All she wanted was a cup of tea and privacy. Of course, her early arrival guaranteed the first scones fresh from the oven, an added bonus.

Funny how she felt more comfortable with the staff than with the rest of the guests. Perhaps embarrassment about wearing the same clothes over and over again. Her grandmother would be horrified at the thought. The members always dressed for each meal, changing clothes several times a day. The amount of luggage that accompanied them each season often required another boat trip from Brunswick to transport it. Had Lexie thought she'd be staying so long, she would've packed a few more things.

Thanks to Mr. Mason, she had learned the names of the dining room staff, along with other facts about them—who had worked there the longest, who was the newest, who was married to whom, and so on. He had also filled her in on which members were new to the club, and their backgrounds as well. Little did he know she might soon be replaced with a new member.

"Good morning, Mr. Thompson." Mr. Mason lifted his gaze past Lexie's chair, pausing before he poured more tea into her cup. "Can I get you anything?"

Lexie's heart skipped a beat as Russell pulled out a chair beside her.

"Good morning, Mr. Mason. Coffee, please." Russell glanced at Lexie, lingering on her eyes. "Good morning, Lexie."

Her face warmed at his twinkle. What a welcome relief to last night's serious mood. She beamed back at him as a ray of early morning sun streamed across the table.

"Good morning, Russell. I didn't expect to see you so early."

"I thought you might be here. I've heard you like having the dining room to yourself."

Memories of the previous evening when he'd left her all alone flooded her mind, and she shot him an angry glare.

Russell drew back and frowned before understanding crossed his face. "I wasn't talking about last night. I was referring to you coming to breakfast early. I'm sorry—I hated to leave in such a hurry last night. Would you forgive me ... please?"

Lexie couldn't stay angry with him, not with that sad puppy-dog look on his face. She relaxed and smiled.

"Sure, Russell. And yes, I do like to be one of the first diners in the morning. I'm not very friendly first thing, and I need time to warm up to the day. After I've had my tea, I'm more hospitable."

"Hey, I can appreciate that. I like to grab a cup of coffee from the kitchen and run up to my office before I deal with the day's business. That time is reserved for God. He and I meet on the balcony and discuss things before I jump into them." Russell studied his cup. "I've discovered the day just doesn't go well if I don't start out right."

Lexie squirmed in her chair. Fingering her pearls, she groped for a response. Russell's relationship to God was so personal, like they were friends, not strangers, like her.

Russell glanced up at her. "You're very quiet. Haven't had enough tea yet?"

"Apparently not." Lexie lifted her cup and took a sip, keeping her eyes focused on the lace tablecloth.

"Oh, I forgot to tell you why I came in here to disrupt your routine." He leaned forward and lowered his voice as he glanced from side to side. "I saw something at Destiny last night."

Lexie's spine stiffened and her breath caught. "You did? You went to Destiny last night?"

Russell went on to tell her about seeing the light from the tower and going to check it out. When he got to the part about running into Abner, her heart slowed.

"So, I think you were right, Lexie. I think Abner is just trying to keep an eye on Destiny and maybe you too. His commitment to your grandfather is remarkable."

"It is. I wonder if the poor man ever sleeps."

"I suppose he has to sometime. But I think he has trouble sleeping— you know, the war. Another man who lives in the dormitory where Abner lives says he often wakes up at night hollering. I think he has nightmares." Russell drained his coffee cup then set it back on the table, pointing to it as Mr. Mason watched nearby. "So, anyway, I asked him to watch the house for us and report to me what or who he sees. I hope you don't mind, but I don't see what harm it can do."

"No, I don't mind. Guess I've gotten used to him being around. But tell me, did you see anyone else last night?"

Russell shook his head. "No. I'm afraid running into Abner sidetracked me. But maybe he will see something now that he's been assigned that responsibility."

The waiter refilled Russell's cup, disappeared behind the kitchen door, and returned with a tray of scones. He set them on the table, grinning at Lexie. "Here you are, Miss Smithfield—warm from the oven."

"Thank you, Mr. Mason. Looks like I've developed a habit. At this rate, my clothes won't fit anymore."

The waiter laughed and stepped away.

Lexie took a scone and bit into it, savoring the sweet taste before speaking again.

"Russell, what was the emergency last night? Can you tell me?"

Russell had a mouthful of scone. He held up his hand motioning her to wait as he took a sip of coffee. "Wonderful scones! I must congratulate the bakery chef." When he acted as though he might leave the table to do so right away, Lexie placed her hand on his arm.

"Wait. You're avoiding my question, aren't you?"

He looked down at her hand, blowing out a breath. "All right. One of our spotters saw a raft or boat with some men last night. It appeared to be heading toward St. Simons."

She gasped. "Oh no. Could they have been Germans?"

"We don't know. We're waiting for the Coast Guard to tell us what they find."

"And when they do, you'll tell me, won't you?" Lexie's heart raced. Maybe she should leave the island now.

He studied her face before answering. "Yes. I will."

Another waiter approached the table. "Mr. Thompson, Mr. Prentice wants to see you in your office."

"Duty calls, I'm afraid." Russell pushed back his chair. "Maybe we'll have an answer."

He stood to leave. "The workmen should be at Destiny today. I'll see you later."

After he left, Lexie decided to go to the cottage while the workers were there. She'd feel safe with others around. And maybe, in the daylight, she'd notice something she'd overlooked before.

She arrived at the cottage in time to see a truck pull up in the driveway and three men dressed in overalls get out. They walked around to the rear of the truck, began unloading supplies, and looked up as she approached.

"Hello. My name is Alexandra Smithfield. This is my house."

"Hello, ma'am." A man with wiry gray hair tipped the bill of his flat cap. "I'm Sam Williams. That's Zeke and Joel." He motioned to the other two men, who greeted her with nods. "You wanna show us what needs to be done? I got a work order here from Mr. Thompson, but I'd rather see for myself, you know."

"I'll be happy to show you. Come on in."

Lexie found the door unlocked, assuming Russell had left it that way for the men. She entered the front foyer and looked each way. Nothing had changed since she'd last been there.

"Most of the damage is upstairs." She pointed toward the stairs in the hallway.

Mr. Williams glanced around and took notice of the water stain over in the dining room. He strode over to it, reached up, and put his hand on the wallpaper in the corner.

"Damp here. You got a leak somewhere."

"Yes, I believe it's coming from the leaky window upstairs."

"Hmm. All right, let's take a look."

Lexie led the men upstairs to the room where she'd found the leak. The workmen entered the room and studied the window, then checked the floor.

"Floor's wet. Yep. Water's been coming in and soaking the floor before running down into the wall below. We need to fix the frame and the window."

They went back down to get their tools and materials. There were some long boards and a couple of sawhorses in the truck bed. "We'll have to cut those boards here. And we've got that pane of glass to carry up too." Mr. Williams looked over at Lexie. "Is there another way to get upstairs so we don't have to carry this stuff through the whole house?"

"Yes, there's a back door off the kitchen. Actually, the lock on that door needs to be fixed too. Come, I'll show you." Lexie motioned for the men to follow and walked down the path that led around the left side of the house to the kitchen.

She found the kitchen unlocked as well.

"In there." She motioned to the screen door and let them enter first, remembering the day Abner Jones had surprised her inside. She followed the men, noticing how they glanced around the room.

"Bet this place used to be nice," the one called Zeke said.

"It was." Like an elderly woman who was beautiful in her youth, but only showed glimpses of her early glory.

Sam pointed to a door. "Them the back stairs?"

Lexie nodded and opened the door, showing them the steps inside. "They lead to the second and third story servants' quarters, but the room that needs repair is across the hall from the second-floor servants' wing."

"What's that?" Joel, the younger man, pointed to the square metal door beside the door to the stairs.

"That's the dumbwaiter." Lexie walked over to it and yanked down on the door handle which squealed as she pulled it open.

Sam approached and studied the small metal elevator. "Needs some grease. It's rusty."

"It hasn't been used for a long time. We used to put luggage in it to send upstairs to the second floor bedrooms."

"Say, you mind if we use it to get our materials upstairs? It'd sure be easier than toting them up there."

"I don't see why not, but the electricity isn't on."

"I can make it work. This house was built around 1900, wasn't it?"

"1899, to be exact. Why?"

"Well, before electricity, these things worked with pulleys. I'm sure the pulleys are still there—just need a little grease, that's all."

Lexie excused herself as the men got to work, coming and going as they worked on the repairs. She tried to stay out of their way and strolled throughout the house. Russell said he'd seen someone in the house the night before, moving from room to room. No wonder there were rumors about the house being haunted. If she believed in such things, it might make more sense.

If only the house could talk to her, tell her who'd been there and what they were doing. Then it would truly be haunted. But she was convinced she had overlooked some clue she hadn't seen yet, something she hadn't remembered. She strained to think, but nothing came to her. No need to hang around and bother the men, though. She went to tell them she was leaving and found Sam back in the kitchen, loading some things onto the dumbwaiter.

"Glad you have this thing here. It sure helps get stuff upstairs. This old back of mine hurts when I have to lift things and carry them up steps."

"So the dumbwaiter is working?"

Sam tugged on the pulley, and the metal basket rose, emitting a soft creak. "Yep. Hardly makes any noise now."

"Well, I'm glad it can help. I'm leaving now. Please let me or Mr. Thompson know if you come across any more things that should be fixed."

"Will do." Sam touched the bill of his hat in reply.

Lexie strolled back toward the clubhouse, enjoying the Georgia sun on the warm winter day. She'd been on the island two weeks already but wasn't any closer to selling the house. If anything, she'd delayed the sale. The time wasn't right yet. The house wasn't ready and frankly, neither was she. She had expected to see the house, sign the papers, and leave within a few days. But she'd discovered she wasn't as afraid of the island as she'd expected, and, in fact, had enjoyed being there, probably due to Russell's light-hearted companionship. If he hadn't been around, her impression of the island might be more somber.

"Hello! Alexandra!" A familiar voice rang out from the grand lawn.

She turned as Floyd hurried over to meet her. Another man fashionably dressed in white trousers with an argyle vest and white shirt followed him.

"Hello, Floyd." Lexie's gaze fell on the guy that accompanied Floyd, her heart dropping as recognition registered. The hatless wavy blond hair, parted and combed to perfection and accenting the chiseled, tanned face, was the same.

"Alexandra, I want to introduce you to my cousin Spencer Bardwell."

Cousin? Oh yes, she knew Spencer but had no idea he and Floyd were related. Hard to believe they were from the same family tree.

"Actually, we've met." Lexie tried to avert her eyes from Floyd's handsome cousin.

"Nice to see you again, Alexandra. When Floyd told me you were here, I couldn't believe my luck!" The man's pearly white teeth gleamed like a movie star poster.

Lexie raised an eyebrow. "Is that so?" Since when would running into her be lucky? He must've forgotten that he had dropped her like a hot potato for her college roommate.

"Say, how about joining us for a bite of lunch?"

Before she had a chance to reply, the two men bordered her on either side and herded her toward the clubhouse. When they reached the front steps, Bernon Prentice approached with an extended hand.

"Spencer! So glad you could make it." He shook Spencer's hand, clapping him on the back with the other. "Our tennis tournament wouldn't be the same without you."

So that's why he was at Jekyll. She should've known the top-ranked tennis player wasn't there for lawn bowling.

"Glad I could come. Uncle Sam doesn't require my services yet."

"Maybe you can get Miss Smithfield to hit a few with you. I've been trying to talk her into a game ever since she arrived."

Spencer grinned at Lexie. "Sure. Why don't we play this afternoon?"

Her head spun. "This afternoon? I…"

"Don't tell me you have other plans. Come on, it'll be fun—like old times." He winked at her and her insides quivered. Like old times.

"I'm afraid I didn't bring my tennis clothes."

Spencer looked her up and down, and Lexie's temperature rose from her toes to her face.

"You look like you're the same size as my sister. I'll send over one of her outfits. What room are you in?"

"Two fourteen, but…"

"Swell! I'll have the concierge go to our apartment in the Annex and tell our man to bring an outfit over. It'll be in your room when we finish lunch."

"And I have plenty of racquets for you to use." Prentice grinned at her, then faced Spencer. "What time do you expect to play? I'll make sure a court is reserved."

Spencer checked his gleaming gold watch. "Two o'clock."

"You got it." Prentice slapped Spencer on the back again and headed off in the direction of the tennis courts.

Despite feeling railroaded into playing, a bubble of excitement forced itself up into her, suppressing the urge to resist. She hadn't played tennis with Spencer since her freshman year, and the former excitement reappeared, hoping to relive itself. What could it hurt?

During lunch, Spencer regaled Lexie with funny tales about his tennis escapades across the country. After transferring from Yale to Stanford, Lexie had only heard bits and pieces of his life and hadn't known what was truth and what was rumor. He'd become the captain of the Stanford tennis team before going pro, earning a spot at the top of the tennis circuit. At lunch, Floyd and Lexie barely got a word in the conversation, but she didn't mind. Handsome as ever, and entertaining as well, he provided a welcome distraction from the troublesome events around her. She detected boredom in Floyd, but he smiled and chuckled while his charming cousin rambled.

Spencer garnered the attention of every female in the room, a fact he was well aware of, making sure he spoke loudly enough for others to hear. Lexie heard giggles coming from neighboring tables as the younger women enjoyed the show he presented. A couple of them were even bold enough to approach him and ask for his autograph. He flashed a brilliant smile at the girls while they tittered and gushed. Had she ever been so obviously smitten at one time? She hoped not. She never would make such a spectacle of herself over anyone. A flicker of pride tickled her conscience though, since she had the privilege of sitting at his table.

When they rose from the table and left the dining room, Spencer grabbed her hand and planted a kiss on it. "M'lady, I'll take my leave now and meet you on yon courts at two bells."

Heat invaded Lexie's face. Smiling, she pulled her hand away and gave him a playful shove. As she turned to go up the stairs, she glimpsed Russell's back disappearing around the landing above. Had he found out anything yet? She checked the grandfather clock in the hallway, noting she had little time to change and get to the courts by two. She'd have to catch up with Russell later.

Right now, she had a handsome man to meet on the tennis courts. A quiver of excitement rippled through her. She hadn't played in a year and was eager to get the exercise. But that didn't explain the feeling of anticipation. Did she expect a chance to renew their relationship? Even though she'd been hurt when he ditched her for another girl, the old attraction still pulled at her.

She found the white blouse and skirt hanging in her room, and Spencer was right—they were just her size. She threw them on and tied a scarf around her hair, then grabbed her sweater and headed out to the tennis courts, perhaps too eager to see her old flame again.

Chapter 28

Russell stomped back up the stairs and slammed the door to his office. Spencer Bardwell was back. Blast it! And back to his old tricks too—trying to dazzle women with his charm and good looks. One glance at him sitting in the dining room jabbering for all to hear had soured Russell's stomach. And Lexie was sitting with him!

Sure, he was a top tennis player and great publicity for the tournament, but his ethics were repulsive. The way he toyed with women was disrespectful, dishonest, and downright wrong. Russell knew of several whose reputation Spencer had sullied. Russell paced the floor, his blood pulsating his temples. And now Spencer had set his sights on Lexie as his next conquest. Russell pounded his fist into his other hand. Surely, she could see through his charade, his flamboyant tactics. Couldn't she?

He opened his desk drawer where he'd stashed a pack of Lucky Strikes. He grabbed the pack and pulled out a cigarette. Although he'd promised Lexie he'd quit, what difference did it make now? Did she even notice? He picked up the matchbook, tore off a match, and struck it on the edge of the book. He watched the flame burn almost to his fingers, then blew it out. No. He wouldn't do it. Maybe Lexie didn't care about his promise, but he knew he'd given his word—and so did God.

Cool air. He needed to cool off. Stepping out onto the balcony, he lifted his head and inhaled the crisp air, then lowered his gaze and surveyed the panorama of the grounds, trying to calm down. He studied the people on the Grand Lawn, calling each one by name in his mind. As he looked to his left, he saw Lexie striding away from the building. Where was she going?

Then it dawned on him. She was wearing a tennis outfit. His gut twisted, knowing she was probably going to play with Spencer. He shouldn't be surprised. After all, she played on her college team, so it was only natural for her to play with Spencer. Plus, it was really none of his business anyway. But it was. He had to protect her from being hurt or mistreated, protect her from wolves like Spencer Bardwell. If Russell had a sister, he'd want someone to keep the creeps away. Robert would want him to do that for Lexie too.

He closed his eyes. *Lord, help me do the right thing for Lexie. Please open her eyes to the truth about Spencer and not let her get hurt.*

But how could he warn her without intruding into her business?

A knock on the door brought him in off the balcony. He crossed the room and opened it to admit two officers from the Coast Guard.

Lexie leaned against the fence, sipping her Coca-Cola.

Beside her, Spencer gulped his drink before lifting the bottle like a toast. "You sure gave me a run for my money. Your game's gotten better."

"Not quite as good as yours, though. Plus I haven't played in a year." Of course, he was the better player and had won, but she'd tried to make him work for it.

"So you ready for another set? I'll give you a chance to even the score." Spencer winked as his grin spread across his face.

Her face warmed. "I'm still pretty rusty, you know."

"Are you making excuses? Come on, you're not giving up yet, are you?"

Lexie put a hand on her hip. "Who said anything about giving up? All right, one more set."

Soon they were at it again, each trying to put more spin on the ball and run their opponent around the court. As Lexie retrieved an errant ball, she noticed Russell standing nearby, watching them. His arms were crossed over his chest like he was assessing the situation. She lifted her hand and waved. He nodded back, a faint smile curving his lips. Wonder if he had something to tell her?

Her focus diverted, she double-faulted her serve. Great. Did she have to look like a beginner while he watched?

When the set was over, Lexie walked over to him.

"Hi, Russell. Sorry you had to see me get soundly beaten."

"I thought you played well."

"She's got great form, don't you think, Russ?" Spencer joined them, boasting a wide grin.

A nerve in Russell's neck twitched. "Hello, Spencer. Welcome back." Russell's voice was flat.

"Do you play tennis, Russell?" Lexie tried to include him.

Russell's face flushed. "No, that's one sport I don't play."

"Guess that bum foot gets you off-balance. Yeah, you better stick to a sport less rigorous, like golf." Spencer laughed at his effort to make a joke.

Lexie jerked her head toward him. How insensitive. She glanced back at Russell, afraid she'd see pain in his eyes. Instead, he stuffed his hands in his trouser pockets and glared at Spencer.

"You don't play golf, do you, Spencer?" Russell challenged the tennis player.

"Oh, I've knocked the little white ball around a few times, but golf's too slow for me." He nudged Russell with his elbow. "I like fast sports, you know."

"So I've heard." The nerve in Russell's neck wiggled.

She looked back and forth as the two men sparred. Neither seemed to think well of the other. She needed to break up this verbal duel.

"Russell, did you have something to tell me—about the cottage?"

Russell didn't answer, as if waiting for Spencer to leave. Spencer took the hint.

"Hey. If you two are going to talk business, I'll be on my way." Spencer grabbed his racquet. "Really enjoyed playing with you today, Alex."

"My friends call me 'Lexie.'" Didn't he know that?

"Right. So, Lexie, I'll see you later. Would you like to play tomorrow?"

She glanced at Russell to see if he had other plans for her, but his clenched jaw didn't move.

"Sure. Let's play before lunch, though."

"Swell. I'll tell Bernon." Spencer flashed his confident grin and strode off.

Lexie and Russell watched Spencer walk away, then she spun around to face him with her hands on her hips.

"What's wrong?"

"Wrong?" Russell stared over her head as if focused beyond her.

"You act angry."

"I'm not angry." He glanced down at her face and his shoulders relaxed.

Lexie blew out a breath. "If you say so. Well, do you have any news?"

"The workmen aren't finished. It could take a while. They had to order some more materials."

"That's not the kind of news I was referring to, and you know it. What about the noise we heard at the beach? What about the men in the raft that were spotted that night? Have you talked with the Coast Guard?"

"I have." He looked into her eyes, searching as if he wanted to say more, but held back.

She tilted her head. "Are you going to tell me anything or just leave me in the dark?"

He eased out a breath. "A tanker was torpedoed about fifteen miles east of here. The raft carried a few survivors. Some more were picked up by fishing boats." He spread his arms. "That's all I know."

"All you know?" Lexie's voice rose.

Russell put his finger in front of his mouth. "Shhh. Lexie, I'm telling you confidentially. The Coast Guard doesn't want the word to get out."

"But why not? Don't we have a right to know?"

He shrugged and sighed. "The authorities believe civilians are better off not knowing these things. It could only cause panic."

"That's ridiculous. What authorities—the Coast Guard?"

"From what I understand, the order comes all the way from the top."

"The President?"

Russell nodded. "That's what I'm told."

"So what do we do? Just wait for the Germans like sitting ducks?"

"We go on about our day-to-day lives and let the military deal with military matters."

Lexie started to argue but clamped her mouth shut. Russell was only doing what he was told, even if he didn't agree with it. And something told her he didn't.

"Nice day for tennis." Russell changed the subject.

"Yes, it is. I haven't played for a long time."

"I must admit, I was surprised to see you out here. After all, you refused Bernon's invitation to play. Guess Spencer Bardwell was more convincing."

Lexie crossed her arms and stared at him. "What are you saying?" Was he jealous?

His face reddened, and he looked away. "Nothing. Just surprised, that's all. I mean, you've been telling me you don't have time to enjoy yourself, but it seems that you are."

Lexie bristled and her temperature began to boil. "You're right. I had no intention of having fun here. My short business trip has gotten complicated, forcing me to stay longer. You just told me there will be an additional delay getting the cottage fixed. So what should I do while I wait to finish the job I came to do? Sit and knit or play bridge with the old ladies? Sorry to disappoint you, but I need a little more activity than that."

She turned on her heel and marched away. The nerve of him questioning her activities. He had carried his over-protection too far. She was an adult and could make her own decisions. Who did he think he was anyway? And she had thought he was such a nice guy. Well, even Russell Thompson had his faults.

Behind her, Russell called out, "Lexie, wait."

But she was tired of waiting. Tired of other people and things controlling her life. She finally had the freedom to do what she wanted to, and nobody better get in her way. Nobody.

Chapter 29

*B*last! That was exactly what he was afraid of. He had overstepped his boundaries. All he'd wanted to do was warn her about Spencer, but his words hadn't come out right. He'd prayed about it, hadn't he? Weren't his motives pure?

Russell strolled back to the clubhouse, studying the ground. *Lord, what should I do now?* He didn't want Lexie angry with him, but she was, and rightly so. As he neared the clubhouse, raucous laughter came from the billiards room, and he recognized Spencer's voice. He gritted his teeth, overhearing the cad's coarse remarks about some woman.

If he talked about Lexie that way, Russell would … what would he do? Challenge him to a duel? Punch him? While it would give him personal satisfaction to deliver justified punishment, such an act would probably backfire on himself. Still, curiosity pulled him to the room. What if he talked about Lexie? Russell had to find out.

Inside, Spencer sat in a leather armchair with his feet propped up on the coffee table as half a dozen other men hovered about, some sitting, others standing. When Russell entered the room, the laughter quieted. Spencer lifted his glass of amber fluid in Russell's direction.

"Well, if it isn't our illustrious superintendent! Come on in, Russ, and pour yourself a drink."

Russell nodded to the other young men present, most of whom seemed too young to drink alcohol. Yet, eager to prove their manhood among their peers, each held a glass. It rankled Russell how Spencer gathered an audience wherever he went. But as he considered those in attendance, he realized how naïve they were. Spencer, the experienced man of the world, represented what they wanted to be—handsome, athletic, popular. They had no idea what he was really like.

"Have a seat and join us." Spencer motioned to the sofa, whereupon a young man seated there quickly rose to his feet.

"Keep your seat, I'm not staying long." Russell stuck his hands in his trousers and rocked on his heels. "Thought I'd see who was winning the pool game, but it looks like no one's playing." Thank goodness, he came up with that one.

"Not now, maybe later." Spencer propped his elbows on the arms of the chair, a cigarette in one hand, and waved the other hand holding the drink. "You looking for a game? I might take you on after I finish this."

"No, no. I'll take a rain check on that." Russell glanced around the room at each of the boyish faces. "Guess you boys won't hear from the draft board for a while."

A couple of faces dropped their gazes down to the floor, but one spoke up.

"I'm joining up when we leave the island. I'm not waiting to be drafted."

Another joined in. "Me too."

Russell knew the boy's family and doubted he'd be allowed to sign up until he finished college.

"What's your hurry?" Spencer said, his words starting to slur. "I have it on good authority this war will be over in no time."

"Is that what you're waiting for, Spencer?" Russell knew Spencer's father was a powerful senator and could probably keep his son from being drafted.

"Well, of course. Aren't you?" Spencer eyed Russell's leg. "Oh, never mind. They wouldn't draft you anyway, would they? They only want *able-bodied* men."

Russell clenched his jaw as heat flushed his body. It took every bit of his strength to keep from walking across the room and knocking out a few of those gleaming teeth. But he wouldn't lower himself. He wouldn't take the bait and give Spencer the satisfaction of knowing he'd gotten under Russell's skin.

Russell forced a smile. "Well, it's a good thing we have you here to protect the home front." He turned to leave, stopping at the door to glance back over his shoulder. "Good evening, gentlemen."

He couldn't get away from there fast enough. Good thing Lexie's name didn't come up. It was one thing to suffer embarrassment over his own shortcomings, but quite another if he'd heard any disparaging remarks about her. He wanted to find her and apologize, but she might not have cooled off yet. He'd never seen her so angry, well not as an adult anyway.

A smile crossed his face at a memory of nine-year-old Lexie stomping away, angry at him and Robert. They were going sailing in Robert's little sailboat and wouldn't let her come with them. She had been furious when they told her she couldn't go. But Robert knew his mother would die of fright if he let Lexie join them. Russell remembered feeling sorry for her but knew it was for her own good—and her mother's anxiety.

So she thought he didn't want her to have fun? On the contrary, he truly wanted her to enjoy life, life without fear. But circumstances since she'd arrived had only contributed to her fears, not removed them. And now he had his own fear—fear that she would be hurt or taken advantage of by Spencer. How could he explain that fear to her—that there were some things one *should* be afraid of?

He glanced up at the second floor of the clubhouse at Lexie's room. Maybe tomorrow he would have a chance to straighten things out. Sighing, he turned the other way and walked to the chapel.

Lexie called for room service the next morning. She didn't want to see Russell and was afraid she'd run into him in the dining room again. She still simmered over yesterday's conversation, and she didn't want to talk to him—yet. So she'd just avoid him for the time-being. Deep down, she hated being upset with him because she considered him a friend, maybe even a close friend. But his words the day before had hurt, and now she wasn't sure he was a friend.

After all, he'd challenged her decision, questioned her, making her feel like a little girl who had to explain her actions to an adult. Why was she accountable to Russell for her actions? For the first time in her life, she didn't have to be accountable to anyone else. Why would he make her feel guilty? And about playing tennis, a sport she really enjoyed. What was wrong with that?

She sipped her tea and nibbled a cold scone. A thought hit her in the chest. Maybe he didn't want her to play tennis because he couldn't. She remembered Spencer's comment about Russell's leg and worried that his feelings were hurt. So he didn't want her to play either? She shook her head. That didn't fit his personality. Selfishness was not one of his characteristics. It just didn't make sense.

She considered how much time they'd spent together since she'd been on the island. Russell was the one who wanted her to stay longer when she said she expected to leave soon. The time had passed quickly, mainly because she enjoyed his company. Could he be jealous of Spencer? Her heart beat faster. Of course, Spencer was very handsome, but so was Russell. Yet the two were so different, she couldn't even compare them.

Someone knocked on her door, and she glanced at her watch. That must be the maid with the tennis clothes she'd dropped off at the laundry yesterday. Still in her chemise and bathrobe, she went to the door and opened it a crack.

The maid Stella held up the hanger with the clothes.

"Your laundry, miss."

Could the woman manage to smile sometime? She'd certainly improve her looks if she tried.

"Thank you, I was waiting for those." Lexie opened the door to admit the maid who barely looked at her. "Just lay them on the bed, please."

Stella did as told and turned to leave, but she stopped and stared wide-eyed at Lexie's gold necklace. Lexie's hand instinctively flew to it as the maid's eyes bore holes through her. Lexie opened the door wide for the woman to leave, hoping she'd take the hint.

"Thank you again," Lexie said, eager to get dressed and meet Spencer at the tennis courts.

Stella made eye contact with Lexie, then glanced away and hurried out the door. Such a strange woman. No doubt her husband, being a boat captain, was on the lookout for Germans. Could he have seen anything?

Lexie hurried into the outfit, excited to play tennis again. She wouldn't feel guilty about that. Russell couldn't spoil one of her favorite activities. She was sorry he couldn't play, too, but that wasn't her fault. Surely, he would understand if he tried. And if he didn't, well, that wasn't her fault either.

Chapter 30

"Atta boy!" Spencer shouted and clapped as Floyd stepped forward to receive his second-place trophy in the lawn bowling tournament.

Lexie, standing beside Spencer, added her applause to the group of spectators witnessing the award ceremony. As Russell had predicted, Mr. Gibbs won first place for the tenth consecutive year. A twinge of sympathy for Floyd squeezed Lexie's chest. Would the poor guy ever win at anything?

Floyd joined Spencer and Lexie afterwards, the small silver trophy at his side.

Spencer slapped him on the back, looking down at Floyd's award. "Let's see that prize!"

Floyd lifted it high enough for them to see, a wry smile working its way across his face.

"Hey, that's swell. Next year, you'll get the big one. The old guy looks like he might not be around next year."

Lexie shot a quick glance at the older gentleman, hoping he hadn't heard the remark. Spencer's lack of tact embarrassed her, but it didn't affect him. He could deliver barbs, laugh them off, and get away with being impolite while no one seemed to notice. She thought Floyd noticed, though, based on the crimson that appeared on his cheeks. He never protested his cousin's behavior, but instead remained a faithful fan like so many others.

Much as she disliked Spencer's manners, she couldn't help but enjoy his attention. Fun and handsome, who wouldn't want to be around him? Russell, for one. She hadn't seen him for several days, not since their disagreement.

"Say, let's celebrate!"

Lexie whipped her head at Spencer's suggestion.

"Why don't we go to the beach—have a picnic?" Spencer called out, garnering everyone's attention.

One of the young men standing nearby responded. "Swell idea! I'm game, are you?" He addressed the others in his group.

Heads bobbed and voices concurred. Before Lexie knew it, she was swept along with a group of other girls and guys away from the Grand Lawn. Spencer gave orders to various individuals to bring food and beverages.

Mrs. Appleton called out to Floyd from the veranda, and he hurried over and handed his mother the trophy. She beamed with pride, showing him off to the ladies and gentlemen beside her. He waved to Lexie and called out to her, "I'll catch up with you later." Poor man—those apron strings were still connected.

"Let's ride bikes!" One of the young women in the beach entourage called out, and several detoured to the bike hut.

"We'll take the roadster," Spencer said to Lexie. "I need to stop at the Annex to pick up a couple of things first anyway."

"Don't you want to ride bikes?"

"Not my style, babe." When they reached the Annex, he said, "I'll be back in a jiffy." Spencer entered one of the ground floor apartments and returned a few minutes later carrying a bottle of liquor in one hand and two glasses in the other. An older gentleman followed carrying a blanket and a basket, which he put in the backseat of the gleaming red sports car parked in front of the building. "Thank you, James." The man nodded and returned to the apartment.

Spencer opened the passenger door of the car and motioned for Lexie to get in. She obliged, and he climbed in the other side.

"Is this your car?" Lexie admired the convertible, one of the few cars on the island.

"It belongs to a special friend who lets me use it whenever I want."

Lexie was curious about the "special friend," knowing Spencer's penchant for name-dropping.

"Would you like one for the road?" Spencer held up a glass.

"No, thank you."

"Suit yourself." He opened the bottle, poured a couple of ounces in the glass, and downed it in a gulp before starting the car. Lexie's stomach tightened at the sight, an unpleasant memory of her father invading her thoughts.

"So, I hear you own one of these cottages now. Nice. So what's it like? Aren't you going to invite me over?"

Lexie jerked her head at his question. "I'm afraid it's not in any condition to have guests."

Spencer laughed. "Bet it's swell. Say, you could fix it up and throw some great parties, couldn't you? Wouldn't have to bother with the stuffy old clubhouse."

"I suppose I could if I were going to keep it."

He looked at her with raised eyebrows. "Why wouldn't you? Hey, not very many single gals own their own place on an island. You could live it up here!"

"I doubt the other members would allow too much partying. Jekyll's not really that kind of place."

"Don't I know? Oh well, just think about it. I'd be glad to help you liven things up around here." He threw back his head and laughed as they pulled up beside all the bikes that were parked by the path to the beach.

The celebration was in full swing when Lexie and Spencer stepped onto the beach. Lexie was amazed at how quickly the party had come together. Scattered blankets and picnic hampers invited the partygoers to relax and enjoy themselves. Several guys carried open bottles of liquor searching for empty glasses to refill. Laughter and gaiety filled the air, accompanied by the gentle sloshing of the waves and cries of seagulls overhead.

The young men removed their shoes and rolled up their pants as they trod into the shallow tide, splashing each other. Some of the guys pulled off their shirts and dove into the chilly water, drenching their undershirts and trousers. The girls tittered and giggled, most of them vying for Spencer's attention. Everyone enjoyed themselves, and increasingly so as they consumed more alcohol. Everyone but Lexie.

She settled on the corner of a blanket, pasting a smile on her face as she listened to the inane chatter around her. The fact that she didn't drink was one thing that separated her. But besides the drinking, Lexie's life had not been problem-free like theirs. The guys bragged and taunted each other while the girls preened. These people never thought about losing their family fortunes or estates—others took care of their important affairs so they didn't have to.

Although Lexie wasn't the oldest in the group at twenty-two, she felt more mature. She was not one of them and felt like a spectator instead of a participant. These people seemed ignorant to the fact that a war was going on beyond this island. Young men their age placed themselves in danger on the battleground while these people cavorted without a care in the world. She glanced around to see If there were anyone who could carry on a real conversation. But there wasn't. She sighed. Where was Russell? Their discussions were real, not fake and meaningless like the ones she overheard.

As she watched Spencer, she wondered why he mentioned her cottage. Was it just coincidence that he suggested she keep it? Or had he and Floyd discussed the cottage? She couldn't imagine why he would be interested in it, unless Floyd put him up to it.

Her face ached from faking a smile, and she was tired of pretending to have a good time. Spencer was preoccupied with entertaining everyone else, so she didn't think he would miss her if she left. She stood up and brushed off the sand from her clothes.

"Hey, Lexie! Where are you going? Aren't you having fun?" Spencer had noticed.

"Just going for a walk." She took a few steps away from the group, studying the sand at her feet. The usually clean beige sand was littered with black slimy blobs. She bent over for a closer look, expecting them to be some sort of jellyfish. But they didn't appear to be living matter. What on earth were they? As far as she could see, the black blobs lined the shore.

"Say, man, what's that on your pants?" A voice behind her made her turn. One of the young men pointed to the pants of another.

"Don't know, but you've got some on yours too." The man touched a black streak on his pants. "It's greasy. Look—the stuff's floating in the water. I'm getting out!"

Everyone in the water dashed out, glancing down at their clothes, all of which bore some trace of the black stuff.

"Must be some kind of seaweed."

"It stinks. Hope it comes out."

Lexie had a sinking feeling in her stomach that the mysterious black stuff was more than seaweed. Farther down the beach, she saw a familiar figure looking out at the water. She strode away from the others and walked up to Abner Jones standing sentinel.

He saw her and nodded. "Miss Smithfield."

"Mr. Jones. Have you seen anything unusual today?"

He shook his head. "Not out there."

"Do you know what this black stuff is on the beach? Is it seaweed?"

"No, ma'am. It's petroleum."

"Petroleum? But, where did it come from?"

Abner Jones pointed to an orange object lying in the debris washed up on the beach. Lexie walked over to it and gasped when she recognized a life jacket, mostly covered with the black slime.

"That tanker that got torpedoed out there."

Lexie's eyes widened. It really happened. And now even Jekyll Island was touched by the war.

Spencer's voice rang out. "Lexie! Come on. We're leaving." She glanced over her shoulder and saw him waving her back.

"Excuse me, Mr. Jones. I must go. Thank you for keeping watch for us."

Abner Jones nodded and Lexie returned to the group, now picking up the remnants of the picnic. Young men in soggy, streaked clothes stamped around as they gathered their belongings.

"We'll see you tomorrow, Spence—at the dance, if not before." They waved as they left the beach.

"Who were you talking to, Lex?" Spencer's glazed blue eyes displayed the effect of alcohol.

Lexie looked back at the lonely figure on the beach.

"That's Abner Jones. He, um, works for my family."

"That crazy old coot?" Spencer made a circle with his finger over his ear. "What could you possibly talk to him about? I heard he'd been in the bughouse." Spencer's grin wasn't as attractive as it had been when he was sober.

Lexie stiffened, holding back the urge to retort or defend Abner Jones. One thing she'd learned from her father—don't try to talk to a drunk. The effort would be a frustrating waste of time. She shrugged and walked toward the car. But when Spencer appeared beside her, she stopped. Did she really want to get into a car with him now? A silent warning told her no.

"I think I'll walk back."

"Wha'? Why? Don't you want to show me around your 'cottage'?"

Lexie crossed her arms. "I just feel like walking, that's all."

Spencer shrugged and hopped in the car, leaping over the unopened door. "Swell. Suit yourself."

She waited for him to leave.

But instead of driving away, he turned to her and said, "Don't forget our date to the dance." He waved and gave her his best smile before skidding away.

Did she really tell him she'd go with him to the Valentine Dance? She didn't recall an invitation. She bit her lip trying to remember and a vague memory of hearing the topic discussed around her came to mind. But although she was there in body, her thoughts had drifted off as they were in the habit of doing amidst the pointless prattle. Either she had agreed unaware, or Spencer had assumed she would go with him.

Yesterday, the idea of spending time with Spencer had been appealing. But now she had second thoughts. How could she get out of going with him? Not that she had other plans, much less another offer. Would Russell have asked her if she hadn't gotten so angry with him? Maybe he had asked someone else. Could he even dance with his bad foot? Her heart twisted, and she realized she didn't care about whether he could dance or not. But she did care if he was there, especially with another woman.

She walked back to the clubhouse, thankful for the peace and quiet—the escape from the boisterous throng of partiers. An image of the oil-covered life preserver came to mind, and she shuddered. What happened to the person wearing it? If only she could talk to Russell, but there was a gap between them that she didn't know how to bridge. She should find out the status of Destiny, too, since she hadn't seen it for a week.

Her heart quickened at the thought of Destiny. Spencer had mentioned her cottage again. Was he really that interested in it? Why?

Chapter 31

Russell paced the floor in his office. Should he go to the dance or not? As the Club Superintendent, he'd be expected to make an appearance. He didn't have a date, but he knew there would be others without dates as well. Of course, he'd hoped to go with Lexie, but she was probably going with Spencer. Every time Russell saw her with Spencer and his group of fans, his gut wrenched. She didn't belong with them—that throng of spoiled rich kids, even if she was rich too. No, she was different. At least he had thought so.

He'd kept his distance, not wanting to interfere with her fun, as she'd accused him. But he kept watch for her from his tower balcony as he agonized over her choice of companions. He was a fool to entertain the notion that she was attracted to him. He wasn't in her league and he knew it, had known it all his life. How stupid of him to think otherwise.

Yet, no matter how busy he stayed, he couldn't get her out of his mind. He had plenty of work to do, much he'd set aside to spend time with her. Yet, he missed her. He really enjoyed being with her and believed the feeling was reciprocated. But he was wrong.

He checked on the progress of repairs to Destiny daily and had been informed that the leak from the window actually originated in the roof. Shingles had been ordered to replace those that were damaged and missing, but with the war, building materials like that were harder to come by. It could take two more weeks before the shingles arrived. At first, he was glad to offer Lexie an excuse to stay longer. Now, he was sorry she'd have more time to spend with Spencer Bardwell.

Russell stepped out on the balcony, hoping to get a glimpse of her. Still early, not many from Spencer's entourage had seen daylight yet. More than likely they were sleeping off last night's celebration. He'd heard about the beach party after the lawn bowling tournament. Some of them returned later to continue their revelry in the billiards room. But knowing Lexie's disdain for smoking and abstinence from alcohol, he didn't believe she'd joined them there.

Every day he sought God's guidance and prayed for wisdom. He didn't get an answer but had the impression that he should wait and not do anything. Wait. Wait until what? He wanted to keep her from being wounded by Spencer's actions. Yet he thought God was telling him to step aside so God could do His work in the situation.

So what do I do in the meantime, Lord? Just keep on doing his job—taking care of other members and guests, the grounds, the buildings, and the employees. That much, he knew. Meanwhile, he had to stay aware of the war's threat to the island. The Coast Guard told him twenty men had died as a result of the attack on the tanker. Some twenty more were unaccounted for, and only five made it to shore in a lifeboat. Russell shook his head. What a tragedy that these men, civilians, were killed simply because they were in the wrong place at the wrong time. Or maybe they just happened to be in the right place at the wrong time.

Because American tankers were being targeted to hamper Allied fuel supply, civilian gasoline supply was becoming limited. Even though the government hadn't admitted the loss of these tankers publicly, it had started a campaign for private citizens to reduce their gasoline usage so the military would have enough. Everyone was encouraged to walk and leave their cars at home. Of course, here on the island, driving was limited anyway and horses were still available. Russell grimaced every time he saw Spencer in the roadster he brought over on the ferry. Sacrifice was not a term Spencer would understand.

When Lexie entered the dining room for lunch, the Maurice sisters waved her over.

"Good morning, ladies." Lexie warmed at the welcome smile of the women. "How have you been?"

"We're just fine." Peg tapped the empty back of the seat beside her, and a waiter rushed over to pull out the chair for Lexie. "Your skin looks a bit ruddy. We've heard you've been playing a lot of tennis."

"Yes, with that professional tennis player, too, no less. You must be very good."

Lexie dropped her gaze to smooth the linen napkin on her lap. "Not as good as he is, I'm afraid. But it has been fun to get some exercise and challenge myself."

The two sisters exchanged glances. "Well, just keep your distance.

That nasty business he was involved in last year was quite a scandal." Marian tapped her finger on the table for emphasis.

Lexie looked from one sister to the other. "I'm afraid I don't know what you're talking about."

Peg leaned forward and lowered her voice. "Oh, it was awful. He was in a terrible traffic accident in California that killed a young woman. They say he was drunk and driving way too fast."

How had she missed hearing about this? She'd been so involved with Mother and the hospital, she seldom read a newspaper. And the only news she heard on the radio last year was about the war.

"Good thing his father has connections or he might've ended up in jail."

"That poor girl's family."

Lexie's stomach tightened as she remembered the day before at the beach, thankful she had refused to ride back with him. And she had agreed to go with him to the dance? Now she really didn't want to go with him. Maybe Floyd would go, too, even drive. No, Spencer wouldn't agree to that. She'd ask the concierge to take her, tell Spencer she had to take care of some business first.

She grabbed the glass of water in front of her and took a gulp.

"Alexandra, are you all right?" Peg laid her hand on Lexie's arm and frowned.

Lexie shook her head. "I'm fine, really."

"So are you going to the Valentine's dance tonight? I'm glad the club is having a social event for the young people. And it's nice that they're even including the staff this year. Of course, you must be going with Russell. We think you make a nice couple, don't we, Peg? Now there's a real gentleman."

One thing she liked about the Maurice sisters was how they treated everyone equally. Despite their wealth, they showed no superior attitude. They saw nothing wrong with Lexie being with Russell, unlike the attitude of some of her peers on the island, namely Spencer. But now she was embarrassed to tell the sisters she had agreed to go with Spencer. Why had she fought with Russell anyway? Where was he? She considered running up to his office to apologize for getting so angry with him, but she couldn't. She might be wrong, but she had some pride.

Her cheeks grew hot when she realized the two ladies expected her to answer. "No, in fact, he hasn't asked me. I haven't seen him much lately."

The sisters raised their eyebrows in tandem. Marian spoke first. "Well, I must admit I'm surprised. You two looked thick as thieves. So, are you going to the dance alone?"

"No. I'm actually going with a group," she lied. But having said it, she decided to make it true.

Lexie ran into Floyd as she left the dining room. "Floyd, will you see Spencer before the dance tonight?"

"As a matter of fact, I'm meeting him after lunch."

"Would you please give him a message for me? Tell him I'll be a little late tonight and not to wait for me. I'll meet him there. Okay?" Lexie tilted her head and gave Floyd her most beseeching smile.

"Sure. If you say so. I'll tell him."

"Thank you so much, Floyd. You're a dear."

A rosy glow spread over Floyd's face, and he smiled before raising his eyes to acknowledge his mother hailing him across the room.

That taken care of, Lexie wandered out on the veranda, hoping to see Russell. Maybe he didn't have a date and she could ride with him. But how, unless she made amends for the last time she'd seen him? Her heart twisted. It wouldn't be fair for her to do that now, just for a ride. After all, she still had a date with Spencer. What would happen if she walked in with Russell? She envisioned an ugly scene between the two men, not to mention disappointment on Russell's face. No, that wouldn't work either.

Two girls that were at the beach the day before strolled out on the veranda. They waved at her and rushed over.

"Hey, Lexie! Aren't you excited about the dance tonight?" Betty, the bubbly blonde with upswept hair, wiggled her whole body as she asked.

"Of course she is! She's Spencer's date." Tina, a petite brunette, clasped her hands together as she rolled up on her toes. "He's so dreamy."

Lexie couldn't keep from smiling at the excitement they displayed, like two little girls anticipating Santa Claus.

"Yes, of course, I'm excited." But not as much as they were. "Who are your dates?"

The two looked at each other and back at her as Betty answered. "We don't have dates, but we're going anyway. I'm sure there'll be guys there without dates. Besides, we just want to dance!"

Lexie expected her to dance right off the veranda, unable to keep her body still.

"Sure, why not? Say, could I ride with you? I need to get there a little later and can't ride with Spencer. Of course, I don't want to hold you girls up if you're in a hurry to be the first ones there." Lexie held her breath, hoping they'd say 'yes'.

"Why no, we wouldn't want to be first, would we Betty?" Tina looked up at her companion. "We should be fashionably late."

Betty's brow crinkled, as if waiting one more minute would hurt. "Yes, of course. Sure, you can ride with us. Sally and Mary are riding with us too. We have to do our part to save gas. Plus, it'll be more fun with all of us!"

"That sounds like great fun." Lexie tried to be enthusiastic, despite the fact that the whole situation reminded her of high school days when her friends focused on boys while she and Robert faced putting Mother in a sanatorium.

"Swell! We're meeting the others here at 6:30." Betty pointed to her watch. "We'll take our time getting there so we won't be too early. Does that work for you?"

"Perfect." Lexie would try to detain them as long as she could to make sure Spencer got there first without her.

"Oh, there's Michael. Michael!" Betty waved like she was flagging a distress call to get the attention of the guy walking across the Grand Lawn. "I want to hear more about last night's party. I had to go home before it was over," she said to Lexie. "Come on, Tina. Let's see what happened. See you later, Lexie!" The two hurried off after Michael, leaving Lexie on the veranda.

Why couldn't she be as excited as they were about the dance? After all, she loved to dance and hadn't had the opportunity for months. Out of the corner of her eye, she saw Abner Jones walking past the clubhouse in the direction of Destiny. He gazed up at her as he passed the veranda and nodded. He must be going to check on the house. It occurred to her that she hadn't thought about the cottage for several days and should go see the progress that had been made. But she didn't have time to go now. If only Russell could go with her next time. Maybe tomorrow, she'd be able to talk to him. Or maybe tonight, if he went to the party too.

Chapter 32

$\mathcal{L}$arge paper hearts hung on strings from the ceiling of the teahouse as red and white streamers crossed the room in opposite directions. Lexie entered at the rear of the herd of tittering females, scanning the room for Spencer.

She was not surprised to spot him on the other side of the room beside a punch bowl filled with red liquid. As usual, he was holding court with the guys. When he caught her gaze, he hailed her, left the others by the table, and hurried over.

"There you are, my late date!" Spencer was the beacon of festivity with a red bow tie adorning his white shirt and reflecting the glow in his cheeks. His white linen suit, accenting his tanned skin and flashy smile, belied the fact that it was still February. No doubt it was always summertime in southern California. Lexie couldn't believe the way he attracted followers as if he were a movie star.

Of course, he was a tennis star, but hardly worthy of the pedestal on which he'd been placed. She had to admit that smile of his could be awfully disarming, and he was very nice to look at … and be seen with. It was easy to see how a girl could fall for him like she had years ago. But the attraction had worn off like gold finish painted on cheap metal, and in its place her dislike of his shallow character grew.

Spencer sidled up to her and kissed her on the cheek, setting it aflame, not because of passion, but because his boldness embarrassed her. However, the action gained his desired response, as cat-calls and whistles rang out, accompanied by laughter. Lexie turned away from the onlookers to face him.

"Hi, Spencer. Sorry I'm late." She didn't mean it, but propriety required her to say it.

"Not as sorry as I am." He patted his chest over his heart. "I've been counting the minutes until you arrived."

Lexie gave him a playful shove. "Sure, Spencer. You looked like you were in the corner crying when I got here."

"Oh, I was—earlier. But these fellows felt sorry for me and rescued me." He lifted his glass of punch as evidence. "May I get you some punch?"

Not sure whether the punch had been spiked or not, Lexie was afraid to find out. On the other hand, she didn't want to be unsociable. It was a party after all.

She nodded. "All right. I'll have a glass."

"Coming right up." Spencer headed back to the refreshment table. Lexie followed a short distance, scanning the room. Was Russell there? A quick search told her he wasn't. Her heart dropped a notch.

Spencer appeared in front of her holding out a glass. "Oh, sorry. Let me get your coat. You can't dance with that thing on."

He put down the glasses and helped her out of her coat, which he tossed over a chair. When he handed Lexie her glass, he held his up like a toast. "Here's to a fun evening!"

The first sip told Lexie the punch contained alcohol. Rather than put it down, she decided to just hold it. A man in charge of the record player stood in front of the room and tapped his glass with a spoon to get everyone's attention.

"Good evening, ladies and gentlemen! Welcome to the Jekyll Island Valentine's Party. Grab your partner and get ready to shake a leg." He placed the needle of the Philco record player on the record and the sound of "In the Mood" by Glenn Miller's band filled the room.

"I'm in the mood, aren't you?" Spencer winked at Lexie, gulped his punch before taking hers out of her hand, and set it on the table.

He grabbed her arm and pulled her to the center of the room which had been cleared of chairs for a dance floor. Lexie glanced around to see if other couples followed suit, relieved to see they did. Soon the room filled with dancers, laughing and swaying to the jazzy tune. When the first song ended, Spencer rushed to refill his glass.

"Boy, this dancing is making me thirsty." He chugged his drink, then held it out to the waiter pouring the punch for replenishment. "Don't you need a refill, Alex?"

Lexie bit back a comment about her name but raised her glass, still quite full. "Not yet." She raised it to her lips and pretended to drink it, wishing it weren't spiked because she was thirsty too. When Spencer strolled over to some guys having a smoke, she approached the waiter serving the punch.

"Sir, do you have anything that doesn't have alcohol?"

The man smiled and nodded, reached under the table skirt, and pulled out a bottle of ginger ale. "Will this do, miss?"

"Perfect. Please take this glass and give me one with that instead."

The waiter obliged, and Lexie savored the cool drink. As she lifted her eyes, she caught Russell's gaze at her from the opposite side of the room. So he did come. Lexie breathed a sigh of relief as she scanned the area around him for a sign of his date. No one stood beside him, but there were many single girls there who might have come with him. She attempted a timid smile, hoping he'd return one. He nodded his head in her direction. Was that a glimmer of a smile?

"Hey, Lexie! Spence said he didn't mind if I took you for a few turns around the floor. What'cha say?" The young man with slicked down black hair and a hint of a mustache grinned from ear to ear as he took her arm. As the Andrews Sisters sang the familiar words of "Don't Sit Under the Apple Tree," she was back on the dance floor. She glanced over his shoulder and glared at Spencer, who didn't even look in her direction. Good thing she liked to dance.

As she began dancing with her new partner, she tried to find Russell again. But he no longer stood in the same spot, and her partner spun her around before she could find Russell. Her energetic new partner insisted they dance the next song as well. Since Spencer seemed to have lost interest in dancing, she saw no reason to refuse. But when she recognized the next song as a slow one, she begged a chance to rest. She was as close to the guy as she cared to get.

She thanked him, searching the room for a quiet spot where she could get away from the crowd. She found one at the back of the room and retreated there, leaning against the wall to watch from a distance. Loud laughter told her where Spencer was—standing in the middle of a group of guys and entertaining them as was his custom. A cluster of girls including Betty and Tina positioned themselves not far from the men, eyeing them and giggling as they vied for attention. No doubt they hoped the guys would ask them to dance, yearning to be held close as they danced to the romantic croon of Bing Crosby's voice.

She would, too, but not with any of those guys. Lexie scanned the couples on the dance floor, watching how they moved in rhythm with each other. Some of the couples appeared to be very much in love, their warm smiles and tender gazes declaring it. She sighed. Would she ever know that feeling?

Then she saw him. And her. Russell danced with the girl Lexie had seen him talking to the night of the movie. Her heart dropped like a rock. So they were a couple.

Why was she surprised? She'd thought he had been seeing someone before she arrived. Why wouldn't he?

Lexie looked away, her eyes growing moist. What did she expect from him anyway? The song finally ended, and Lexie decided to refill her ginger ale. As she made her way back to the refreshment table, Spencer turned around and waved to her before trotting over.

"Say, Lex, where'd you go? I lost you."

As if he'd been looking for her. His eyes sparkled, but Lexie suspected it was the liquor's effect on him and not her.

"Ready to dance some more?"

The strains of "Boogie Woogie Bugle Boy" blasted out, and all the guys hooted. Each one grabbed a partner and headed to the dance floor. Everybody loved the Andrews Sisters' song, its jazzy rhythm compelling a person to move his feet. Lexie and Spencer boogied along with the rest of the crowd, remaining on the dance floor when Duke Ellington's band played the next few songs. When the tempo slowed again with the next song, someone tapped Lexie on the shoulder.

She turned and her breath caught.

"May I have this dance?" Russell gazed down at her, his eyes searching her face. He glanced over at Spencer, who nodded and shrugged.

"Sure, Russ. I need a new drink anyway. Take care of my girl." Spencer strode away and Russell took Lexie's right hand in his before slipping his left arm around her waist.

Warmth radiated from his touch throughout her body.

"Are you having a good time, Lexie?" His words spoken so close to her ear fluttered her stomach. "I hope Spencer is taking good care of you."

She leaned back to look up into his face to see if his expression was serious or teasing. It was obvious Spencer took care of no one but himself. And he'd called her "his girl"! She started to protest, but the soft glimmer in Russell's eyes told her it wasn't necessary. Then she remembered the other woman she'd seen Russell with. She turned her head to scan the dance floor and spotted her with another man. Glancing back to Russell, she found his eyes still on her and not on the other woman. Was the other woman his date or his girlfriend?

"Sure. It's a nice party, and I've enjoyed dancing." No need to discuss Spencer. "And you? Your date's a pretty girl." Lexie looked sidelong at the other woman.

Russell's eyebrows rose as he followed her gaze and laughed. "Jean? We didn't come together, if that's what you mean. We're just friends."

Relief lifted the weight in her heart, and she resisted the urge to grin. They danced without talking as Lexie fought the desire to lean into him and melt into his arms, a place that offered safety. She closed her eyes and soaked in Bing Crosby singing "It's Always You." Wouldn't it be wonderful if someone felt that way about her? Someone like…

The song ended, and she came out of her trance. She lifted her gaze to Russell's green eyes while he still held her close.

Breathless, she began, "Russell, I'm sorry…"

But Russell began speaking at the same time.

"Lexie, I'm sorry…"

They stopped and stared at each other, then smiles crept across their faces before they broke into laughter.

"You first," Russell said.

"I shouldn't have gotten angry with you and acted so childishly."

"Hey." He squeezed her right hand as his other arm fell from her waist, leaving a cold vacancy where it had been. "We're friends, right? No need to let a silly spat get in the way of our friendship. Truce?"

Friends. Of course, that's what they were. And he was one friend she didn't want to lose.

She exhaled a deep breath. "Truce."

Spencer reappeared beside them and slapped Russell on the back. "All right, old chap. I'm back to take over." He stepped between Lexie and Russell. "Ready for a foxtrot?"

Russell gave Lexie a wink as he stepped away, leaving her with her date. A sense of abandonment swept over her as she watched him go. As Count Basie's orchestra began to play, Spencer dragged her to the center of the dance floor, looking disheveled with his tie hanging loosely around his neck and his collar open. The first time he stepped on her foot, she winced.

"Sorry, babe," he said with a laugh.

But he stumbled a few more times, bumping into another couple, showing the liquor's effect on his balance. She glanced at the people around them. Had they noticed? Heat flooded her face, revealing her embarrassment. She had to stop him before he fell down or made a complete spectacle of himself.

"Spencer, I'd like to sit this one out if you don't mind. I'm kind of tired."

"Sure." He tugged at his collar. "It's getting hot in here, isn't it? Let's go outside for some air."

She welcomed the chance to get him away from the alcohol. Maybe the cold air would sober him up some. But on the way out the door, he grabbed another glass off the table and carried it with him. A gust of cold air hit them as they stepped outside onto the porch facing the ocean. Lexie shivered and wrapped her arms around herself, focusing on the incoming waves. The temperature had dropped significantly since the balmy afternoon. Now, dark clouds rolled across the sky, concealing the moon and preventing its light from illuminating the deserted beach.

Russell retreated to the other side of the dance floor, no longer needed as Lexie's partner.

Those few moments with Lexie in his arms were like a dream. His first glimpse of her that night had stolen his breath away. Waiting for an opportunity to speak to her, he'd started toward her when Spencer walked away. But that other guy jumped in and stole her back to the dance floor.

It had felt so right to have her close to him, so natural, but not long enough. He'd tried to keep from staring at her all night, dancing with Jean just to get close to Lexie. She didn't know how pretty she was, dressed in a simple white chiffon blouse and gray skirt. Her customary pearls reminded him of the club's traditions, but that red ribbon around her golden curls was Lexie being herself.

He could still smell the scent of her, like she was his very breath. "Thank you, God, for giving me those moments with Lexie," he prayed silently, closing his eyes in gratitude. He hadn't wanted the song to finish, the experience to end, but knew it had to. But he needed to apologize first. What a relief to know she, too, wanted to restore their friendship.

Too soon, Spencer had returned and taken her away from him. Again. The fool was drunk and looked ridiculous as he tried to dance. Poor Lexie, she must be so embarrassed. Russell held himself back from rushing over to rescue her and send the show-off packing. But that wasn't his place or responsibility. Lexie seemed okay. She was a strong woman, stronger than even she realized. Surely, she was strong enough to hold Spencer at bay. At least she didn't throw herself at him like the other girls did. She didn't need to.

"Hi, Russell." Dorothy, one of the maids, appeared at his side, beaming up at him. "What'cha doin', standin' here all alone? Don'cha wanna dance?"

"Sure, Dot. Would you like to?" Not that he wanted to dance, but he needed to get his mind off Lexie. Besides, Dot wanted to dance, and he was available. Why not?

As they made their way onto the dance floor, he saw Lexie and Spencer go out the back door. She hadn't put on her coat, despite the falling temperature. Why didn't Spencer get it for her—that selfish buffoon. She'd be freezing, and … he stopped. No doubt Spencer could warm her up if he tried. The thought burned in his mind, and he was unable to put the fire out.

"So what do you think about that?" Dot was talking, but he hadn't heard a word.

He shook his head. "I'm sorry, what did you say?"

"A penny for your thoughts. Your mind was a million miles away."

Actually, it was only a few feet. He struggled to focus on his dance partner without counting the minutes since he'd seen Lexie and Spencer leave.

"Please forgive me. I'm afraid I was thinking about business. Now, what were we talking about?"

As Dorothy began talking again, his mind went back to Lexie. What if they left? *Dear God, please don't let her get into a car with him.* Russell knew about Spencer's reckless driving history, but did she? The song ended, and Russell thanked Dot for the dance, not asking her for another. He excused himself and drifted toward the back door, hoping to get a glimpse out the window nearby. Not that he was nosy, just concerned. But what if he saw them in an embrace? His stomach churned at the thought. He should just stay out of her business. That's what he had promised himself after the argument.

He took a glass offered by the server and sipped it. What was this stuff anyway? Someone had spiked it, and he was pretty sure who it was. The club would never serve anything so vile-tasting and strong. So this was what Spencer had been drinking. And everyone else, apparently. There would be some hangovers tomorrow.

Russell checked his watch. How long had they been out there? The roar of the wind off the ocean whistled through the window pane behind him. No moonlight shone through the black skies. Uneasiness hovered over him. On nights as dark as this, many things could go unseen. The guards would only have their flashlights to get around the island, which would not only aid them but highlight their position to anyone else. He felt pangs of guilt being at a party while others were on duty. Maybe he shouldn't have come.

Yet the opportunity to share those moments with Lexie made the effort worthwhile for him. Did it mean anything to her as well? He cast an anxious glance out the window. Where was she?

Chapter 33

$\mathcal{L}$exie shivered and moved back against the building, trying to stay out of the wind.

She should have grabbed her coat. Maybe she could go back in to get it, but Spencer might follow. No, if she could hold out a while, the cold air might help clear his head. He walked to the edge of the porch, guzzled the contents of his glass, and plunked it down on the railing. Turning his back to her, he leaned on the porch rail facing the dark ocean. She shuddered as waves splashed onto the shore amid the roar of wind gusts. How long could she stand it out here?

Spencer spun around and looked at her. "Hey, Lex. How about a walk on the beach?" He waved his arms toward the shore.

Her teeth rattled when she answered. "No, it's too dark. And cold."

She wished she hadn't mentioned being cold since he hadn't noticed before, oblivious to the chill himself. Now, he strode toward her with his arms outstretched.

"You're cold? Why didn't you say so? I can warm you up."

She pressed her back against the wall to avoid his embrace. He stood before her, waiting, she assumed, for her to accept his offer. When she didn't respond, he leaned forward, placing a hand on either side of her and trapping her where she stood. His breath reeked of alcohol as he drew close, causing her stomach to roil, and she turned her face away.

"Come on, Lexie. What's the matter? It's Valentine's Day, for crying out loud."

He sounded like a whimpering puppy, but she had no sympathy for him.

"Spencer, I don't know what you think, but I'm not interested."

"You're not interested?" Anger replaced the whimper. "Not interested in what, Lexie? Me? So why have we been spending so much time together?"

She questioned that herself, especially now. But a rational conversation with him in his current condition was impossible. She should have gone back in. How was she going to get away from him now?

"We've had a swell time together, Spencer. I've really enjoyed playing tennis with you." Perhaps she could sweet talk him back inside.

"Well, we can't play tennis all the time you know. There are other ways to spend our time together. Even more enjoyable ways. Don't you feel romantic?" He pressed in closer.

"Spencer, please don't. I want to go back in now." Like an animal caught in a snare, her heart raced with the urge to get free.

"Well, I don't. You at least owe me a kiss."

Her body tensed as her temper flared and she lashed out. "I don't owe you anything, Spencer! How dare you?"

"How dare I? Like this." He mashed his lips against hers, suffocating her breath and pinning her against the wall.

She put her hands on his chest and tried to push him away, but he grabbed them, holding them down as he pressed his chest against her. She jerked her head to the side to avoid another painful kiss.

"Stop, Spencer! You're hurting me!"

He tried to kiss her again as she struggled against him. *Dear Lord, what have I gotten myself into? Please help me.*

Unexpected relief rushed through her as his weight lifted from her. She sucked in a breath of air. In the darkness, she watched two people struggle. Spencer flailed his arms, trying to wrest himself from another man. Gradually, she recognized the man who held Spencer's arms, pinning them behind him. Russell.

"Hey, what are you doing? Can't a guy kiss a girl without being interrupted?" Spencer thrashed around, trying to free himself from Russell's grip.

"Sure, Spencer. But not this time." He looked at Lexie. "Are you all right?"

When she nodded, he said, "Go on inside and get warm."

She moved to the door but couldn't take her eyes off the two men. When Russell released Spencer's arms, he raised a fist, but Russell caught it.

"You don't want to do that, Spencer. You wouldn't want to have a black eye at the tennis tournament."

Spencer relaxed and shrugged. "Hey, she's not worth the trouble." He jerked away from Russell, hopped down from the porch, and stalked off.

Lexie's whole body trembled, partly from the cold, but mostly from Spencer's assault.

Russell closed the space between them and put his arms around her, warming her inside and out. "Let's go in."

Lexie wanted to stay inside the snug refuge of his arms and was thankful he kept an arm around her as he opened the door. Then he guided her inside with his hand pressed on the small of her back.

The crowd had thinned out in the room. Slow music played on the record player and only a few couples remained on the dance floor. Russell strode to the punch table and told the waiter to pour the rest out.

"If anyone complains, send them to me. Or offer a non-alcoholic beverage."

Lexie wanted to applaud but wished he'd done that sooner—before Spencer got so disgustingly drunk.

From the front of the room came the announcement of the final dance.

Russell turned to Lexie and with a gentle smile that melted her insides, gestured to the dance floor. "Would you do me the honor?"

Lexie nodded and returned to the haven of his arms. Guilt washed over her with the realization that Russell had tried to protect her from Spencer. She should have known he wasn't trying to interfere. How could she ever doubt him? He was the most honest, responsible, stable person she knew. Not to mention a smooth dancer with not even a hint of his limp. They swayed with such synchronization, as if they'd danced together for years, moving in silence before she relaxed enough to talk.

"I hope he doesn't try to drive. Somebody could get hurt," Lexie said, remembering the story the Maurice sisters had told her.

Russell grinned as he reached into his pocket and pulled out a set of keys. "That won't be a problem, since he's lost his keys."

Lexie allowed a smile to cross her face as she gazed into his eyes. Russell never ceased to amaze her.

"Have you seen Destiny lately?" he asked.

"No, I'm afraid I haven't, but I thought about going over there today. How's the progress coming?"

"Slowly, I'm afraid. A leak in the roof caused the leak upstairs, so we had to order some custom shingles to match the rest of the roof. With the war diverting supplies and manpower, it will take longer to get them."

The war. For the past few hours, she had forgotten about the war. No doubt the rest of the partiers had too.

"I feel guilty for enjoying myself while our soldiers are fighting."

He pulled her close and rested his head against the top of her hair. "I know. I've had those feelings too. But they're fighting so we can keep these freedoms. What else can we do? We can't bring the party to them."

"Good thing there's the USO to entertain the soldiers. And celebrities like Bob Hope who take the shows to them overseas."

"That's true. I'm sure the soldiers who have the opportunity are very appreciative."

The song ended, and when Lexie looked around, she and Russell were the only couple left.

"May I offer you a ride back?"

The girls she had come with were nowhere in sight. They probably assumed she had left with Spencer.

"Please. It appears my ride has left without me."

"How fortunate for me." Russell winked at her, his dimple teasing.

"Excuse me a moment, please." He strode over to each member of the staff who worked the party, thanking them for their service, before returning to her. No wonder they respected him.

He and Lexie gathered their things, and he helped her with her coat. They donned their hats and gloves before heading outside to the car. Lexie glanced at the roadster Spencer had driven, sitting in the same spot with no Spencer in sight.

"I suppose one of his buddies gave him a ride back," Russell said as he opened his car door for her.

"Or maybe he walked. A long walk in this cold might do him good."

Russell chuckled as he got in the driver's seat. "So if we see him walking down the road, do you want to give him a lift?"

Lexie jerked her head. "Would you really offer him a ride?"

He laughed out loud. "That would be the Christian thing to do, wouldn't it? Treat others the way you'd like to be treated?"

"You must be a very good Christian, then." She knew she wouldn't extend the offer.

"No, Lexie. I'm not good, just forgiven." He reached over and patted her hand. She cocked her head and studied him. How could he do Spencer a favor after the way he'd acted? Personally, she never wanted to see Spencer Bardwell again, and quite honestly, didn't care if he *did* have to walk home.

Russell pulled up in front of the clubhouse, got out, and came around to get her. They hurried up the steps and into the warm building.

"So would you like to go see Destiny in the morning? I can meet you at breakfast. Are you planning to be there early as usual?"

Lexie glanced at the clock showing midnight and stifled a yawn. "I don't think I'll get up as early tomorrow."

"Me, either. Why don't you come up to my office when you're ready, and we'll have breakfast there?"

"Sounds swell."

He leaned over and Lexie closed her eyes, ready for the kiss she expected. But he brushed her on the cheek with his lips instead.

"Good night, Lexie."

"Good night, Russell."

She plodded up the stairs in a daze as the evening's events swirled through her head. The irony that she had to fight off Spencer's kiss but couldn't get one from Russell was difficult to grasp. Russell had referred to their 'friendship'. Why did she want to believe their relationship was more than friendship?

Lexie dressed quickly in the morning, anxious to be with Russell again. Seemed like it'd been ages since they'd spent any time together. She studied herself in the mirror, twisting her mouth at the reflection. She wore the same pants and one of the three blouses she'd brought with a cardigan buttoned over it. Russell must be tired of seeing her in the same things. Good thing for the laundry at the club. Besides, Destiny didn't care what she wore.

Years ago, she would have been able to call home and have one of the maids pack up some clothes for her and ship them down. Not anymore, though. All the former servants had either retired or died, and no one had been hired to replace them. The housekeeper only came once a week, since the house didn't need much cleaning—not with just Lexie there. And Lexie questioned if she needed to come that often.

Lexie grabbed her hat, coat, and gloves then hurried out the door and down the hall to the stairs. When she reached Russell's fourth-floor office, the door was open. She peeked in the door and saw him at his desk on the telephone. He motioned to her to come in. Lexie entered and put her things down on the chair across from him. A fire glowed in the fireplace, spreading its warmth through the room. As she strolled over to the windows to look out, shafts of golden sunshine pierced the glass and played with the colors of the Persian rug on the floor.

Outside, the branches of the surrounding trees whipped back and forth in the gusty wind. She peered down on the Grand Lawn, empty of people, possibly due to the early hour or the brisk weather. It would be a cold walk to the cottage. Behind her, Russell hung up the phone.

She turned to see him approaching.

"Good morning, Sunshine," He lifted her hands and clasped them together in his as he gave her a cheerful grin. "You look lovely today, Lexie."

She crinkled her brow. She didn't look any different today than any other day, as far as she knew. "Thank you, Russell. Good morning to you too. You seem to be in a happy mood."

"I am. Happy to see you!"

A surge of hope bubbled through her as she realized the feeling was mutual. She couldn't help but smile back. How could anyone resist his enthusiastic good nature?

"Come have a seat. They've already brought breakfast." He motioned to the silver tray on the coffee table. She walked over, picked up the coffee pot, and glanced at him.

"May I pour your coffee?"

"I've already had a cup, but I'd love to have more, especially if you're serving." He picked up his cup and saucer from the desk and held it for her to fill. When he motioned for her to sit on the sofa, she obliged and took a cup and saucer for herself, placing a tea bag in the cup before filling it with water from the silver teapot. She dunked the bag several times before adding honey and lemon. Russell sat beside her and helped himself to a scone from the tray.

"It looks pretty windy out there." Lexie nodded to the windows as she sipped her tea.

"Yes, it is. Perhaps we should take the car instead of walking to the cottage."

"Whatever you want to do. We might warm up during the walk." Lexie eyed the ladder going up into the turret.

Russell followed her gaze. "Would you like to take a look through the telescope?"

"Sure, I've always wanted to do that." A ripple of excitement tickled her stomach.

"Okay. Get some more hot tea in you first. It's probably pretty chilly up there."

After she finished her tea, she hopped up from the sofa. "I'm ready."

Russell smiled with his eyes and set his cup down. "Swell. Good thing you wore your pants. Climbing that ladder in a skirt would be rather difficult, I'd think."

Lexie took the rungs of the ladder and climbed, Russell right below her. She reached the top and pulled herself up. Russell did the same and stood beside her in the small turret room of the clubhouse.

"Wow. The view up here is spectacular!" The cloudless azure sky was breathtaking in the brilliance of the winter sun, adding crispness to the objects below.

"There's St. Simons Island. See the lighthouse?" He pointed to his right.

"May I?" She tapped the telescope which sat on a tripod.

"Of course. And if you look over there, you can see the dock at Brunswick."

"I had no idea you could see so far."

"On a clear day like today, you can see quite a ways."

"No wonder you could see the launch coming from Brunswick."

"It helps to know when to look for it too. That way, we have time to assemble the staff to meet the guests at our dock."

"You've always done that, haven't you?"

"Well, someone has. I haven't been here forever. Even though sometimes it feels like it."

She glanced up and studied his face. A muscle twitched in his neck as he gazed out the window.

"I don't think I'd ever get tired of this view. It's so exhilarating!" She moved the telescope around to get different perspectives of the panorama, then stood and straightened her back.

He shifted behind her and raised his arm, pointing. "See the marsh across the river? A man could get lost in there, with so many waterways winding through it." He put his other hand on her waist and steered her to the left. "Over there is Moss Cottage, the Vanderbilt house."

Her stomach danced as the close warmth of his body sent electricity through hers. She struggled to focus on the objects he pointed out, resisting the urge to lean back against him. But no, that wouldn't be fitting for "friends".

She returned her gaze to her right, trying to see Destiny's roof.

"Do you think the workmen are at the house now?"

"No. It's Saturday, and they're not working today."

"Russell, have they seen anything else suspicious?"

"No, not really."

She tilted her head. "What does that mean?"

"Well, they said they thought some of their tools may have been moved around, but I wonder if they're imagining ghosts. After all, who would want to bother their tools?"

"Who would want to prowl around the house in the first place?" Lexie said, with her hands on her hips.

Russell shook his head and shrugged. "Are you ready to go there now?"

"Sure." At least no one would be prowling around in the daytime, especially on a gorgeous day like today.

He swept his arms toward the ladder. "After you."

Lexie backed down into the office and Russell followed.

"Another cup to keep your insides warm before we go?" He motioned to the tea.

"No. I'm rather anxious to see the place now."

"Okay." He assisted her with her coat, grabbing his hat and coat off the coat rack by the door on the way out.

When they stepped outside the clubhouse, a gust of wind almost blew Lexie down.

"Looks like we better take the car," Russell said.

Lexie thought about the view from the tower as they drove to the cottage, still invigorated by the experience. Somehow, just being above the world removed her from the problems below. Even a glimpse of the tennis courts, a reminder of her ordeal with Spencer, failed to dampen her spirits.

As they pulled into the driveway, Lexie spotted one of the guards riding a horse down the road toward them. Russell hailed him when they got out of the car.

"Lexie, I need to talk to the guard a minute. He's been riding watch this morning. Go on into the house and get out of this wind. I'll be there in a jiff."

He handed the keys to Lexie. She glanced at the rider, wondering if he had news to report.

As if reading her mind, Russell added, "I'll let you know if he saw anything interesting."

She smiled and nodded, then hurried to the porch to get out of the cold. The door opened easily, apparently serviced by the workmen. The scent of fresh-cut lumber greeted her as she stepped inside. The place looked better, cleaner and spruced up— such an improvement over her first visit.

The back door banged against the house and she jumped. Did someone come in there? She froze and listened. The door banged again and again. Of course, the wind must be creating the problem. Why couldn't they ever fix that door? She headed to the kitchen to try to latch it tightly. As she rounded the corner past the dining room, she saw him. From somewhere deep inside of her, an unearthly sound emerged, and she screamed.

Chapter 34

$\mathcal{A}$ spine-chilling scream ripped the air, sending shock waves through Russell. He jerked his head toward the house as the screams continued. Lexie!

His heart pounded as he sprinted toward the house, ignoring the pain in his foot. He leaped up the front steps and rushed to the door. The screaming continued, coming from the rear of the house near the kitchen. Racing to the dining room, he turned the corner and found Lexie standing over the body of Abner Jones.

He pulled her into his arms. "I'm here, Lexie." She sobbed into his shoulder while he hugged her close. As he stroked her hair, he stared at the unmoving form lying on the floor. "There, there."

Abner Jones lay crumpled face first on the wooden floorboards, a trail of scarlet blood from a gash in the back of his head had run down his neck to a dark puddle beneath. Whoever did this hit him from behind.

Shaking uncontrollably, Lexie murmured, "He's dead, isn't he?"

The guard rushed into the kitchen and knelt by the body. "He's still warm. But from the look of this dried blood, it must have happened during the night."

Lexie turned her head to look at Abner and began sobbing again.

"It's my fault! He was looking after me! I'm the curse, Russell. It's me. I got him killed!"

"Shhh, Lexie. It's not your fault."

"It is! It is! I should never have come back to the island."

The guard lifted Abner's hand and gripped his wrist. "Hey, I think I feel a pulse!"

Lexie stopped crying to look at the guard's face. "Are you sure? He's alive?"

"Yeah, I think so, but just barely. He's hurt pretty bad."

"Thank God. Let's not move him. We need to get the doctor here right away. Would you mind staying here until the doctor comes?"

Russell put his arm around Lexie and led her back to the dining room. "I need to get her to the clubhouse. I'll call the doc from there."

"Sure, boss." He regarded Abner. "Poor old guy. Who would do this to him?"

Who indeed? Whoever it was, they weren't just trying to scare someone. They were dangerous and not afraid to hurt anyone in their way. This had gone far enough. He had to find out who they were and put a stop to it before someone else got hurt. What if it had been Lexie? His heart wrenched at the thought. If anything happened to her, he'd never forgive himself.

Overcome with shock, Lexie trembled as Russell ushered her into the car. He needed to stay with her, comfort her, and protect her. But he was also anxious to find out who had done this to Abner. For now, though, he didn't want to let Lexie out of his sight.

When they reached the clubhouse, he left the car parked in front, helped Lexie out. He put his arm around her as they climbed the steps and entered the lobby, hoping to avoid curious stares from anyone watching.

"Do you know where Dr. Hoover is?" Russell addressed the clerk at the front desk.

"He left the dining room about an hour ago, sir. Perhaps he's at the infirmary."

"Ring it for me, please." The clerk complied while eyeing Lexie as he handed Russell the phone. Russell turned his back on the clerk and covered the receiver.

"Dr. Hoover, Russell Thompson here. I need your help. Abner Jones has been injured. He's at Destiny cottage—head wound … unconscious. Please get there right away. He'll need to be taken to the infirmary … Yes, one of the guards is with him now … Thank you, sir. Please let me know how he is after you examine him. I believe he's lost a lot of blood. Good-bye."

He handed the phone back to the clerk. "Have the kitchen send up some fresh coffee and tea to my office, please."

Russell kept his arm around Lexie's shoulders as they made their way up the stairs. Lexie appeared dazed, lifting each foot as if it were a heavy brick. Times like this, it would be nice to have the elevator that had been discussed numerous times. Finally in his office, Russell took Lexie's coat and led her to the couch.

When Lexie shivered, he re-lit the fireplace and added another log, then came back to sit beside her. His heart wrenched seeing her in so much pain. If only he'd had someone else watch the house, someone who might be more alert, or younger than Abner. Poor old man. Why hadn't he taken the situation more seriously?

He took Lexie's hands in his and gently rubbed them. She stared across the room with red-rimmed eyes, acting as if she didn't know he was there.

"Lexie, the doctor is on his way. I'm sure Abner will be all right." He hoped so, anyway, but he wasn't really sure.

She shifted her gaze toward him. "Do you really think so? He looked so … pale." Her lips trembled as a tear slid down her cheek.

He withdrew his handkerchief from his coat pocket and handed it to her. "Lexie, I'm praying so."

She shook her head and wiped her eyes, releasing a heavy sigh. "Russell, I was at a party having fun, dancing, while Abner…" She buried her face in her hands. "Oh, I feel so terrible!"

"It's not your fault, Lexie."

"But he was there because of me! He was hurt because of me!"

"No, Lexie. That's not true. Abner's devotion to Destiny goes back a long way, before you were born. Remember, he was keeping an eye on the place before you ever arrived?"

She nodded. "But I think he wanted to protect me too."

"Maybe so, but only because he cares about you. You didn't force him to be at the cottage. He wanted to be there."

A choked sob. "He cared about me even though I had misjudged him." More sobs.

Russell pulled her into his arms and held her close. A soft knock on the door signaled the waiter's arrival. Russell hated to let go of Lexie, but slipped her out of his arms to answer the door and admit the server. When he left, Russell poured Lexie some tea and coffee for himself. She held the cup with both hands, staring into the liquid as if expecting an image to appear.

Russell strode over to the window and glanced down at the Great Lawn, noting how the wind whipped the trees around the perimeter. The temperature had dropped dramatically, quite a change from yesterday. He gazed across the room at Lexie, still focused on her cup. His stomach knotted with anxiety and a desire to make her happy again, to restore the happiness they'd enjoyed only hours ago.

He returned to sit beside her again. "Lexie, I don't think you should be alone. Whoever did this to Abner is dangerous, and he might not hesitate to harm you too."

She gazed up at him with sad eyes. "What am I supposed to do, Russell? I have no one here to stay with." Her eyes filled with tears again.

"I've thought about that, and I believe the Maurice sisters would be happy to let you stay with them at Hollybourne."

"I don't want to impose on them."

"Then *I* will." He leaned forward and closed his hands over hers. "Lexie, I care about you." He searched her eyes, wishing he could tell her how much. But no, not now, if ever. "And I know the Maurice sisters do too. After they hear what happened to Abner, they'll be eager to have you stay with them."

Lexie looked away and muttered. "Everyone will know there really is a curse on us now."

Russell sat up straight. "What are you talking about, Lexie? What curse?"

She stared at him, eyes wide. "Didn't you know? Our family is cursed, the island has cursed us. First it took my little brother Kenneth when he drowned, then Grandmother and Grandfather, Father, Robert, Mother, and now Abner, because he was close to our family. Mother always said the island cursed us. I didn't want to believe her, but she was right, Russell, she was right."

"The island cursed your family? Lexie, the island is just an island." Surely she didn't believe in an island curse. She was too smart to believe in such things.

She glanced away, her face coloring.

"So why else would all these things happen to us, to our family?"

"Lexie, bad things happen to people everywhere. That doesn't mean they're cursed. Sometimes people just get sick, or accidents happen."

She jerked her head toward him. "And what about Abner? Was that an accident?"

Russell shook his head. "No, I don't think so. Look, sometimes people make bad decisions, and they affect other people. Unfortunately, there is evil in this world—people sin."

The phone on Russell's desk rang, interrupting their conversation. He rose from the couch and grabbed the receiver. "Hello … yes, Doctor. I see … Thank you for calling." He jotted down a number on a pad, glancing over at Lexie.

"Abner's at the infirmary. The doctor managed to stitch up his head wound. Abner's still unconscious, but he seems to be better. Dr. Hoover's going to call when he regains consciousness."

Lexie jumped up from the couch. "I must go see him." She crossed the room for her coat.

"Lexie, wait. He's unconscious. He won't know you're there."

"But I'll know, Russell. I need to be there for him. Who else does he have?"

"Okay. I'll go with you. But I'm going to talk to the Maurice sisters about you staying there."

The nurse pointed to the side of the room behind the curtained screen.

"Just a minute, Lexie. I want to speak with the doctor a moment." Russell waited outside the door as the doctor approached. As the men began discussing Abner's condition, Lexie wandered into the room and over to the bed beside the window.

The man lying in the bed looked so different than the Abner she knew, and for a moment, she thought it was the wrong person. Gray hair thinned across the top of his white head and disappeared beneath a thick bandage wrapping around his skull. It occurred to her that she'd never seen him without his cap.

He also appeared so much older than before, and thinner. His baggy clothes had concealed how skinny he really was. Lexie watched his chest rise and fall. He was really alive. She lowered herself into the plain wooden chair beside the bed, staring at the patient. She owed him. But what could she do for him?

Russell appeared at the foot of the bed, his brow creased with worry as he looked at her.

"Are you okay?" He spoke in soft tones as he came over and rested his hand on her shoulder.

She nodded. "I'm fine."

"The doctor says his vital signs are improving. He should regain consciousness soon. We'll have to wait and see how the blow affected him."

They watched Abner in silence for a few moments, then Russell patted her shoulder.

"Ready to go? I'll take you to Hollybourne. The sisters are expecting you."

When did he talk to them? The last few hours were a blur.

"No, I'm staying here. With him." Lexie kept her eyes fixed on Abner.

"But, Lexie, you can't do anything here. Come on, the doctor will call when he regains consciousness."

"You go on, Russell. I'm staying here. I need to talk to him, need to be here when he comes to."

Russell studied her a moment, then sighed. "All right, but don't leave here alone. Have them call me at my office when you're ready to go, and I'll come get you." He leaned over and kissed her on the forehead before walking out of the room.

Alone with Abner, Lexie recalled the hospital where Mother had stayed. The sanatorium had been much nicer than this plain room. Of course, the sanatorium was a real hospital, a mental institution that had been Mother's home for several years, like most of the other patients. What kind of place had Abner been put in by his parents? She shuddered to think he might have been in one of the notorious "hospitals" for the insane.

She studied the veins standing out so prominently on the back of his hands, freckled and tanned by years of exposure to the sun. On impulse, she reached out and touched the one nearest her. The hand was cool to the touch, so she began to gently massage it. Tears trickled down her face as once again the heavy burden of guilt overcame her.

"Abner, Mr. Jones, I don't know if you can hear me or not. It's Alexandra Smithfield, and I just wanted to tell you how sorry I am that you got hurt." She sniffed and wiped her nose with the handkerchief she still had in her coat pocket—Russell's handkerchief. She had forgotten to give it back to him. Poor Russell. He must wish she'd never come back, since she'd caused so much trouble for him. As if he didn't have enough to deal with already. Between the club responsibilities and the threat of German submarines … Alarm raced through her as she remembered that threat, followed by fear as she considered the implication. What if Abner had seen a German at Destiny and the man had hit him, tried to kill him?

Her heart pounded. Did Abner see his attacker? Would he remember if he did? If he knew who it was, he could identify them. No wonder he was hit. And if they found out he was still alive, they might come looking for him to finish him off. Lexie scanned the room, large enough for two patients, but only Abner occupied it at present. The first floor window could be accessed from the outside with a ladder.

As a nurse came around the screen, Lexie jumped, gasping as her hand covered her mouth.

"I'm sorry, ma'am. I didn't mean to startle you. I just needed to check Mr. Jones. Would you excuse us for a moment?"

Lexie didn't bother telling her she'd assisted doctors with patients before. Besides, it might be embarrassing to Abner if he knew she saw him being examined. She stepped outside the room, eyeing everyone with suspicion. Were any of these people capable of harming Abner?

She felt conspicuous standing in the hall. When the nurse came to the door, she studied Lexie. "You can go back in, ma'am."

"Is there anything I can do for him?"

"No ma'am, except pray. That's about all we can do now besides keep him comfortable."

Pray. If God really cared about Abner, why did he let him get hurt? On the other hand, Abner could have been killed, but he wasn't. She went back into the room and plopped back down beside the bed. Abner looked comfortable enough—the nurse had adjusted his covers.

All right, God, if you don't mind listening to me, even though I haven't been around you much for a while, I need to talk to you—not about me, but about Abner.

She leaned forward, resting her forehead against the bed, and prayed.

Chapter 35

Lexie awakened with a start as a hand shook her shoulder. Groggy, she lifted her head from the bed and slowly turned to see who had touched her.

"Hey. I didn't mean to scare you." Russell stood beside her, his hand still resting on her shoulder.

"I must have fallen asleep." She straightened and looked to her right at the man on the bed. "He's still unconscious."

"Yes, the doctor said it's probably best that he is. They say that lying still will help his wounds to heal."

"Is there a chance he might not regain consciousness?"

Russell shrugged. "I suppose so. We just have to wait and see. And pray he recovers." Russell studied the motionless figure and blew out a breath. Facing her, he reached for her hand. "Are you ready to go now? It's been a while since I left and I got worried when you didn't call for me, so I came back."

"I—I guess so." She stood and stretched her back, then jerked her head toward Russell, lowering her voice as she stepped away from the bed. "Russell, I've been thinking. What if Abner could identify his attacker? If they find out he's alive and is here, they might try to kill him—again."

"The thought crossed my mind, too, so I've asked the staff to keep Abner's room off-limits to all visitors except you and me. I also asked them to let me know if they see anyone suspicious lurking around."

Lexie glanced over at Abner. "Good. Thank you." She went back to the bed and patted Abner's hand. "I'll be back tomorrow, Mr. Jones. You feel better, okay?"

As she walked away from the bed to the other side of the screen, Russell eyed her. "Do you think he heard you?"

"Maybe, maybe not. Who knows? But if he can hear, I want him to know someone is here for him."

Russell's tender smile sent warmth pulsing through her. He took her hand and led her out of the room. As they walked down the hallway, Lexie saw the maid named Stella hurry out of the building.

"Wonder what she was doing here?"

"Maybe Jack or her daughter is ill."

A vision of the cute little blonde girl came to Lexie's mind. She'd only glimpsed her once since she'd arrived. The fair-haired child was like sunshine compared to her sullen mother—so different, they scarcely seemed related. Hard to imagine Stella as a cheerful child.

"Oh, I hope it's not the little girl. She's so adorable. How old is she?"

"I believe she's about nine or ten, a real sweetheart." Russell pointed to the desk ahead. "I'll check with the nurse and see if she's here."

They stopped at the nurse's station where Russell inquired about the child.

"Oh yes, Evie was here—had a fever for a couple of days, but she went home today."

"Well, I'm glad to hear she's better now." Russell patted the counter. "Thank you."

In the car on the way to Hollybourne, they passed the chapel.

Russell glanced over at Lexie. "You know, tomorrow is Sunday. Would you consider coming to church?"

Lexie didn't know how to answer him. "I prayed for Abner today."

"You did?" Russell's smile showed he was happy with the news. "That's good to hear. Abner can use all our prayers."

"But I'm not sure God really listened to me. I haven't been keeping in touch with him, and he probably thinks I'm a complete stranger."

Russell laughed as he gripped the steering wheel and focused back on the road. "Lexie, I'm sure you're not a stranger to God. He's been keeping tabs on you even though you haven't talked to him lately."

"Well, I hope he listened, for Abner's sake."

"I'm sure he did. So, does that mean you'll go to church tomorrow?"

"I'm not sure yet. I'll think about it, though."

They pulled into the driveway of Hollybourne and stopped in front of the steps.

When Russell knocked on the door, the quick response of footsteps on the other side conveyed expectation. The beveled glass door swung open and Peg appeared. She gave a quick glance to Russell, grabbed Lexie's hands, and pulled her into the house.

"There you are, dear! We've been expecting you. When Russell told us about Abner's accident, we knew you'd be upset."

Accident? Lexie shot a glance at Russell, who nodded. So he didn't tell them someone hit Abner. Why wouldn't he? She'd play along, though, if that was what he wanted. It was far too distressing to try to explain what really happened. Especially since she didn't know.

Marian met them in the foyer. "Come in, come in. Oh, we heard about how you found Abner at the cottage. What a shock that must have been. Poor man. Too bad he stumbled and fell, hitting his head like he did on the dumbwaiter. How is he doing?"

Lexie resisted the urge to look at Russell, lest she give away his fib. Obviously he had reasons to keep the truth quiet. No need getting the island buzzing about poor Abner.

"He's still unconscious." At least that much was true, though she wished it wasn't.

"Dr. Hoover says Abner should come out of it though," said Russell, the eternal optimist. "Lexie's been sitting with him at the infirmary all day."

"Bless your heart." Peg gazed at Lexie with compassion in her eyes, then faced Russell. "Is the doctor going to move him to the hospital in Brunswick?"

"Not yet. At least not until he regains consciousness."

Lexie glanced at Russell. He hadn't mentioned that Abner might be moved. What would she do then—go to Brunswick every day to visit? One thing for certain—she wasn't going back home until she knew he was well enough to go home himself. Her heart ached at the thought of his home—a dormitory room for workers on the island.

"Oh good, here comes Hazel with the tea." Marian watched the maid carry the tray with the silver service and set it down on the coffee table. The maid poured each a cup of hot tea, but Russell held up his hand to refuse.

"Russell. You don't want any? How about a tea biscuit?"

Russell smiled and accepted one of the dainty cookies from the plate the maid offered. He held it up and nodded. "Thank you, this is all I need right now."

"Alexandra, one of the housemaids from the clubhouse brought your things over, so you don't have to go back for them." Peg spoke over the top of her tea cup.

"Oh?" Lexie raised her eyebrows and looked at Russell.

"Yes, I took the liberties. I hope you don't mind."

"No, I guess that's all right. I didn't bring that much with me anyway."

She fingered the pearls at her neck, glad she wore all her jewelry. A thought jarred her mind. "Did you notice who brought them?"

Marian glanced at Peg for an answer.

"Yes, it was that unfriendly woman, I believe her name is Stella, that brought them. She acts like a smile would crack her face."

"Peg! That's not a very nice thing to say. Please excuse my little sister. She seems to have forgotten her manners."

"Perhaps not, but it's true, and you know it."

Lexie glanced back and forth at the sisters.

"Well, maybe she has her reasons, and we don't know what they are. Judge not, Sister."

Peg twisted her lip, a crease between her brows.

Russell rose from his chair. "Ladies, I hate to leave such lovely company, but I must go. Will I see all of you at church in the morning?"

Lexie knew his emphasis on the word *all* was directed at her.

"Well, of course, you will!" Marian stood, as did the other ladies.

"Please don't get up." Russell motioned for them to sit. "I can see myself out."

Lexie moved to his side. "I'll walk you to the door."

Russell grinned as he looked down on her. "If you insist."

They paused at the door, Lexie looking down at her fingers. Russell put his hands on her arms and squeezed them gently. "The sisters will see to it that you're taken care of. Let them—they enjoy doing it."

Lexie peered up at him, gazing into his eyes, so inviting as they twinkled at her. "Russell, I just want to say 'thank you' for all you've done for me."

He kissed her on the forehead. "You can thank me by coming to church tomorrow."

She managed a slight smile. "All right. I will, just for you."

"Fantastic. But it's for you, too, Lexie. I think you'll find it better than you remembered as a child."

"I hope so, Russell, I really do."

Sunday morning was overcast and chilly as the women scrambled up the front steps of the church, clasping their coats together at the necks.

"Oh, I do hope the sun comes out and warms things up," Marian said to Lexie and Peg.

"It could be worse, Sister. At least we're not stuck in the snow back home."

An usher held the heavy wooden barnlike doors open to the cedar-shingled building and the women bustled inside. Lexie stared at the interior, trying to remember how it looked when she was a child. Although somewhat dark due to the rich stained wood of the walls and pews, the room reminded her of a winter cabin. Deep scarlet carpet covered the floor, lending a cozy touch to the rustic atmosphere.

"Here's our seat." Peg motioned to Lexie to follow and headed down the center aisle, entering the third pew on the left. Lexie complied, sitting between the sisters. She scanned the front of the room, noticing the arch over the altar where the pulpit was. Behind the pulpit, a beautiful stained glass window covered the wall. A memory of sitting there as a child trying to count the panes of each color drifted into her mind. Warmth filled the room and spread from one club member to the other as they came in and took their places in the pews. Everyone nodded at Lexie and smiled as if they were happy to see her. How odd.

Lexie remembered there was another Maurice sister that had been married in the chapel. She pictured a bride and groom standing under the arch, and the image sent a thrill through her. What a cozy place to get married, so unlike the gaudy, extravagant weddings her college classmates had. Some of them had more attendants than would fit in this small chapel. As she pondered the differences, strands of a hymn emanated from a piano, barely visible in an alcove off to the left in the front. She caught a glimpse of the pianist's back, a man, and her heart leaped. Russell?

She glanced at the sisters on either side, whose eyes were closed, their heads bobbing to the tune. Her attention diverted to the reverend who approached the pulpit. When the music stopped, he welcomed the guests then invited everyone to stand and sing along with the next hymn. Each of the sisters picked up a hymnal and Lexie looked on with Peg. Not wanting to appear heathen, she attempted to sing along. As she sang "Nearer my God to Thee," the words pricked her, asking her if she really meant them.

The hymn ended and the minister began his sermon. She watched Russell move from the piano bench to a place on the end of the first pew where he could face the altar. Their eyes met before he sat down and the grin that spread across his face made her heart do a little dance.

Her face warmed, and her own smile eased onto it. Knowing she had made Russell happy made her happy in return. She still couldn't believe he was the pianist. No wonder she'd seen him coming from the chapel before. He must have been the person playing the piano the day she went for a horse ride.

Her mind drifted to the events of that day, the day she'd found Abner on the beach looking for Nazis. Her heart wrenched, knowing how the man had frightened her. Before she knew more about him. She had been so wrong to judge him, so wrong to judge his motives. He wasn't the person to be afraid of, yet someone was. Someone who didn't mind hurting him. It angered her now that Abner had been unfairly attacked. How dare they? They shouldn't be allowed to get away with it. The words of the minister yanked her attention back to the present when he said, "All have sinned and come short of the glory of God."

All? Her eyes flitted to Russell, his gaze fixed on the minister. Even Russell? So, no one was perfect, not her, not Russell. Then the minister said, "Yea, I have loved thee with an everlasting love: therefore with loving-kindness have I drawn thee." And God still loved her. Even though she had ignored him. Her eyes misted as Russell returned to the piano bench and began to play another hymn. This one sounded familiar. The one she heard when she passed the chapel the day of the horse ride. The sisters opened the hymnal and began singing, "It Is Well with My Soul." As the words and the music swept over her, Lexie wanted that to be true.

When the minister finished the benediction, the congregation began to shuffle out. Russell caught up with Lexie and greeted the women.

"Good morning, ladies. So glad to see you today." He leaned over and kissed each of the sisters on the cheeks. "I see you brought my girl." He clasped Lexie's hands in his and kissed her on the forehead.

His girl? Although she wanted to argue his claim of possession, she didn't, not caring to spoil the joy that bubbled inside her. She'd discuss his reference later.

"Good morning, Russell. I didn't know you played the piano."

"You didn't? Sorry, I thought everyone here knew that. Yes, I've been playing since I came back from college and our former pianist retired."

"And we're so glad he was here to take her place, "Aren't we, Sister?" Marian nodded to Peg.

"Certainly." She leaned forward and lowered her voice. "Maybe we can talk him into playing for us next time he comes over. That piano of ours doesn't get enough use."

Russell laughed as the sisters turned and walked up the aisle to the rear of the sanctuary, which led to the front door. As they did, Russell put his hand on Lexie's back and ushered her along.

"So how do you feel about being in the chapel after all these years?"

"It's lovely. I really enjoyed the service, and the chapel was more welcoming than I expected. I was afraid God was angry with me for staying out of church so long."

"Well, you see, God isn't angry with you. He's even happier to see you here than I am, which is saying a lot."

Her gaze fell on the stained glass window at the rear of the church, the sunlight filtering through, sending streaks of color across the floor.

"How lovely. I'd forgotten about this stained glass window."

"This is the one commissioned by Tiffany for the chapel."

Lexie studied the picture, marveling at the image of people standing before a king on a throne. As she took another step, she had the sensation of being watched. She glanced around but saw no one looking at her. When she looked up, her breath caught.

There they were—the object of her mother's fears and the source of her paranoia.

Chapter 36

*T*hank God, she came to church today. Russell's heart almost leaped out of his chest when he saw her sitting there in the pew between the Maurice sisters. She looked so innocent, so angelic, but a little bit timid. He chuckled to himself. Timid was not a word he would normally use to describe her. Feisty maybe, independent yes, but the last couple of days had changed her. First the ordeal with Spencer, then finding Abner had sobered her, perhaps even humbled her.

He smiled, remembering the look of surprise on her face when she saw him at the piano. Her eyes were big with wonder when he joined her after the service. Yet she seemed comfortable, even appeared to have enjoyed the service. Maybe now she could put the past behind her.

But when she glanced at the ceiling and stopped, her eyes filled with terror. "Lexie, what is it? What's wrong?" Russell followed her gaze to the carved wooden animal heads that adorned the ends of the exposed beams.

"Those." She pointed up. "I remember now how they frightened me as a child."

"But now that you're an adult, you know they're just decorations. Surely now, you're not afraid of them."

Lexie studied the six different animal heads, their features contorted into grimaces, above her. "Why would they put such hideous things in a chapel?"

Russell shrugged. "It goes with the gothic architecture of the building, like the gargoyles outside."

"Mother said they represented the six faces of death, and that they cursed our family. Each time one of our family members died, she said it was the curse."

"Do you really believe that, Lexie?" Russell peered into her eyes, hoping she didn't.

"The sensible person in me says it's just superstition. Yet, it's uncanny, don't you think, that our family deaths have paralleled the six faces?"

Russell noticed the Maurice sisters waiting at the front door with the minister.

"You ladies go ahead. We'll be along shortly."

"Will you join us for lunch at the clubhouse, Russell?" Marian said.

"Thank you, yes. I'd love to."

"Reverend, would you like to accompany us?" Peg addressed the minister.

"It'd be my pleasure." He grabbed his hat and coat, which were lying across a chair in the corner, and followed the sisters out.

"Please. Sit down a minute." Russell motioned to the pew. "Let's talk about this. You say your family was cursed. How is that?"

"Well, my little brother Kenneth drowned when he was only three, so I guess that fits the curse of flood. Next Grandmother Smithfield died from typhoid fever, which she got here, they said, so that's the curse of pestilence. Grandfather had a heart attack, so that's the curse of disease. Robert died at Pearl Harbor, so that's the war curse, and you could say Mother died of starvation because she quit eating and just wasted away in the hospital. But Father's accident—I don't know where that fits, but he died here too. There's only one curse that hasn't gotten us, the curse of fire."

Tears ran down Lexie's cheeks, breaking Russell's heart. There was a reason her father's accident didn't fit, but he couldn't tell her. Not now. Not ever. What good would it do? Only upset her more. He reached for her and wrapped his arms around her slim shoulders, stroking her silky hair with his hand.

"Lexie, it's true your family has had its share of trouble. But not because of a curse from these things." He pointed overhead. "Lots of people have problems, and they're not connected to the island in any way. Maybe in your mother's mind it made sense, but did you believe everything she said?"

"No." A muffled voice spoke against his chest. "She was sick, mentally, and had been for a long time. I think it started when Kenneth died, then she just got worse with each relative's death. After Father's death, she never wanted to return to the island."

"Lexie, sadly, there is evil in the world—everywhere—the Germans and the Japanese represent evil to us now because of the war. But there's evil here, too, and, unfortunately, Abner ran into it. And don't tell me it was because he was in your cottage."

She relaxed against him and sighed. Then she sat upright with a start.

"Abner! I haven't checked on him today. I need to see him, find out how he's doing."

"All right, we'll go to the infirmary after lunch."

"No, Russell. I can't eat until I see about him. Don't you understand?"

Determination flashed in her eyes, and he knew he was beaten. Shrugging, he said, "Sure Lexie. We'll go see him first." His stomach growled, but he told it to wait. There were more important things than food.

When Lexie and Russell entered Abner's room in the infirmary, they walked to the other side of the screen. But he wasn't there. The bed had been made up, and the room was empty.

Lexie covered her mouth as her heart plummeted. She stared at Russell. "No, Russell! He couldn't have died!"

"Surely someone would have sent word." Russell took her hand and pulled her toward the door. "Let's find the doctor."

At the nurses' desk, Lexie breathed a sigh of relief to discover Abner was still there and still alive but had been moved to a private room, per doctor's orders.

"He's in room six." The nurse pointed two doors down the hall to her right.

The room at the end of the hall was smaller than the first, with only one bed instead of two. They walked in to find Abner propped up in a sitting position. Lexie glanced at Russell before hurrying over to the man.

"Mr. Jones, can you hear me? It's Alexandra Smithfield."

The old man's eyes opened slowly. He stared at Lexie, then found his voice.

"Miss Smithfield."

"Oh, you're conscious! Thank God!" Maybe God had listened to her after all.

"Yes, ma'am. Got a bit of a headache though." He pointed to his bandage-wrapped head.

"I'm so sorry this happened to you."

Russell stepped forward. "Abner, good to see you awake. You had quite a gash back there."

"The doctor said you found me and called him. Thanks."

"Abner, I hate to bother you, but can you remember anything that happened? Did you see anybody?"

He shook his head slowly. "I've been racking my brain to remember, but so far, nothing. Guess whoever hit me was behind me, and I couldn't see them."

Russell touched the man's arm. "Don't worry about it, Abner. You just rest up and get better."

"Thank you for coming to see me. Think I'll take a nap now." He closed his eyes, and Russell took Lexie's arm and led her from the room.

"Not much more we can do here. He needs to rest. Are you ready for lunch?"

"I guess so. I still hate leaving him alone though." Lexie twisted her lips.

"He'll be fine. Let's go."

On the way to the clubhouse, Lexie turned to Russell. "Russell, why didn't you tell the Maurice sisters what really happened to Abner? Why did you say he fell?"

"Well, first of all, we don't know what really happened. I had to tell them something though, to explain why I wanted you to stay with them."

"Russell Thompson, you told a lie."

Russell winced. "You're right. But Bernon knows what happened, and he asked me to keep it quiet. He doesn't want the other members to get upset. The truth will come out—it always does." He ran his finger around the inside of his collar.

"Just like the Germans, right? Just pretend everything is all right, keep up appearances."

Russell's face glowed crimson, and he shifted his shoulders. His customary smile disappeared. Instead, deep lines furrowed his brows and drew his eyebrows together.

"It's a vacation spot, so it's our duty to keep the worries of the world away."

"Except that some of them are right here."

He nodded slowly. "You're right, Lexie. But I must do what my boss tells me. Do you understand?" He faced her and stared into her eyes, as if trying to instill comprehension.

"Yes, Russell. I guess I do understand." And in a way, she did. But she didn't like it. She didn't like any dishonesty, especially from Russell, the one person she thought she could trust. But something in his eyes bothered her. He was used to keeping secrets, but was he keeping a secret from her? A chill shook her body, but she didn't think it had anything to do with the weather.

Chapter 37

"You know our nephew Albert Jr. and his family are coming to visit next week." Marian lifted her glance over her cards. They were playing bridge again, which Lexie and the sisters had done every day she'd been there, vastly improving her game. "I know you'll enjoy them."

"I really should go back to the clubhouse. I've taken advantage of your generosity too long already." Lexie made the opening lead to start the hand.

"Nonsense!" Peg turned to Lexie. "We love having you here, don't we, sister? And we certainly have plenty of room for all of you here, with nine bedrooms."

"We always have room for company," Marian added. "Mother and Father enjoyed opening their home to guests, and we take pleasure in continuing the tradition."

"Well, I thank you. You've been wonderful hostesses."

Lexie did enjoy being with the sociable sisters, but she was getting restless. The island had been inundated with a week of chilly rain. The clouds hovered over the treetops, refusing to let the sun penetrate. Russell came by daily to take her to visit Abner Jones, who had yet to remember anything else about his attack. But the doctor said his wound was healing and his memory might return as well, respecting his patient's desire to stay on the island instead of being sent to the Brunswick hospital.

"If this rain doesn't let up by tomorrow, the tennis tournament might have to be cancelled. The indoor courts at the Morgan Center don't offer any room for spectators."

Peg's remark startled Lexie. She'd completely forgotten about the tournament. Thankfully, she hadn't seen Spencer again but heard through the sisters that his attention had shifted to the daughter of another member. She hoped somebody would warn the girl and her family about the cad. Somebody, but not Lexie. She wanted to sever all ties to the man.

When Russell picked her up later, he told her the tournament had indeed been cancelled.

"Just as well," he said. "I don't think it would have been well-attended. With the war going on, people aren't traveling as much."

So Spencer would be gone. Lexie breathed a sigh of relief that he wouldn't be around to run into, and his next "victim" would be spared. Good riddance.

A few minutes passed in silence as Lexie stared out the side of the car watching raindrops hit the window and form rivulets that ran down the door.

"Russell, I think I should move back to the clubhouse."

"Why? Do you think the sisters want you to?" He looked her direction while he gripped the steering wheel.

"They haven't said so, but they're going to have more relatives at the house next week."

"Yes, I believe Al and his family are coming. But that shouldn't be a problem. The Maurice family has always had guests at Hollybourne."

Lexie didn't answer and continued staring out the window, her mood reflecting the gray weather. Truth was, she was bored. She wanted to be productive, not just sit around all day and play bridge. Maybe she should go back to the hospital where she was needed. Here, she was no use to anyone, not even Abner Jones.

When they arrived at the man's room, his color looked better, not gray like it had been.

"Good afternoon, Mr. Jones," Lexie said, as she and Russell approached the bed and stood on either side.

"How're you feeling today?" Russell offered a smile at the old man.

"Almost normal. Maybe I can go back to work next week."

Lexie and Russell exchanged surprised glances.

"I don't think you better rush things, Abner." Russell patted the man on the hand. "We need you to get well. Besides, you can't do any gardening in this weather."

"No, sir. But I could stand guard. Anybody seen anything out there lately?"

"No, nothing."

"You know, I think I remember something from that night I got hit over the head." Abner jabbed his finger at the air.

Lexie sucked in a breath waiting for his next words.

"What, Abner? What did you see?" Russell asked.

"I seen somebody go in the house, so I followed them."

"Did you get a good look at them?"

"Not too good, but one of them was a man—wearing a hat and coat. He went up the back stairs, and I was gonna go up after him, but somebody hit me from behind."

"One of them? So, did you see two people, Abner?" Russell leaned toward the man.

"Yep, the other'n was smaller. He must've been the one what hit me. Guess he saw me coming and hid till I got in there."

So at least two men were in the house. If only Abner could describe them.

As they left the infirmary, the sun squeezed through gaps between the clouds, trying to brighten the dreary day.

Russell peered up at the sunlight peeking in the windshield. "Looks like the rain might be over with, finally. And just in time too."

"What do you mean, just in time?" Lexie cocked her head at him.

"Just in time for Sunday. You know it's not supposed to rain on *Sun*days." He turned and gave her a wink.

"Is that a Jekyll Island rule?"

"Absolutely!" He laughed, and Lexie's mood lifted with the clouds. "Say, if you don't mind being early, I'll pick you up and take you to church tomorrow. You know, I need to warm up a little before the service."

"Sure. You can give me a private concert."

"It'll be my pleasure."

The sun wasn't the only thing shining the next morning. Lexie was radiant when Russell picked her up, and she seemed genuinely happy to see him. His heart did a jig when she smiled and said "Good Morning" to him.

"Looks like you're right about the sun shining on Sunday," Lexie said as she got into the car.

"Of course. Did you doubt me?" He gave her a wink and covered his heart with his hand. "I suppose we could have walked. Maybe after church when it's warmer we can take a stroll."

"Sounds great. I've been cooped up in the house way too long."

On their way to the chapel, they saw one of the island guards on horseback. He waved as they passed and Russell waved back.

"Too bad they have to be on duty this morning."

"I know. That's why I'm going to take a shift this afternoon and relieve one of them. They shouldn't have to work on Sunday."

"So why do they have to? Does someone have to be on duty all the time?"

"Unfortunately, yes. The Coast Guard has asked us to have someone continually. They simply don't have the manpower to assign to the island full-time."

"So I guess they still think there's a threat."

He nodded, which was all he could do for now. He couldn't tell her the Coast Guard was putting pressure on the management to close the island early and send everyone home. Last he heard, even President Roosevelt worried about his friends on Jekyll being unprotected. Prentice was holding off as long as possible. The club needed the money to survive, and now that both the tennis and golf tournaments had been cancelled, the revenue was far below the season's normal income.

When they reached the chapel, he unlocked the back door and let Lexie in, turning on the lights as he entered. She waited for him, then followed him over to the piano.

"Why don't you sit over there and get comfortable?" He pointed to the first pew. "It'll be at least an hour before the minister arrives."

Lexie seated herself in a spot where he could see her if he glanced to his left. Her gaze fell on the stained glass window behind the altar as he sat down on the piano bench and began to play.

Lexie focused on the rich blues and reds in the stained glass image while the piano music resonated through the small chapel, carrying her back through the years.

"Grandmother, what are those people doing in that picture?"

"They're coming to worship the Christ Child."

"The baby?"

"Yes, dear. That's the baby Jesus, the Christ Child."

"Is that his mother holding him?"

"Yes, Alexandra. That's his mother, Mary."

"Are those other people his friends?"

Grandmother's tender eyes smiled down on her, warming her heart. *"Yes, dear. They were his friends so they brought him presents."*

"I want to give him a present too."

"You can, Alexandra. You can give him your love."

"But how can I give him that? I can't wrap it in a box."

"No, but you can give it to him by praying to him every day."

"I can do that!"

"Of course you can, sweetheart."

Lexie's eyes misted remembering the child who sat here looking at the picture with her grandmother. Somehow, she had forgotten the conversation. But the years between vanished as Russell played hymns that struck a chord of familiarity in her heart.

When did her mother's fear of the chapel erase the comfort she remembered now? Why did she accept those fears as truth? Mother had been wrong. And now she knew Mother had been ill, mentally, until she had completely lost touch with reality. Mother's beliefs were not hers, and neither was her illness.

She closed her eyes, letting the music penetrate the walls the years had built, the soothing rhythm saturating her with peace. She hadn't proved to be much of a friend to the Christ Child, having given up her habit of prayer for many years. Was He upset with her for forgetting Him? Would He let her make it up to Him if she started again?

Lord Jesus, please forgive me for forgetting you. I truly want to know you again. I don't have a family anymore, so I'd really like to be part of yours, if you'll let me. I'm scared, because there are bad people around, and I don't know who they are or what they want, much less why they'd hurt an innocent old man like Abner Jones. Could you please help me understand what they want at the cottage? And dear Lord, please make Abner well.

Before she opened her eyes, another image appeared. A secret hiding place. Only she, Robert, and their father knew about it, and now she was the only one left.

Chapter 38

"The wind has picked up." Russell glanced at the sky as they walked to the clubhouse for lunch after church. Occasional strong gusts pushed the palm trees sideways and whistled around the building. "Looks like there's another cold front coming."

"And it was so pretty and clear this morning too." Lexie held on to her hat as the wind whipped her hair. "I had hoped to enjoy the fresh air today after last week's dreary weather."

"Well, you know our winters in the South. Cold one day, warm the next. This one might blow through pretty fast, and afterwards it'll probably be cooler, but clear again."

They entered the dining room where the Maurice sisters waved them over. Lexie didn't recognize the other people at the table. Marian introduced Lexie and Russell to her nephew and his wife and invited them to join.

Lexie wanted to talk to Russell about what she remembered in the chapel, but privately. However, it was rude not to accept the sisters' invitation after staying there the past two weeks. The newly-arrived relatives caught everyone up on the rest of the family back home in Pennsylvania. Like so many others, the people in their community were involved in the war effort, with more and more men volunteering for the military.

The government had stopped the sale of new cars, which especially annoyed the couple, who wanted to purchase a new model. Apparently, giving up that opportunity proved too much a sacrifice for them. Lexie bit her tongue, afraid she might offend the guests if she revealed her true feelings about their selfishness.

After the meal, Russell checked his watch and pushed back from the table.

"Please excuse me. I have some business to attend to."

"On a Sunday? My dear, don't you ever take a day off?" Peg said, shaking her head.

"Not during the season, I'm afraid." Russell smiled at the group and stood. "However, I don't mind. It's my favorite time of year, since I get to see you lovely ladies."

The sisters giggled. "Russell, you charmer. Run along now, if you must."

Lexie gazed up at Russell, wanting to go with him. She had really hoped to spend the day with him but then remembered he was relieving one of the guards that afternoon. She almost offered to ride patrol with him but suppressed the urge. No doubt the idea wouldn't be met with approval. But maybe he had time to visit Abner before he went on duty.

"Russell, I'd like to check on Abner. Will you be going by there?"

He glanced at his watch again. "Sure. Are you ready to go now?" Lexie looked at the others at the table and smiled. "Please excuse me. It was a pleasure to meet you. I'll see you later at Hollybourne."

On their way to the infirmary, they talked about the newcomers and the news they'd brought. Before Lexie had a chance to tell Russell what was on her mind, they had arrived. She'd have to wait until later.

Abner sat on the side of the bed staring out the window as they walked in.

"Good day, Abner. You going somewhere?" Russell teased the older man.

"I'm ready, if they'll let me. Tired of lying around here."

"How's that head doing?" Russell placed his hand on the man's sloped shoulder. The bandage wasn't as thick as it had been.

"Doc says it's healing up. Guess my head's pretty hard."

Russell laughed, and Lexie thought she saw the hint of a smile on Abner's face.

"Well, thank God for that!" Russell chuckled, patting Abner's shoulder.

"Mr. Jones, can we get you anything?" Lexie moved closer to the bed.

"No, miss, but thank you. I just wanna get out of here."

"You will when you're all healed up." Russell stepped away from the bed. "Sorry Abner, but we need to go now. Good to see you looking better."

As Lexie turned to walk away, Abner put his hand on her arm. "Miss, I just thought of something."

Her heart halted. What had he remembered?

"Yes?"

"Do you think you could get me a radio? It's pretty quiet in here, and I don't read much."

She blew out a breath. "Of course. We can find one, can't we, Russell?"

"Sure. Be right on it."

When they left the room, Lexie turned to Russell. "For a minute, I thought he had remembered something."

"Yeah, me too. Well, maybe he still will at some point."

Outside, the overcast sky had darkened to gunmetal gray. Russell checked the time again. "Lexie, I really need to get to the stables. Do you mind walking back alone? I think you can get to Hollybourne before the rain starts."

"No, of course not. You go ahead. I'll be fine."

"I'm really sorry. I'll make it up to you later. Promise." He winked and gave her that endearing dimpled smile.

"I hate for you to be out in a storm on horseback. How long will you be on duty?"

"Should be at least eight hours. But don't worry. I've got some dungarees to change into and a slicker in the barn."

"Take care, then. I suppose I'll see you tomorrow?"

"Absolutely!" He kissed her on the forehead and walked away.

Although it was windy, the air was balmy and tropical, the way southern weather feels just before a storm. Lexie hiked along the road with her head lowered against the wind. An occasional strong gust pushed her hard enough to make her stagger. What would it feel like to be here in a hurricane if this was just a cold front?

Even though she'd pass right by Hollybourne, Lexie had to make another stop first.

Destiny looked lonely sitting by itself at the end of the compound, or did she just feel guilty about not going there since she found Abner? She shuddered at the memory of him lying on the floor in his dried blood. She shook her head to get the image out. Abner was fine, thank God.

She looked up at the roof and noticed some new shingles, indicating the workmen had replaced the damaged ones. Was the work on the house finished yet? She didn't have a chance to ask Russell about it. When she stepped onto the porch, she noticed the trim around the door and windows had been painted. She hadn't requested that work, but it definitely improved the appearance of the exterior. Based on the odor, the paint was still fresh, maybe even wet. A glance to her left confirmed her suspicion. A can of paint sat beside the wall next to another can holding brushes. The workers must've tried to get some painting done yesterday after the rain quit but left everything to resume on Monday.

Not wanting to get any paint on her clothes, Lexie decided to use the back door instead, assuming it probably hadn't been painted. The wind whipped the trees back and forth as she hurried around to the rear. She was right. The back door still looked as aged and weather-beaten as it had before. She pulled it open and stepped in, hearing thunder rumble in the distance. The smell of paint and new wood greeted her as she entered the kitchen. A quick glance around assured her she was alone. Not that she expected anyone to be there on Sunday, but she didn't want anyone else to see the secret place if it still existed.

She walked over to the dumbwaiter and pulled up on the handle. The metal cage inside was empty of any worker's tools. Good. They wouldn't be in her way. She leaned in and looked around, but what she looked for would be difficult to see from where she stood. She would have to climb inside. Her heavy coat was too bulky, so she dropped it on the floor. Getting in a space just big enough for trunks and suitcases wasn't as easy as it had been ten years ago when she was a good bit smaller.

Lexie strained to see in the dim light of the small elevator, dark and quiet, with very little light coming from the opening—like a tomb. She shuddered. Strange that she ever thought it was a fun place to hide.

She raised her fingers to the top of the cage and ran them along the openings until her fingers hit solid metal. Peering up into the shaft, she saw the shape of a box. It was still there. She and Robert had found it one day when they were playing. When they asked their father what it was, he said, "a secret hiding place."

She never saw the inside of it, but always wondered what was hidden there. She'd imagined all kinds of things when she was a child— did Father keep a souvenir, a favorite rock, or maybe even gold coins, like a pirate? Father never told them anything else, and she never saw him remove it. Surely it was empty now. But maybe there really was something important inside it. And maybe it was what someone else wanted.

How could she get to it though? It was on top of the outside of the cage. She groped around the inside edge of the dumbwaiter. At the edge where the top and side joined, she felt a latch, one like that on a jewelry box. She pushed it this way and that, heard a click, and a small hatch door creaked open, creating a gap which appeared large enough to get the box through. She reached her hand up through the space, but the box was attached firmly by a clasp on each end. As she struggled to unhook one of them, a deafening clap of thunder shook the house. She jumped and her hand pushed the clasp open. Her arms grew heavy while she worked to free the box over her head.

The back door slammed and she jerked, cutting her wrist on the metal opening. "Ouch!" came out in reaction to the sudden pain. Was someone there? Did they hear her? Her heart beat wildly in her chest as she listened for more sounds. But all she heard was the roar of the wind and raindrops pelting the house. The wind must've caught the door again. Why hadn't they fixed that yet?

She couldn't stop yet, not before she got the box. Trying not to think about the rusty cut on her wrist, she worked until she finally got the other clasp open, then maneuvered the box to fit through the opening. As it tilted into the space, she grabbed its edges and pulled it inside. Was this what they'd been looking for? The metal box was heavy, but she couldn't tell if it contained anything. She shook it, but nothing rattled. She tried to open it, but couldn't. She could barely see anything now since it had become so dark outside. She'd have to get out of the cage and carry the box to a window for a better look.

She climbed out and straightened, her back relieved to be out of the confining space. As she walked to the dining room bay window, she heard the floorboards creak.

"I'll take that." A male voice behind her made her jump.

Lexie spun around to find a man with an overcoat and hat on, reaching out for the box. She strained to see his face, and as a bolt of lightning flashed, the features of the boat captain came into view.

"You!" She hugged the box against her chest as a tremendous boom rocked the whole house.

He took a step toward her, his arm outstretched. "Just hand it over, Miss Smithfield."

"No! Why do you want it? It doesn't belong to you." Lexie's heart raced.

He glanced around before taking another step forward. "Look, I don't want to hurt you. Just give me the box."

"You mean like you hurt Abner Jones? Guess it was easy to hit an old man from behind."

"I didn't … look, I don't want no trouble. Just give it to me."

Lexie caught the acrid smell of something burning but didn't dare take her eyes off the man in front of her. *Lord, please help me.*

"Tell me why it's so important to you, why you've been trespassing on my property to look for it."

A female voice approached from the kitchen. "I'll tell you."

Chapter 39

$\mathcal{R}$ussell hunched his shoulders against the wind. He pulled his hat lower over his head as cold heavy raindrops slapped his face. What an awful time to be on a horse. But somebody had to be there, so it might as well be him.

Soon the rain made it impossible to see toward the ocean, and the roar of the wind across the water rendered any other noise unheard, except for the ear-splitting thunder. Good thing Lexie got back to Hollybourne before the storm arrived. But too bad they hadn't had more time together. He had noticed a change in her recently. She acted comfortable in church now, not frightened like she had been at first. She had made peace with God and seemed to be making peace with her past. Was he preventing that process?

He turned back toward the clubhouse as the horse whinnied, spooked by a violent clap of thunder. Perhaps the weather would be more bearable on the other side of the island by the river. As he came around the Grand Lawn, he saw a plume of black smoke rising above the treetops down the road, probably from the chimney at Hollybourne. However, the closer he got, the greater the smoke cloud grew, but it was farther away than Hollybourne. Destiny?

A flame shot above the trees. Something was on fire. He kicked the horse and galloped toward it.

Stella sauntered across the room to stand beside her husband. Her eyes gleamed like daggers pointed at Lexie, and her crooked smirk dripped with derision.

"It's about time you heard the truth about your father."

Lexie's pounding heart dropped a notch.

"What are you talking about?" She hugged the metal box tighter.

"Eleven years ago, your father seduced me. You're shocked, aren't you?"

"I don't believe you."

"Ha! Well, it's true. And I've got proof too."

Lexie glanced at Stella's husband Jack, noting the pained expression on his face.

"What proof?"

"Remember that little girl on the boat ride with you? The one that liked your fur coat? That's his daughter Evelyn."

She tried to breathe, but the acrid odor of smoke filled her nostrils. She shook her head. "No, that's not possible."

Pointing her finger at Lexie, Stella said, "Oh yeah? Guess I should know, huh? Yeah, he got me pregnant, and when I told him, he promised to take care of me and the child. But then he went and killed himself. Coward."

Russell burst in the front door. "Lexie! The house..." He stopped mid-sentence and stared at the scene before him. "What's going on here? Jack? Stella?"

"You tell her, Russell." Stella glanced sideways at Russell and nodded at Lexie. "He knows all about it."

Lexie jerked her head at Russell. "Is it true, Russell? Did my father have an affair with this woman?" *He killed himself* echoed through her head.

Before he could answer, Stella took a step closer to Lexie. "*This* woman?"

"Russell, tell her she's a liar."

Russell moved toward Lexie. "The house is on fire! We have to get out, now!"

"No!" Stella screamed. "That's mine, and this house is mine! He told me he kept his most valued possession in a safe place here. I figure he hid the lease here, and it belongs to my daughter, his heir."

"But he already had heirs."

Stella gave her a sinister smile. "You're the only one left, besides Evie." Looking at her husband, she motioned to Lexie. "Get it from her, Jack."

Jack grabbed hold of the box and tried to wrestle it from Lexie's arms as Russell lunged across the room. He knocked Jack down and seized Lexie by the arm while the ceiling above began to crackle and split apart as the fire made its way into the first floor.

"Stop or I'll shoot!" Everyone froze and turned to face Stella holding a gun and aiming it at Lexie. "Give me the blasted box!"

"Lexie, give it to her." Russell tried to pull Lexie toward him.

"No! Whatever is in this box belonged to my family, like this house."

"Then I have no choice but to kill you." Stella lifted the gun and pointed it at Lexie's head.

"No, Stella. This has to stop." Jack reached out to his wife. "You almost killed Abner. I won't let you do this. Give me the gun."

Parts of the ceiling fell around them, filling the room with smoke.

A startled Stella turned the gun toward her husband. "But Jack, it belongs to us, to Evie."

As a chunk of ceiling fell inches away, Jack lunged for his wife and the gun went off.

Russell grabbed Lexie and raced out the front door with her, not stopping until they reached the street. They looked back at Destiny as the roof fell in, with flames shooting out the top and the sides of the building.

Lexie stared at the inferno, her trembling hands covering her mouth in horror. Russell put his arm around her shoulders, and together they watched the fire devour the house, while the dwindling rain did little more than sizzle as it hit the flames. Movement on the porch caught their attention as Jack stumbled out of the smoke holding Stella. He struggled down the steps and into the yard where he collapsed.

Russell rushed to the couple and helped pull them farther away from the fire. Lexie ventured near the man sobbing over his wife's still form. "I told her to stop, to give up. She just wouldn't listen." A red stain spread across the woman's chest. Lexie's heart went out to the stricken husband despite his threats to her just moments earlier. He was a victim, too, and Lexie pitied him. The urge to pray for the couple grew inside her, so she did.

A resounding crash turned their heads to witness the final surrender of the house to the flames. Destiny was a smoldering pile of rubble.

Chapter 40

Lexie stared out the window from Russell's office, trying to come to grips with the secrets of her family's past so long hidden from her.

"I can't believe my father had an affair with another woman."

"Maybe he didn't. No one knew for sure except Stella and your father, since no one else was around. And Stella could have been lying, but Robert made sure she kept quiet by sending her money every month. He didn't want your mother to know, or you or anyone else, for that matter."

Lexie turned to face Russell. "But how did Robert know?"

"The day of the hunt, Jack confronted your father in front of the hunting party. Jack was angry because he was in love with Stella and planned to marry her. Your father was drunk, which was his usual state after the stock market collapse. When Jack threatened to expose him, your father raised his gun at Jack. Robert and I rushed him, the gun went off and the bullet hit my foot, taking a couple of toes with it."

Lexie's eyes widened. "*That's* what happened to your foot?"

"Yep. Robert took me to the infirmary, and your father stormed off."

"What did Stella mean—'he killed himself'?"

"That's not true. When they found his body, the question was raised, considering his state of mind—drunk and upset. But the doctor ruled out suicide. It was obvious that he tripped on his gun and caused it to go off. It really was an accident."

"But why didn't you tell me about this, Russell? Didn't you think I had a right to know?"

"Robert swore me to secrecy. I wanted to tell you when you came back here, but I thought it was better to leave the past in the past. I had no idea the past would rear its ugly head again."

Lexie strolled to the picture on the wall showing her father, her brother, Russell, and Jack in their hunting attire. "Was this the day he died?" She crossed her arms and stared at the faces, shaking her head.

"Yes, the day that changed so many lives."

She spun around and faced Russell. "So Stella sent the telegram."

"Either she or Jack, under her orders."

"She was pretty desperate."

"Obsessed is more like it."

Russell tapped the metal box on top of his desk.

"Looks like we'll have to get a crowbar to open this."

Lexie had forgotten all about the box, the one that almost cost her her life. She studied it, then an idea struck her.

"Maybe not." She lifted her gold necklace with the heart and key out of her blouse. "Maybe this will fit."

Russell lifted an eyebrow as Lexie unhooked the necklace and handed it to him. The key slid in and the box clicked when he turned the key.

"Are you ready?" He studied her face.

Lexie sighed. "Yes, go ahead."

The lid creaked as Russell pushed it open. Inside was a faded red construction paper heart with a doily glued to its back.

"I made this." Lexie picked up the paper heart and looked into the now-empty box. "I made it for Father. Is that all that's in there?"

Russell spread out his empty hands. "That's all. Wonder why he put that there?"

"Me too." Lexie frowned. His most valued possession was a paper heart? Then she burst out laughing. "Of course. Father told me this was the key to his heart."

Russell frowned. "So where's the lease?"

"It must be with our accountant. I can't imagine why Father would leave it here." Shaking her head, she replaced the heart she'd crafted all those years ago back into the box. All of that for a piece of paper. Yet warmth filled her knowing Father loved her so much.

Russell shook his head. "Stella must have gotten desperate after Robert died and her money stopped coming. So she sent you the telegram, hoping you'd lead her to her fortune."

"I wonder why she thought she'd find something valuable in the house."

"Your father had an ironic sense of humor. He may have teased her about having treasure hidden in the house."

"But his treasure wasn't valuable to her."

"No, only to him."

Lexie's tears trickled down her face, and she turned away to gaze out the window. "I hope she can get the help she needs at the mental hospital. Thank God, the bullet missed her vital organs."

"Poor Jack. She must've been driving him crazy."

Lexie's heart skipped, and she spun around. "Russell, I have a sister!"

Russell drummed his fingers on the desk. "Maybe, and maybe not."

"But what do you mean? If Evelyn is Father's daughter…"

"*If*, Lexie. We can't be sure. Jack might be her father. After all, he married her as soon as she got pregnant, and no one knows but God who the father of the child is. Your father was drinking heavily, and he probably made passes at Stella. But she could've made the whole thing up, just to blackmail him."

"Well, I want to get to know the little girl anyway. I know what it's like to have your mother in a hospital, especially a mental hospital. I can at least be her friend. Besides, I've always wanted a little sister. Russell, maybe it was really God that brought me here so I could help her."

"Jack would like that. He dearly loves that little girl." Russell studied her, a tender smile easing across his face.

"What are you looking at?" Lexie put her hands on her hips.

"You. You know Evelyn looks a lot like you."

A knock sounded on the door and before Russell could answer, Bernon Prentice entered the office.

"Excuse me, Russell. I'm sorry to interrupt you, but this is important." He remained standing, glanced at Lexie, and nodded. "Miss Smithfield, you can hear this since it affects you too." Lexie sank down into a chair in front of Russell's desk as he continued.

"The Coast Guard, based on orders from the White House, has ordered the island to be evacuated. We need to tell all our members and guests they must pack up and leave as soon as possible."

Lexie glanced at Russell to see his reaction, knowing he'd expected the news for a while.

Russell nodded. "How would you like to do that, Bernon? Visit each one? Call a meeting?"

"Both. You and I can divide up the members at the cottages and the annex. We'll post a sign about a meeting in the dining room for tomorrow afternoon." Prentice put both hands on the back of the chair facing Russell's desk.

"All right. And the staff—they have to leave, too, I suppose?"

"Yes, everyone, even those that live here year-around. We'll have a meeting with them today before the rumor mills start flying."

"Thankfully, I believe they all have relatives in Brunswick. I hope they can stay with them."

Prentice shrugged. "I hope so too. We can't afford to find housing for them."

"I'll take the cottages on the north side of the clubhouse." Russell pointed in the direction of Hollybourne.

"Fine. I'll take the rest." Prentice faced Lexie. "I hate to end your stay this way, Miss Smithfield. I'm so sorry about what's happened to you and Destiny. I wish you'd had a more pleasant visit here."

Lexie smiled. "That's quite all right. My time here has been exciting, for sure, but enlightening as well."

Prentice raised an eyebrow. "Very well, then. I'm off to spread the news."

They watched him leave, then Lexie turned to Russell. "So you're finally going to tell the members."

"Yes." He nodded. "Finally."

"Where will Abner go? Who will take care of him?"

"His roommate at the dorm has already offered his family's home in Brunswick for Abner's recuperation."

"What about you, Russell? What will you do? Where will you go?"

"I have relatives on both coasts. But California is warmer than New England right now."

"California?" Her heart sank. She hadn't expected him to go so far away—from Jekyll Island or from her.

"Sure. Why not? I'll need to get a job somewhere."

"Will you look for a hotel or another club to manage?" Lexie made a sweeping movement with her arm, trying to keep her lips from trembling.

Russell smiled and rubbed his chin, his dimple teasing her. "I don't know, maybe I'll get a gig playing piano. You know, I play all types of music. That's how I've picked up some extra money during the off-season."

Lexie tried to imagine Russell playing piano professionally. What a different lifestyle that would be than managing the island club. Just when she thought she knew him, a picture of another Russell emerged.

Russell leaned forward, his elbows on the desk. "So I guess you'll return to work at the hospital back home?"

She nodded, letting her gaze drop to her hands. "Yes, I guess so." Tears filled her eyes. No one waited for her back home—no one that mattered. Would she ever see Russell again?

Russell got up from his chair and came around the desk, took Lexie's hand, and kissed the back of it, pulling her to her feet. Her heart fluttered around inside her chest as he put his finger under her chin, lifted her face, and gazed into her eyes.

"Maybe I should move to New York instead. I'm sure there are jobs for piano players there." His eyes twinkled as he studied her, running his finger down her face, stopping to push a curl away from her mouth.

She nodded, holding her breath.

"Swell. Because I don't want to be too far from you. I love you, Lexie."

He leaned down and pressed his lips against hers. She melted into his embrace and allowed herself to be swept away to another dimension— one that was safe and filled with love.

After blissful moments passed, they parted to catch their breaths.

"Do you think you could marry a piano player?"

Lexie smiled and nodded as tears trickled down her cheek, then she tilted her head. "Guess that depends on who the piano player is."

Russell laughed out loud and pulled her close. "This one." He kissed her with such intensity, it took her breath away.

"Oh, then the answer is yes," she whispered when the kiss ended.

He wrapped her in his arms and held her. "I'm sorry about Destiny, Lexie."

She glanced up at him. "It was just a house, Russell, but God had other plans for my destiny."

Acknowledgements

Thanks to ongoing preservation, the "Millionaires' Village" at Jekyll Island is being restored. Guests are still able to stay in the beautiful Victorian hotel, known as the Jekyll Island Club. I am thankful to all those who work to keep this historic area preserved.

I especially want to thank Gretchen Greminger, curator at the Jekyll Island Authority, for her long-suffering patience with my many questions and emails. Gretchen was immensely helpful in giving me information and pointing out references for me to use.

It was a rare privilege to stay in the hotel and imagine what it had been like a hundred years ago. Our hotel tour guide, Gail Rumble, was very informative and entertaining. I was thrilled when she let us tour Russell's office, now the Presidential Suite, and climb the spiral staircase (which replaced the ladder) into the tower where the telescope is. What a thrill it was to see what Russell saw when he looked around the island from his tower office.

Of course, I have to thank my husband Chuck for taking me on these research trips, helping me take notes, and gathering information for my book. What facts I missed, he didn't, and I so appreciate him being my partner in this endeavor.

Thank you to my patient, understanding critique partners Sandra Barnes, Kiersti Plog, and Sarah Tipton for their time and effort to help me make this book better. You ladies provided me with special support and encouragement through the writing process.

I'd like to also thank my beta readers for accepting the role of reading the book before publication and offering suggestions to improve it.

Thank you to Dan Walsh, whose book *The Discovery* opened my eyes to activities off our shores during World War II and inspired me to research that era in depth.

Thanks to my agent Joyce Hart, who encouraged me to write the book; to Leslie L. McKee, whose diligent editing polished all the rough places; and to Ann Tatlock, managing editor of Heritage Beacon, who saw the beauty in my story.

Discussion Questions for *The Gilded Curse*

1. Lexie Smithfield is afraid she'll inherit her mother's dementia. Have you "inherited" any traits from your parents? Are they good or bad?

2. Lexie's fears make her suspect everyone, even Russell. Who did you suspect was behind the unusual activities? Were you surprised by the ending?

3. Russell is 4F due to the shooting accident. Spencer likes to make fun of his handicap. Have you ever known someone with a handicap? How did they handle it? How did others act toward them? Were they treated like they were inferior?

4. Russell struggles with a promise he made to Robert, Lexie's brother, not to tell her about the situation between Lexie's father and Stella. Do you think he should have told her sooner? Have you ever been in a situation where you wanted to tell someone something but had promised not to?

5. Lexie grew up afraid of the grotesques in the gothic chapel on the island because her mother was superstitious about them. Do you have any superstitions? Why?

6. Lexie thought God would be angry with her for ignoring him for so many years. Have you ever thought God was mad at you? Was it because of things that happened to you that you thought God was using to punish you?

7. Lexie was attracted to Spencer because he was handsome, popular, and flamboyant. But his character was flawed, and she ignored the warning signs until it was almost too late. Do you or have you ever known anyone like Spencer? Were you attracted to him or appalled? Did you find out too late what he was really like?

8. While Lexie is at Jekyll Island, Nazi submarines are off the coast torpedoing American ships. Did you know this really happened in 1942? Did you know the government tried to hide the reality of the situation from its citizens? Do you think that was right or wrong?

9. Lexie's family suffered a lot of losses. Some families seem to have more tragedy than others. Does that mean God didn't care? How do you explain those situations to nonbelievers?

10. Lexie's mother suffered from mental illness, but she was fortunate to get the best treatment available at the time. Abner Jones suffered from PTSD, post-traumatic stress syndrome, as a result of his experiences in WWI and was put in a mental institution until Lexie's grandfather got him out. Both were misunderstood. Do you think mental illness is still misunderstood? Do you know anyone who suffers from it? How are they treated? Can they get help?